Barbara Dennison

Novels by Ethel Carnie Holdsworth

Miss Nobody (1913)
Helen of Four Gates (1917)
The Taming of Nan (1919)
The Marriage of Elizabeth (1920)
The House that Jill Built (1920)
Down Poverty Street (1921)
The Great Experiment (1923)
General Belinda (1924)
Equality Island (1925)
This Slavery (1925)
The Quest of the Golden Garter (1927)
Barbara Dennison (1928)
Eagles' Crag (1932)

Barbara Dennison

Ethel Carnie Holdsworth

with an Introduction by
Jess Samuel

Kennedy & Boyd,
an imprint of
Zeticula Ltd,
Unit 13,
44-46 Morningside Road,
Edinburgh,
EH10 4BF
Scotland.

http://www.kennedyandboyd.co.uk
admin@kennedyandboyd.co.uk

Frst published in 1928 by Stanley Paul, London
This edition published 2025
Copyright © Estate of Ethel Carnie Holdsworth 2025
Cover photograph © Helen Brown 2025

Paperback ISBN 978-1-84921-248-9

Introduction

Jess Samuel

Since the 1980s, the dedicated efforts of the
community which has sprung up around poet,
journalist, activist and author Ethel Carnie
Holdsworth (1886-1962) have enabled an extensive
remapping of the life and career of this remarkable
literary figure. Thus far, the publication of Carnie
Holdsworth's *Collected Poems* (2020), and reissuing
of six of her novels have offered insights into the
development of both her socialist-feminist politics,
and what Nicola Wilson identifies as the 'generic
eclecticism' which characterises her work.[1] Carnie
Holdsworth's participation in the 'long cultural
tradition … of socially committed writers incorporating
popular forms into their fiction' enabled not only the
author's dramatization of the twofold oppression
faced by working-class women, but also her rendering
of escapist visions in which characters from this
demographic variously experience liberation from
poverty, exploitation, and alienation.[2] Roger Smalley
ventures that her later and lesser-studied long-form
fiction — *Barbara Dennison* (1929), *All On Her Own*
(1929) and *Eagles' Crag* (1930)—was written during
a period of the author's life during which she became
increasingly disillusioned by what she perceived as
'her failure to prevent capitalism and fascism from
flourishing' after 1925. Consequentially, Smalley
suggests, the ideas espoused in these texts are

expressed with less clarity.[3] While I argue that the reissuing of *Barbara Dennison* provides evidence that the author's desire nor ability to communicate socialist-feminist ethics via the form of 'popular' romance ever wavered, this is certainly a novel in which her ofttimes revolutionary polemic is tempered by a profound scepticism about just how much most women could expect from their 'real' (p.173) lives.[4]

Biographical information

Ethel Carnie was born in Lancashire on New Year's Day in 1886, though she was primarily raised in the 'growing textile town' of Great Harwood after her family moved there in 1892.[5] Both of her parents were cotton weavers, and after a brief stint in full-time education an eleven year old Carnie herself became a 'half-timer' at the Delph Road Mill.[6] Just two years later, she began labouring full time as a 'winder' at St. Lawrence Mill.[7] The young girl passed the time structuring her thoughts in 'rhythmic forms', and began developing this creative impulse through taking 'evening writing classes' at a local technical college.[8] She also regularly attended 'political meetings' with her father, who was a member of the Social Democratic Federation and an important influence on his daughter's burgeoning radicalism.[9] At nineteen, she gave a reading of her poem 'The Bookworm' in front of the Blackburn Author's Society. The group was 'astonished' by her verse, and went on to sponsor 'five hundred' and then 'a thousand' copies of her collection *Rhymes from the Factory, by a Factory Girl* (1907).[10] Her work was also published in both local papers and an array of progressive periodicals, and her accomplishments soon captured the attention of *Clarion* editor Robert Blatchford.[11] He scouted the twenty-one-year-old Carnie to write for his periodical *The Woman Worker* in the summer of 1909, an opportunity which saw her move to London.

Carnie's stint as contributor to Blatchford's paper was short-lived – just over six months—but her output during this period proved her to not only be a talented writer but a person of powerful convictions. Her outlook was internationalist, her allegiance not to any official party but to the people, her politics rooted in a recognition of the specific plight of working-class women. While her 'clear-spoken' message resonated with many readers, it seems that by 1910 her unflinching analysis of both politics, culture, and media had aggravated Blatchford on a personal level.[12] Her writing began to appear less and less frequently in the *Woman Worker* and its rebranded successor *Women Folk*, with Blatchford eventually instructing his manager Alec Thompson to 'drop her off' the paper.[13] In February 1910, 'An Open Letter to Miss Ethel' — probably penned by Blatchford himself— appeared in *Women Folk*, claiming that Carnie had 'floated' out of London 'upon a tempestuous and saline sea of tears', the result of an 'acute form of home sickness'.[14] While there may have been some truth to his explanation, Deborah Mutch argues that Blatchford's 'controlling' tendencies were also likely to have played a role in Carnie's abrupt return to Lancashire.[15]

Following this turbulent period in Blatchford's orbit, Carnie Holdsworth did not return to writing full-time for a few years. However, the connections she had formed to a plethora of publications in London meant she continued contributing to periodicals alongside spells of employment in the factory, as a teacher, and selling ribbons at markets. A thriving British periodical culture would eventually support Carnie Holdsworth's first foray into novel writing. Her debut *Miss Nobody* first appeared as a serial in the *Christian Commonwealth* over the summer of 1913, providing the first-time author both financial support and access to a 'mass reading audience'.[16] While there are no figures which can offer an indication of the commercial success of *Miss Nobody* (1913) when it was first published as a book by Methuen, subsequent publisher Herbert Jenkin's deemed the 'early reception' to Carnie Holdsworth's work good enough to offer her a six-book contract deal.[17] This saw the re-release of *Miss Nobody*, followed by publication of *Helen of Four Gates* (1917), *The Taming of Nan* (1919), *The Marriage of Elizabeth* (1920), *General Belinda* (1924) and *The Quest of the Golden Garter* (1927). A notable exception from this sequence is the novel for which Carnie Holdsworth is 'most often remembered', *This Slavery* (1925).[18] Wilson suggests that the book's explicitly revolutionary stance likely meant it was rejected by 'specialist purveyors of light romantic fiction' Herbert Jenkins, and following its serialisation in the *Daily Herald* it was published instead by 'left-wing press' the Labour Publishing Company.[19] The success of these novels, particularly *Helen of Four Gates*, facilitated Carnie Holdsworth's purchase of former inn the Long Tail in 1919, where she and her family enjoyed a period of relative stability.[20] However, during the next decade the first Labour government fell, the anti-fascist periodical she had founded and edited with her husband Alfred Holdsworth, *The Clear Light* (1923-1925), folded having 'consumed all she had earned', and her marriage resulted in separation in 1928.[21] Her final two novels *Barbara Dennison* (1929) and *Eagle's Crag* (1931) were published by Stanley Paul.[22] Despite the groundbreaking achievements her prolific career evidences, Carnie Holdsworth's 'literary celebrity' was swiftly forgotten following her death in 1962.[23]

Plot Overview

As *Barbara Dennison* is currently one of Carnie Holdsworth's lesser-known novels, I will provide a brief overview of the plot here. The narrative juxtaposes the London lives of Barbara and Crichie Dennison and their acquaintances Flora and Fred Peachley with rural Rimton, where Barbara's long-time companion and village blacksmith Dave Reid resides with the pair's foster parents, Sarah and Dan Farmer. Book One introduces the Dennisons, who, despite being newly married are already aware of a widening chasm between them. Barely suppressed frictions are only exacerbated by the arrival of Dave in London, who is privately harbouring romantic feelings for Barbara. In Book Two, the reader meets the Peachleys, whose marriage is also in crisis following the loss of their savings in the collapse of Dinkermanns bank. At the behest of his wife, Fred takes on extra work as a translator to pay the rent on their house in the upmarket Hendon. When he leaves the house to post an advert for his services, the largely disparate lives of the Dennisons and Peachleys collide when Crichie calls by the house and is compelled by Flora's polished femininity and staunch conservatism. The pair begin having an affair, with Crichie gifting Flora a fur coat from Goffers Emporium, where he works as a clerk. On a subsequent trip away together, Flora tells Crichie that she is deciding whether to leave Fred and their three children to enjoy a better quality of life with him.

Crichie's absence afford Barbara a trip to Rimton. On a walk with Dave, the pair have a heated argument about the romantic tension between them, and the state of Barbara's marriage. This fight strengthens the protagonist's resolve to return home to Crichie and try harder to make their relationship work. Yet, upon arriving at Goffers to surprise her husband,

Barbara discovers his purchase of the fur, which she then sees Flora wearing, thus revealing their infidelity. In Book Three, a heartbroken Barbara once again returns to the Farmer home, only to be drawn in to an argument with Sarah in which it is revealed that Barbara's biological mother, Ruth Delling, is still alive. Barbara briefly stays with Ruth before being persuaded by Dave to return to Rimton with him. In a quiet moment on a secluded lane, the reader is primed to expect Dave and Barbara to submit to their desires and begin a new life together. However, upon overhearing Sarah and Dan discussing Barbara's predicament, the pair learns Goffers has collapsed. The Farmers clearly expect Barbara to return to Crichie, and she leaves Rimton the next morning. Upon her arrival home, the Dennison's maid Mary breaks the news that Crichie has died, to which Barbara quietly responds: "'Thank God!'" (p.222).

Carnie Holdsworth's attitude(s) to marriage

The themes of 'oppression and romantic love' prevalent across Carnie Holdsworth's writing are primarily examined in relation to marriage in *Barbara Dennison*. [24] Marriage was an issue the author had been writing about since the days of her *Woman Worker* column, in which Smalley describes her as taking 'uniformly hostile' stance on what she viewed as an 'inimical institution' that was nearly impossible for working-class women to escape from.[25] In Carnie Holdsworth's fiction, however, marriage was treated inconsistently, utilised more frequently as a literary device rather than a topic for discussion in its own right. As Smalley notes, marriage actually provides 'happy endings' to *Miss Nobody*, *The Taming of Nan*, *The House That Jill Built*, and *General Belinda*.[26] In both her serial *Iron Horses* (1915) and her 'propaganda' novel *This Slavery*, hasty nuptials between vulnerable working-class women and villainous upper-class capitalists enable explorations of class conflict.[27] In *Helen of Four Gates*, the union of Helen Mason and the 'sadistic' Fielding Day is one of 'myriad' ways the heroine is brutally exploited by the men in her life.[28]

The renewed focus on the institution of marriage in *Barbara Dennison*, could, as Smalley suggests, be explained by Carnie Holdsworth's own experience of separating from husband Alfred the year before the novel was published. The pair had met at a 'literary club' in 1915, married 'secretly' shortly thereafter, and chose not to go on a honeymoon.[29] Just two years in to their marriage, Alfred was conscripted, and was reported 'killed' in 1918.[30] Carnie Holdsworth 'thought she was a widow', but Alfred was eventually discovered alive in a British hospital, having spent time as a prisoner of war in Germany.[31] Once reunited, the couple worked together on *The Clear Light,* which became the 'mouthpiece' for the National Union of Combatting Fascism in 1924.[32] By 1928, though, Carnie Holdsworth's doctor had advised her to leave Alfred if she wanted to 'retain her sanity'.[33] She moved away with the couple's children, Margaret and Maud, and Alfred never saw any of them again.[34] I note here that the specifics on the breakdown in Holdsworth's relationship are ultimately unknown. I do not suggest that any aspect of *Barbara Dennison* is autobiographical in nature, but rather that the author's experience of a thirteen-year marriage and seemingly acrimonious split reignited her concerns regarding the situations married women could easily become trapped in if they did not have sufficient means, support, or self-confidence to leave.

Marriage in *Barbara Dennison*
A particularly noteworthy feat of the novel is Carnie Holdsworth's attunement to the ways 'mental rather

than physical cruelty' constituted a commonplace
– if more misunderstood – form of spousal abuse.[35]
While the narrator notes that central characters
Barbara and Crichie endeavour to be 'patient'
(p.80) with one another, small and seemingly trivial
incidents contribute to the total degeneration of their
relationship within the suffocating legal and socio-
cultural confines of marriage. In the opening scene,
Barbara notes that it is the morning of their first
wedding anniversary, and Crichie attempts to mask
the fact he has forgotten with exaggerated affection,
pleading for a kiss. However, when he pulls away, he
notices

> big tears on Barbara's lashes ... Was it possible
> that those tears of hers had been caused by the
> suspicion that he had forgotten their anniversary
> morning? He hoped not. But—it was Barbara's
> usual smiling face that returned his look. (p.12)

While not entirely obvious to Crichie, it is
transparently clear to the reader that his lapse in
memory is the cause of Barbara's emotional pain –
a pain she immediately tries to disguise so as not
to upset him. Crichie blames his forgetfulness on
his manic schedule at Goffers Emporium – 'enough
to make a man forget anything' (p.9). Yet, as the
narrative progresses, it becomes clear that his failure
to recall this milestone date is not a singular, stress-
induced incident, but symptomatic of his growing
apathy toward his wife. Gradually, everything that
Barbara does irritates Crichie; he is incensed by
her 'tap[ping]' (p.80) her fingers on the table, but
'equally' (p.80) angered by her total deference to him
when he tells her to stop. He criticises everything
she does, from the way she rubs her eyes, to her
choice in décor, to the shine on her nose when it

is unpowdered. What makes Carnie Holdsworth's rendering of Crichie's abusive tendencies particularly insightful, though, is her ability to identify the ways it is rooted in his internalisation of capitalistic and patriarchal ideologies.

Indeed, Carnie Holdsworth demonstrates the role of mismatched politics in corroding curiosity, empathy and respect in both the Dennison and Peachley marriages. While the Dennison marriage is obviously strained from the outset of the novel, Barbara is initially more resilient to her husband's demeaning critiques. For example, the heroine reads both Shaw and H. G. Wells (p.18), and playfully scolds Crichie for trying to 'censor' (p.18) her literary diet when he expresses his displeasure. In time, though, their relationship will emulate the more mature Peachley marriage, wherein these moments of light-hearted sparring give way to resentful coexistence. Crichie himself notes the similarity between his wife and Fred Peachley, warning that both spend too much time 'thinking' (p.18). Fred, like Barbara, is also a reader. He engages with 'Socialist' ideas through literature (p.114) and can consume Socrates and Montaigne 'in the original' (p.97) owing to his study of languages. He is also an affectionate father to his three sons. Flora Peachley, by contrast, is an admirer of futurist art (p.94) and a strict disciplinarian. She views her husband's love of languages as 'a waste of time' (p.93), demanding in the wake of the Dinkermanns collapse that he utilises his skill to find additional work as a translator to pay the rent on their home on the aspirational 'Avenue' (p.108) where they live. Fred tries to appeal but is cut off by Flora's 'contemptuous silence' (p.96). In the case of both the Dennisons and Peachleys, it is evident that, as Smalley summarises, 'circumstances have paired the wrong individuals'.[36] However, while Crichie and Flora's mutual disregard for 'emotionalism' (p.146) allows them to pursue their extramarital romance without any guilt, their more progressive counterparts do not have the 'cruel trick of fate' which led them into their marriages resolved. [37] Instead, Carnie Holdsworth further investigates the ways that her heroine's internalisation of the same values which drive her husband's abuse and infidelity also prevent her from escaping what she comes to clearly conceive of as the hollow 'masquerade' (p.174) of their relationship.

While she is characterised as a perfect match for Fred, Barbara's love interest takes the form of her foster brother Dave, a fellow lover of nature and music whose affections she comes to reciprocate over the course of the novel. Yet, despite their sharing a 'passionate' (p.176) kiss in a climatic scene on Ridgley Fell, Barbara quickly decides to return to her 'real' (p.173) life. The heroine explains to an incredulous Dave that while this choice will necessitate the sacrifice of both she and her husband's 'individuality' (p.173), marriage provides women's only route to fulfilling 'Nature's end' (p.173) of furthering the human 'race' (p.173). The way that Barbara interprets Nature's doctrine marks a considerable shift from the kind of relationships other Carnie Holdsworth heroines share with the natural world, which Patricia Johnson argues functions consistently as a space for these working-class women to 'see and define themselves outside the delimiting structures of society'. [38] In *Helen of Four Gates* in particular, the eponymous protagonist's affinity with 'Nature' is fundamental to the formation of her 'creed' – that her love for Martin Scott, her true 'mate', displaces her desire to conform to the social mores which saw her marry violent sadist Fielding Day. [39] The 1917 novel ends with soulmates Helen and Martin reuniting romantically, but not through marriage. In *Barbara Dennison*, this radical 'exalting' of free love has dissipated.[40] After both her kiss with Dave, and a brief period of separation from Crichie after discovering his unfaithfulness, Barbara ultimately returns to what she comes to see as her 'own place' (p.179) as a middle-class housewife. Completely demoralised by the way she has been treated within her marriage, she is unable to act as an agential party in its termination. Instead, the narrative releases the heroine from her 'prison' via the shocking revelation of Crichie's death at the end of the last chapter, the revival of her consciousness immortalised through her final murmured words.[41]

The reissuing of *Barbara Dennison* not only lends expansive insights into the ways Carnie Holdsworth's critiques of marriage remained consistent throughout her life, but also reveals a text dense with discussion of the broader 'tensions' in class and gender relations to which the author frequently returned in her fiction.[42] Productive areas of focus for future study could more closely examine the novel's representation of masculinity, or its attention to popular perceptions of the rural working-classes, to offer just two examples.

Endnotes

1   Nicola Wilson, 'Ethel Carnie Holdsworth: Genre, Serial Fiction, and Popular Reading Patterns', in *A History of British Working Class Literature*, ed. by John Goodridge and Bridget Keegan (Cambridge University Press, 2017), pp. 311–326, p.323.
2   Wilson, 'Ethel Carnie Holdsworth: Genre, Serial Fiction, and Popular Reading Patterns', p.323.
3   Roger Smalley, 'The Life and Work of Ethel Carnie Holdsworth, With Particular Reference To The Period 1907 to 1931' (University of Central Lancashire, 2006), p.312.
4   'Mrs. Holdsworth's Novel', in *Nelson Leader*, 1 November 1929, p.n/a.

5   Edmund Frow and Ruth Frow, 'Ethel Carnie: Writer, Feminist, Socialist', in *The Rise of Socialist Fiction 1880-1914*, by H. Gustav Klaus (The Harvester Press, 1987), pp. 251–266, p.251.

6   Frow and Frow, 'Ethel Carnie: Writer, Feminist, Socialist', p.251; Smalley, The Life and Work of Ethel Carnie Holdsworth', p.ii.

7   Patricia E. Johnson, 'Finding Her Voice(s): The Development of a Working Class Feminist Vision in Ethel Carnie's Poetry', *Victorian Poetry*, 43.3 (2005), pp. 297–315, p.298.

8   Preface to *Rhymes from the Factory by a Factory Girl* (1907) qtd in Frow and Frow, 'Ethel Carnie: Writer, Feminist, Socialist', p.252; Pamela Fox, 'Introduction', in *Helen of Four Gates*, by Ethel Carnie Holdsworth (Zeticula Ltd, 2016), pp. ix–xxxiii, p.x.

9   Frow and Frow, p.252.

10 Frow and Frow, p.253; Smalley, p.56.

11 Smalley, p.57.

12 Gertrude Higham, 'Chums', in *The Woman Worker*, 18 June 1909, p.n/a. Over the course of Carnie Holdsworth's time spent contributing to *The Woman Worker*, several readers wrote in to express their appreciation of her 'charm[ingly]' frank approach to political and cultural commentary, particularly as it pertained to both women's issues and women's activism.

13 Robert Blatchford, undated letter from Rome, Robert Blatchford archive Manchester Central Library, MS F9205 B72, 3, qtd in Smalley, p.89.

14 Pa B, 'An Open Letter To Miss Ethel', *The Women Worker*, 15 December 1910, p.685, qtd in Frow and Frow, p.259.

15 Deborah Mutch, 'Making Space for Women: The Labour Leader, The Clarion, and The Women's Column', in *Women, Periodicals and Print Culture in Britain, 1830s-1900s: The Victorian Period*, ed. by Alexis Easley and Clare Gill (Edinburgh University Press, 2019), pp. 365–378, p.374.

16 Nicola Wilson, 'Ethel Carnie Holdsworth: Genre, Serial Fiction, and Popular Reading Patterns', p.317.

17 Smalley, p.8.

18 Nicola Wilson, 'Introduction', in *This Slavery*, by Ethel Carnie Holdsworth, ed. by Nicola Wilson (Trent Editions, 2011), pp. vi–xxiii, p.xx.

19 Wilson, 'Introduction', p.xix.

20 Smalley, p.133.

21 Roger Smalley, 'Introduction', in *General Belinda* (Kennedy & Boyd, 2019), pp. ix–xix, p.xvii.

22 Smalley, p.133.

23 'Ex-Mill Girl Who Became Literary Celebrity', qtd in Wilson, 'Introduction', p.xii.

24 Pamela Fox, *Class Fictions: Shame and Resistance in the British Working-Class Novel, 1890-1945* (Duke University Press, London, 1994), p.127.

25 Smalley, p.78.

26 Ibid, p.298.

27 Fox, *Class Fictions*, p.136.

28 Ibid, p.134.

29 Smalley, 'The Life and Work of Ethel Carnie Holdsworth', p.79; 'Mill Girl Poetess: Marriage of Miss Ethel Carnie', *Blackburn Times*, 10 April 1915, p.n/a.

30 Smalley, 'Introduction', p.iii.

31 Ibid, p.xiii.

32 Ibid, p.xvii.

33 Smalley, p.216.

34 Ibid, p.xxxiv.

35 Smalley, p.309.

36 Smalley, p.300.

37 Ibid, p.311.

38 Patricia E. Johnson, '"For God's Sake, Women, Go Out and Play": Nomadic Space in the Work of Ethel Carnie Holdsworth', in *Locating Classed Subjectivities: Intersections of Space and Working-Class Life in Nineteenth-, Twentieth-, and Twenty-First-Century British Writing*, ed. by Simon Lee (Oxon, 2022), pp. 61–76, p.63.

39 Ethel Carnie Holdsworth, *Helen of Four Gates* (Kennedy & Boyd, 2016), pp.110-200 quoted in Pamela Fox, 'Introduction', p.xx.

40 Fox, 'Introduction', p.xx.

41 Smalley, , p.78.

42 Fox, *Class Fictions*, p.128.

Book One

Chapter One

An arrow of gold, sped from Day's fair hand, touched the Venetian glass bowl which held the powder Barbara used to take the shininess off her nose. Crichie hated shiny noses.

"Barbara!"

Crichie Dennison had just come along the landing, in brown dressing-gown and with cigarette in mouth. He looked in at the doorway of the mauve room, with its thinning shadows, its rainbow-gleamings and glintings of prismed light which would soon give way to the broad white flame of morning.

All was hushed within the mauve room. From outside came the chatterings and chirpings of the roof sparrows, who were shaking brown, cramped wings and perhaps discussing if Spring was really near, at last.

"Barbara!"

He had advanced into the room, and seated himself in the wicker chair, which yet creaked with newness.

Barbara moved slightly, but did not awaken. She was dreaming, and in the dreaming followed a clear, brown stream which frothed and murmured and tumbled over a pebbly bed where trout floundered up and out of sun-lustred pools which reflected a dawn sky; trout, with crimson spots, flashing the water in crystal spray. She and Dave were after a beauty, at least nine inches long. They were jumping bare-headed and half-dressed from stone to stone, holding their breaths almost, in the silence of a dawn which flamed the sky from Rimton to Carbridge, wavering, quivering bands of orange and ruby fire, great banks of purple clouds, were changing with each moment. All was so still, there was only the chatter of the stream over its pebbles, only the soft whispering of the willows, with their thin, long leaves, leaning over the bank-side. She had just jumped that bank, helped by Dave, and had alighted on a moss-covered boulder, and now in the distance was Dave, beckoning to her to "come on", holding in his hand, this Nimrod in comically-patched pants, a peeled willow-stick, as sceptre.

Crichie—suburbia—food prices—Kreisler about to visit London—the latest novel—all the life which interested her when she was awake was as though it had not been, as though it were some casual life which had not touched the spirit that was revelling so in this day-dawn, this stream, these willows, with their quivering reflections interset with skyey beauties. Every still reach of the stream lay reflecting the dawn glories. She was helping Dave catch a wary, red spotted trout, hearing him calling from his boulder at intervals, "Come on, Barbary. Come on," and the morning echoes repeating the words.

"Barbara, get up, please. It's after seven."

So Crichie, his cigarette half-smoked, in the room out of which objects now appeared, half their surfaces shadowed, half in light, a chiaroscuro from which a modern artist might have created a dozen studies, from the bed, under whose rich eiderdown lay the figure of Barbara, to the dressing-table with the Venetian jar, and the carpet, whose corner nearest the window made a strip of mauve, patterned with large, white vine-leaves, while a big pouffe of crimson velvet stood near-by, on which rested Barbara's silver-glinting slippers with Cuban heels.

Barbara did not move.

She was near him—-yet far—a creature fleet as the winds and free as the dawn, running with Dave down the course of a stream two hundred miles away.

Crichie sat back again. He was looking around the room with that appreciation which can only be known to one who has worked hard to buy everything in it.

Barbara's arm, like shadowed ivory, moved almost imperceptibly.

Dave had caught the trout—caught it just where the oak-tree's roots and a big stone made an enclosing pool. Dave, shirt-sleeves rolled up, had leaned down and got it in his hands. Dave had caught the trout. She was dancing with delight on a mossy boulder in mid-stream, a tattered frock, made from one of her foster-mother's, swinging round her bare, brown legs.

"No woman has a more comfortable home," mused Crichie, with appreciation of the fact that it been got at cost price. Eighteen-eighteen, that satin wood wardrobe with the deep-bevelled mirror which reflected his figure in the dressing-gown now distinctly brown, reflected the hazy rings of smoke from the cigarette old Peachley had given him as they had met, to be rattled through the tube, last night. A yawn.

Barbara's arm moved again, then lay still as though nestling deeper into the soft warmth of the eiderdown, which had been contributed to by thousands of little eider-ducks, who had lived and died, merely to so contribute to the world's comfort—where the world could buy comfort. Crichie's rings of smoke from Peachley's cigarette drifted towards the fireplace, where the porcelain screen stood, whereon some unknown worker, who had never known Barbara, had painted autumn leaves, and possibly would toil the bulk of a lifetime away painting autumn leaves on porcelain. Seven, six and eleven, that screen. Crichie watched the smoke-rings curling across its opaque whiteness. A good line that, and—it had been fortunate for them he worked at the Emporium and could get things at rock-bottom prices. A few years and he would be junior-partner. There, there would be scope. He squared his shoulders as to some larger air. Scope, that was the thing to aim for, when a man had brains. Poor Peachley! Rather a good cigarette, this. Must have been one of a Christmas box. Always struck you as trying to make things last as long as possible, Peachley did. Tragedy, Peachley was. Crichie always recalled Peachley, not as he met him in train and club, but as he sat on Sundays, watching his three little boys play with a miniature railway on the scrubby little lawn outside the dingy little sitting-room, and jumping up jerkily, almost as though apologizing for his existence, when Flora Peachley said: "Can't you stir the fire?" or "Fred, you've pulled the table-cloth awry." No. Never would get anywhere, old Peachley. One of those bewildered dreamers caught in the cog-wheels of life's grind.

The cigarette-end burned Crichie's fingers as he stood, mentally looking down on Peachley.

He laid it on the bronze ash-tray.

He came back to Barbara, who so persistently refused to wake up.

"Barbara!" he entreated, emphatically, firmly.

She opened and began to rub her eyes.

"Barbara, don't do that," he expostulated, aggrieved. "I've told you often. It flattens the eye-ball or something. It's bad for the eyes."

"Very well, dear."

Barbara, who always woke up placid, yawned and stretched herself. Her fair hair, with its almost moon-glinting paleness, streamed about her shoulders. Yawning, she put up a rather stubby hand to a large but fine mouth, and her wedding-ring, new and broad, caught the light. Her eyes, almost too large for beauty, and browny-green as a Rimton summer pool, awoke to Crichie, to the mauve room, the Venetian jar and the wardrobe, the vine-leaved carpet and the porcelain-screen—drank in Crichie with avidity, and took the rest of the paraphernalia casually. Things had never had a hold on Barbara. People—always.

"I've come all the way from Rimton to London in a flash," she informed Crichie. "Give me time to fit in again."

"Barbara—it's after seven," Crichie told her.

"'Morning's at seven, the hill-side's dew-pearled,'" quoted Barbara. "Pull the curtains back, dear. There's the gurgle of a northern stream in my blood yet. Is it another grey-city morning? Now, where are my stockings?"

He watched her hunt for them.

She hung half out of bed and found them on the floor.

Lazily, and still thrall to a northern dawn, and stream, and the willows, and Dave, she pulled a stocking over her arm.

"Gee! A ladder!" she lamented.

"Barbara, you're careless. Those were the best the Emporium had in stock, double-heeled, best woven—"

"Yes, dear," agreed Barbara. "But they always ladder. You might as well get me cheaper ones. Do draw the curtains back."

She was yet hemmed about with the fresh, wonderful beauty of that morning which was pouring over Rimton, where Dan and Sarah and Dave would be awakening. She tried, as she pulled her stockings on, to visualize all the billions that were waking up all over the world. Light was flowing into the room now, despite the curtains—was pouring, pouring, and all becoming wide flame of day. The golden beam which had heralded it had fled. Flecks and spatters of colour, glimmerings and gleamings, chiaroscuro of departing shadows, filled the room. They could hear the prosaic sizzle of an English breakfast—eggs and bacon—below. The pleasant aroma penetrated appetizingly to their nostrils. Up from the street came the whistling of a citizen of London. They had never seen him, and probably never would if they lived there twenty years. They knew him clairaudiently. Always, at this very moment, each morning, at this very spot, he burst into whistling the same melody, a delicate, joyous minuet of Beethoven's; Always, as he passed, they were reminded of sunlit groves, with light, delicate leaves, dappled paths and French gardens by the water's edge, reflecting the light-hearted grace of a generation that had danced its minuet, and vanished, sleeping now, with powder-wigs, and Snuff-boxes, and velvet-patches, and head-feathers, all laid by.

After the first bars they stared at each other unbelievingly.

Barbara's eyes were so round they worried Crichie. "Don't stare so, Barbara," he told her.

"He—he isn't whistling the minuet," she said.

"No."

They had lived here a whole year, and had got used to that citizen of London, whom they had never seen, whistling that delightfully joyous minuet, and—he was passing whistling the 'Dead March'.

"Got his income-tax papers, possibly," Crichie told Barbara.

"Well, it's not nice of him to pass whistling the 'Dead March' for the first time—on our anniversary morning," said Barbara.

"It isn't. I was thinking the same," said Crichie. "He might have whistled it on some other morning, Beautifullest, we've been married a year."

He sat staring at her. It was the anniversary of their wedding-day; and he had forgotten, till she had reminded him. A week since he had recalled that in seven days it would be the anniversary. But the stock-taking at Goffers's had been intense. Never had he seen old Goffers in such a driving mood. Crates and crates of new goods coming in, too, at the same time. Enough to make a man forget anything. He hoped Barbara had not noticed that he had forgotten.

"Yes, a whole year," said Barbara. "Do pull the curtains back, Crichie. Let the blessed light of commonplace day in."

She had not noticed, he thought, with relief. He was glad. What had they said, that wonderful night, when moonlight lay over a world of solemn peaks crowned with eternal snows? That never would they forget the anniversary as some did, poor, purblind mortals! And—well, it was all the Emporium's fault, and Barbara, who had remembered, did not go out to work in an Emporium, with hundreds of clerks to supervise and with the goal of partnership to achieve.

"Crichie, you're sitting on my undies—and you've not pulled the curtains back," she told him.

"I'm sitting on a cushion; nothing else," he answered.

"Then they're under the cushion."

"Barbara, and they cost—"

She leaped out of bed, suddenly, went over to the window, and flung the curtains back, impatiently, as though her spirit ached to see the sky—the width of the world—and get out of this sheltered room.

Then she waited whilst Crichie took the things reproachfully from under the cushion.

"In Rimton," she told him, "they wear coarse, white, linen underclothes, which they dry on hedges or on the grass, fastened down with little stones when its windy. They make them themselves, and change once a week—after cleaning-day in the houses. Funny that I should be living here and being so extravagant."

He was watching her scramble into the billowy, soft silk and lace and net, with the embroidered appliqués. Jumping Jehoshophat! He expected her to tear them, so savagely was she getting into them. She was huffed about something.

"I want you to have beautiful things, Barbara. But you might take care of them," he said, conciliatingly.

"Yes, dear. I know."

The huffiness went out of Barbara swift as a flash.

Their voices, quiet, good-humoured, fell on the air of the mauve room. Outside, the voices of the sparrows now had a full, morning tone in their chirps, and the little brown birds during all this had many times darted down into the street for crumbs and darted back again. A boy went past, calling "Milk", and managing to make the word sound like anything but milk as he rumbled it out of his interior. The sound echoed and rumbled along the street.

"I'll try to learn to take care of them," said Barbara, with answering conciliation.

"Ting-ting."

Their faces lit up and beamed at each other. It was the little Swiss bell they had brought home from their honeymoon, calling them to eggs and bacon, to the marmalade Crichie never sat down without, to the *Morning Post*, and letters, and all the mosaic-like details of life. Barbara, standing by the window, staring at the roofs over the way as she dressed, and seeing them sierra-like against a sky that looked like grey-wool ravelled, recalled that gorgeous week as she heard the Swiss bell. They had only had a week. Crichie could have had longer, but thought it best to get back to the Emporium. He had explained to her that when a man was away too long, well, they might find they could go on longer without him, and she had admired the shrewdness and common sense which meant to take no risks—not even to have a longer honeymoon—yes, she had admired it very much a year ago.

And Crichie, in the wicker-chair which creaked as they said in Rimton things creaked when unpaid for, hearing the Swiss bell, was recalling how he had tried to give Barbara an insight into the indexing system at Goffers's Emporium, and how patiently Barbara had listened—sitting on a rock, with her feet swinging over what appeared to be the edge of the world, and then had surprised him by saying, irrelevantly, as she pointed over a wide, sunlit valley, whence came the ringing of cattle-bells: "Oh, Crichie—look at those clouds. Aren't they like Arabs in white cloaks, riding over the desert?" And he had come back from his attempt to interest her in his world, to see her world, and, as though a veil had been rent, he had caught the emotional thrill which was hers, and which she had passed on from her spirit to his. A sudden splendour had hung for a moment over everything, and he had wished irrationally they could remain there for ever, with Barbara's hat on the rock on which they sat, with the ragged goats moving about, magnified where the mountain mists caught them, with that wide, sunlit valley below them, its meadows a green mist over which cattle moved, like specks, and above, when he looked up, the torch of the rising sun flaming peak after peak into glory of ice-billows, frozen for ever into immobility, and here and there the light touching a sombre, storm-matured pine to green-black beauty. How they had indexed at Goffers had seemed a small thing. There on the rock which overhung the valley Barbara had made Goffers and the Emporium seem nothing at all, for a day—a year ago.

"Ting-ting."

Mary was ringing with gusto.

"Barbara, one kiss," begged Crichie, rising from the chair.

She met him, half-way across the carpet, and tumbled suddenly into his arms, with a little cry that was half a sob, half a laugh. Their lips clung together, honey and fire still, though a year had gone And then he saw there were big tears on Barbara's lashes and a gentle, sad smile on her mouth—and whilst he looked she tore herself away, laughing, and said, casually: "Let's get down to breakfast quickly. It's really a shame the way we've kept Mary waiting about. We must settle down."

Before he could recover from his astonishment at Barbara caring whether Mary waited or not, and at Barbara's idea that they should settle down, she had gone, and the door closed. He heard the cheerful ripple of water from the bathroom-tap and—she was humming a song.

Then he heard Mary's footsteps.

She handed him his shaving water, and he carried it. to his room, cheerful room with fishing-rods on the wall and the bookshelf holding light literature, his recreations symbolized, a good "thriller" or comedy for winter, and summer-time, the reaches of the Thames beyond the water that was darkened by commerce and merchandise, and both these pleasures looked on not so much as pleasures as exercises, to keep him fit for the Emporium.

They met on the landing, Barbara in her rather gay morning-dress, Crichie ready for the Emporium.

Was it possible that those tears of hers had been caused by the suspicion that he had forgotten their anniversary morning? He hoped not.

But—it was Barbara's usual smiling face that returned his look.

"In memory of those mountain stairs," he said, taking her hand.

They walked downstairs to breakfast, in memory of that glorious dawn-walk from glaciers to the valley, without guides, a year ago, a long, short year ago. They walked between walls in shining paper, guaranteed to wash down each spring, the best that the Emporium could give for money, and their feet were on the thick mossiness of Axminster of a green colour Barbara had chosen because it held a shade of that wonderful green of a wonderful valley when "a new Heaven leaned over a new earth".

"Carters are giving us poor meat, latterly, for the price," said Barbara, when Mary had gone, after bringing in the dishes.

Crichie received his bacon and eggs, shook out the morning paper, whose rustling mixed in with the chirping of the sparrows on the little lawn outside, where Mary had thrown the crumbs from the cutting of the new rolls.

"Are they? Then speak to them about it," Crichie told her.

She saw the top half of his face above the paper.

"I shall."

There was a new, emphatic note in Barbara's voice. Crichie heard it, as he skimmed his paper over and gulped hot coffee. Skirmishings in Afghanistan. He received an impression of uncivilized, turbaned savages riding with spears through sand-storms. Always there little skirmishings going on. A seat won by Labour. Huh! Labour! And what had that ever done? Nothing, nothing at all but cause trouble and disturbance and unrest, and shake the fabric of society, which was all right. Suicide of unemployed man. Nothing much in the paper this morning, really. Dash the Labour by-election. Where were the brains of the working-classes going, to elect men with no knowledge of statecraft, who just talked about the rights of the workers? He heard the clink of Barbara's Shelley cup on the Shelley saucer. World was all right if they'd leave it alone. Great financier blows his brains out. He turned the page over, and heard Barbara talking.

"Yes, quite stringy it's been latterly," she was saying, still referring to the meat Carters had sent. "Perhaps they thought we should not notice, being newly married, and—but I shall let them know."

"S-sh, Barbara!" exclaimed Crichie, tensely. He sat bolt upright with a look of shock.

"What is it? Another war?" asked Barbara.

He looked aggrievedly at her.

Really, Barbara did sometimes say the most senseless things! Absolutely ridiculous things. For how could there be another war when the Germans were beaten?

He gave something almost like a groan.

"There's an amalgamation going on—an American firm lining up with Goffers! Big finance, you know—no, of course, you don't—Rotten, I call it. They're extending. It's going to be like a trust. Well, I wouldn't have thought it of Goffers. I wonder—"

He was staring at his plate.

He was wondering how this would affect him.

"Had it been an English amalgamation—" he said.

"But, Crichie—aren't Goffers Germans?"

He looked at her in weary frenzy.

"Of course they are, but commerce is international—"

Then he stopped, realizing his own inconsistencies.

Barbara's hazel eyes, clear and thoughtful, were regarding him, and gave him a feeling of —

"Women don't understand these things," he said, loftily.

She picked up the bell and rang for Mary.

Mary appeared.

"You've forgotten to bring us marmalade," Barbara told her, smilingly. "Mr. Dennison alwavs has marmalade.

"Bother the marmalade!" ejaculated Crichie Dennison. Goffers—amalgamating with Americas capital. And last year old Goffers had hinted at a junior partnership for him, and the amalgamation would mean—Goffers run by a board—all the old system of Goffers's swept away and reorganized. And she was bothering him about marmalade.

"My hat and coat, Barbara," he told her.

"With it affect your—partnership, Crichie? she asked him.

"Bound to do. Rotten it is. Six years of my life gone in Goffers, and then an amalgamation come along; rotten, I call it."

He stalked down the hall.

Barbara followed and reached his hat off the peg, whilst he stood in deep gloom.

Always it was different in the hall from any room in the house, somehow. Always, as she stood here, with Crichie, reaching his hat and coat for him to depart from her, it was different. Always there hung about the hall an air of commercialism, of conflict and bivouac—as though the world and its turmoil reached into the hall, where the highly-polished hat-rack stood, one amongst the millions of the city's hat-racks. And she got a little creepy, unhappy sense of more than bivouac as she stood in the hall this morning. Supposing—this atmosphere which she had often felt in the hall, that ante-room between home and the street which led to the Emporium, should flow like a tide from the hall into all the other rooms, gradually submerging their peace and security and comfort and—harmony!

"You've reached me the wrong hat, Barbara," grumbled Crichie. "This wants sending to the renovators. I told you last week."

"I'll send Mary with it this morning," she told him.

He looked at her.

Damn——it was the anniversary of their wedding-day, and he had allowed himself to get piqued, first by a silly Labour victory and now by this amalgamation, which, after all, might not materialize. And—the sight of Barbara, patiently standing with his coat over her arm and soothing him down because he had got angry over her reaching him the wrong hat, touched him suddenly with a little sting of pain.

"Well, bother Goffers," he said, suddenly, stooping to kiss her, hurriedly, because he must get that train.

Barbara smiled.

The smile did not reach her eyes, as it usually did, so that they danced like wells of clear water with sunlight on it.

"Crichie—" she said, gently, and paused.

"Well?" he asked.

But she helped him on with the overcoat.

"Oh—", she told him, as he faced round to her. "It isn't worth saying. But I was wondering—don't you rather let the Emporium swamp everything? And—I've seen men who confronted life's odds all the time without getting peevish about it."

He stared at her, dumbfounded.

"I don't say they didn't get angry," said Barbara. "I've seen them get very angry. But anger and peevishness are quite different. One's big and the other's little. A boy gets peevish. A man gets angry."

"Barbara!"

They looked at each other in the bivouac of the hall.

"You mean to say I'm—only a boy? gasped Crichie.

"Just that," Barbara told him in a pained voice. "You've met your first crisis—and I don't care a rap whether you get a junior partnership or not, but I did care—tremendously—how you'd stand in a crisis. It's all the difference between being some thing and getting something. You—you even fell out with the marmalade-jar because of Goffers."

"Couldn't you see—I didn't want bothering about marmalade, just then?"

Crichie was stunned.

"Why shouldn't you have been bothered with the marmalade?" asked Barbara.

"Because it was a small thing," Crichie told her.

"Then you could have treated it as such—and taken it as usual," she told him.

"Well, I'll have to get that train," he said.

She followed him to the door, and he opened it.

They saw the front garden, the grey sky, the grey houses, the stretch of lawn with the golden-privet hedge, and—their tree.

"Crichie!"

Barbara's voice danced suddenly, and her eyes danced, and Goffers, and Crichie falling out with the marmalade-jar, and with her for reaching the wrong hat, worried because he was so small—all faded.

"The almond's out," she cried. "Look there!"

And away at the far end of the garden, all in a world of grey, they saw a single pink bloom, like pink snow fallen on a barren world of mist that dragged like a ravelled woolly cloud across the houses, clinging there as it had clung there many weeks.

She walked down the garden path with him.

"And I'll get tickets for us for somewhere—" said Crichie. "Perhaps it'll not turn out into an amalgamation. Sorry I got angry."

"Peevish!" corrected Barbara, smiling, and with her usual gentle placidity.

"You see—you don't understand. If I don't get the partnership it means—no scope. That's more than the money. Scope. To feel you've elbow-room, initiative, a chance to get to the top, to prove that you've brains. You understand, perhaps, now, Barbara, why I fell out with the marmalade-jar?" he appealed boyishly.

His egotism had got a shock.

"To get a partnership would be to have to meet a crisis all the time," she told him. "I can't see old Goffers falling out with marmalade-jars. He'd go on eating in any crisis—and no one would know there'd been one till it was over. He might be a bit more brusque. That'd be all. And then he'd go down to Richmond and forget himself there'd been one, and catch a pike and be as pleased over that as over getting the order he'd nearly missed. Those who believe in competition should be able to bear it, Crichie."

She was looking at him with almost an inscrutable smile.

He got a sudden panic.

"Barbara—what are you reading? he asked, peremptorily.

Barbara laughed.

"Never you mind. I must have scope, too—"

"Barbara, you mustn't—" he paused, not quite knowing what he was going to finish with.

"Think—" prompted Barbara, and laughed again mischievously. "There—don't miss your train, Crichie. I'm really getting quite a collection of mental furniture. I find the destructiveness of Shaw and the constructiveness of H. G. Wells entertaining. And it's fifty years since women allowed men to censor what they read."

He pulled out his watch, presented to him by old Goffers after they had got an order once which had almost slipped them.

The train would certainly not wait.

"But, but what can you do with all this reading and thinking?" he asked a little feebly.

She gave a despairing sigh.

"Isn't it better to be intelligent?" she asked.

"I shall have to go," he said loftily. "Barbara, it's stuff. And it won't make you happier, that I can see. Most people who think—well, look at Peachley. Best join the tennis club."

He swung the gate open and passed through—looking back at her as she stood in the morning-gown, the light catching her fair hair, her pale, clear complexion, the glow and life of her, the vivid darkness of her eyes. He waved his hand and she waved back, just as thousands were waving to each other, those going out to the world's work, those staying behind to the world's work within four walls. Scope he had said he would have to have. Barbara, by the gate, thought of it with gentle irony. She had lived an active life for twenty-two years. What was there for her to do to-day? They had no need of Mary, none whatever, but had her because she; Barbara, must not be seen washing the doorstep or doing any real work. After making out the menu for luncheon and dinner at night, calling at Carters to reprove them about the meat, or sending Mary in her stead, dusting and arranging flowers, there was nothing to do. Mary would be chagrined should she help, even. Scope! And away in little Rimton women were doing everything, working as hard as their men—and she, with nothing to do, felt the wretched nothingness of such futility. Her upbringing by Dan and Sarah had been such as had ingrained a fret against frittering time away. And she was doomed to fritter. Hundreds of thousands frittered time away pleasantly, She— could not.

She walked slowly into the hall.

"Letters, Mrs. Dennison," Mary told her.

"Thanks, Mary."

She took them off the tray.

Rimton! Her heart leaped at the sight of the postmark. Two letters with Rimton post-mark. What a time since she had written to Rimton. She stood, appalled at the thought of what must have seemed to Dan and Sarah neglect on her part. Why had she not written? She pondered with puckered brow. Why? Was it that she had been too happy? No, that did not seem the solution. Rather it had been that all had been lost in Crichie, who was lost in—the Emporium. The world felt to surge back at her, as she held the letters, Crichie to pass into just one person in the world, and not the world in one person—a metamorphosis which a year had brought. He had even forgotten their anniversary. She knew he had. Forgotten the first anniversary! She reached the end of the hall and looked back. The hat-rack stood immutable, an insensate thing. Barbara shivered suddenly. The hall—it always had looked, and did look, different. That morning she and Crichie had almost quarrelled there. If ever there was conflict, she knew it would be there, by the hat-rack, first thing in the morning. Or—was it—was it only that great sprawling, gloomy wall-paper which had come by mistake instead of that they had ordered, had got on her nerves?

She hurried away from the hall.

Rimton.

To think of it—its clear stream, the old bridges, the willows, the white, sun-glistening roads, and of Dan and Sarah and Dave—was to feel yesterday's peace fall on the heart. Of course, she and Crichie had been very happy. She stood, as one looking backwards on it, that year behind them. They had not had one quarrel. That was certainly a feat. Not one quarrel and no bickerings. They were still always profoundly conscious when each entered a room—both of them; Nothing had worn away; They had the same quivering, emotional sense of physical nearness and dearness, that delightful sense of being one flesh, newly-made one. No, nothing had worn away, mused Barbara, nothing had been torn down by passionate conflict of will against will. All was secure. And yet—

"The butcher will want his order, Mrs. Dennison," said Mary, appearing on the threshold, ready to entray the breakfast remains.

Barbara nodded.

"Yes. I'll write it out," she told Mary. "You'd better call and tell them that the meat has been rather stringy lately, We pay top price and ought to get the best. If they can't give it we shall go elsewhere."

Mary almost gaped.

Then she said: "Yes, Mrs, Dennison, I'll call."

Barbara moved into the hall.

She had remembered the hat that had to go to the renovators. She took it from the peg. She eyed the wall-paper with dissatisfaction. Yes, it was certainly getting on her nerves. It howled at one—that paper. Perhaps if she was like Mrs. Peachley, with several children, she would not worry about wallpapers! A smile curved her mouth and her eyes danced—then she recalled that Crichie did not care about children, not for a long time he had said. Still, nothing had worn away—their hands often trembled when touching accidentally, after a whole, long year. They had been very happy. She found herself insisting on it. She walked into the sitting-room and opened Dave's letter. And as she read she was standing back in Rimton, with the stream-lighted meadowlands, the northern dykes with their brambles and leaves and rushes, the sunlit and shadow-dappled roads that swept up to the uplands and moors. And he did not say why he was coming. He was coming for a week, and would they put him up? And Sarah's letter also asked her to "put our Dave up".

Her eyes filled suddenly with warm tears, pleasant tears, which somehow washed the dryness out of them, the aching pain which had throbbed behind them as she had stood in the hall staring at the hat-rack, for a moment, wondering if Goffers would finally make Crichie an automaton who would forget life and love.

Dave would be here on the morrow on the three-thirty into Euston.

She would hear of everybody, hear of the old places, northern names sweet in the ears. Yesterday they had seemed a long way off—yesterday she had stood quite apart, in Crichie's world, lost in it, and this morning she had hurled the curtains back, as though she gasped for air, for the world back again— for all the people in it, which had for a year all been almost forgotten for Crichie, who took the place of them all, who had been her passion, as his was— the Emporium. As she put the letters back into their envelopes she touched the little Swiss bell, which toppled over and jingled. The jingling jarred on her.

"I'm getting nerves," she thought ruefully. "Oh, for a five-miles' tramp over Ridgely Fells."

Chapter Two

Dave Reid had tossed about all night on the feather bed which was his foster-mother's proudest household possession. Years and years it had taken her to gather all those feathers, when they had eaten poultry Dan's customers did not buy, in the hard, early days before he had hit on the great idea of stocking the best potatoes in the dale, even though he had little out of them, and so building up trade on the excellence of one much-wanted line. And then, in thanks for the success that ensued, he had purchased at a sale the picture of Raleigh which still hung over Sarah's dresser.

Barbara had slept in that feather-bed and in that room before she went away. Now Dave slept there and had left the pokey, chill box which was over the outhouse.

Occasionally, as he had tossed about, he had heard Sarah wheezing and coughing in the next room, whilst Dan, tired with fresh air and his "round", which covered many miles of up and down road, slept like a tired ox—slept, as Sarah often told Dave, whilst she coughed fit to burst herself, not, as she would add swiftly, that she blamed him for that, for he had the right to it, the way he worked.

The sound of Sarah's coughing in the dead silence of the night had echoed through the small house, with its old-fashioned wooden window-shutters, which Dan painted green every spring, after the blisterings of summer and the whips of sleet, rain and snow of the long northern winters. About three, he had guessed it to have been, the wind got up and the valley back of the house had been filled with one hollow roar. He had lit the candle and, carrying it to the one unshuttered window in the house, had seen the flickering yellow flame of light reflected, as in the darkness outside— slashed ghostily with a zigzag snow-curtain whirling in all patterns as the wind blew in higher, thinner notes. A real northern blizzard, and no mistake, he had mused, and, half-frozen, had slid back between the blankets, pulling them up round his ears. Then he had lain staring at the shadows on the wall, had tried to count sheep, and, falling to sleep still, had entertained himself picturing the black blankness and void of the moors as they would stretch under that dancing, mirage-like curtain of snow, weaving and unweaving itself every moment, flying zigzag over pools black amidst the moor's blackness. Whilst the storm had gathered in all its force, rising, rising, and he had wondered if Barbara was asleep through it, or if the window-sashes were raffling in that vast, far-away city, and she was recalling how the winds made their wurthering music in this wilderness of the hills. Then, passive, he had listened to the growing crescendo of wind. It had become to him a paean of sonorous music, almost orchestral in its splendour, almost with a rhythm and melody of its own, with the notes of fife and drum, piccolo and pipe, and wailing violins, and long, skirling chords of harmony which baffled description. Dave could picture things best in sound.

At five the storm had abated. By five-thirty it had sunk into hoarse mutterings, then to faint whimpers, a very child in its weakness, and silence had fallen over the snowy earth.

He crept downstairs quietly, stepping two down to avoid the step that creaked, lest he should awaken the old folk, so that Sarah would sleep on till daybreak and

Dan get another hour or two in, for, snow or no snow, he would have to go miles along the roads this day with his fruiterer's cart and the old, brown horse, which had only one fault. Dan called it a fault even whilst he was proud of it. Tommy would let no other horse pass him on the road, if he could help it, when going.

Dave built a great fire half-way up the chimney. He hung the kettle over it, filled to the rim and hooked high on the "rackan" so that the water would not boil away. Then, as Sarah would have .expressed it, he "snidged out".

What a world!

People were sleeping, mundanely sleeping, and missing all this. He felt sorry for them, even as he recognized humorously they would have said that the boot should be on the other leg—that he was a fool to have tramped all this way before daybreak to stand five miles from the cottage on Ridgely Fells's highest point.

Stars hung in the sky, though they were dimming. The Pole Star, the Great Bear, Cassiopeia, burned bright still. The moon had sunk, but a wan, silver glimmer yet haunted the horizon.

And below—

Snow and mist, mist and snow—the hills pale, enchanted hills which made earth look to have taken on the nature of light and to have made the sky darker by contrast. Nothing was distinct. There was a faint light in the east, which told that the sun-god would soon stride through the star-littered meadows of the Heavens. But even under the eastern sky the landscape was vague, glimmering, anarchic.

He stared, face upturned to the glory of the Milky Way. His spirit bounded at the glory of it, the beauty of that path of sun's-worlds in the making. He even forgot he was going to London, an obscure northern player who might make a "hit". He forgot he was on

Ridgely Fells until he lurched, dizzy and drunk with staring into that starry glory, and he laughed to think he might have rolled down the snowy slope below.

Worlds in the making. He felt very small. Even a "hit" would be small. How large the universe was. He wished he knew more about astronomy, but the forge took all his day, and evenings—his 'cello, and he had to talk sometimes to Dan and Sarah.

He had stood star-gazing till his feet were chunk of ice, almost frozen to that bit of Ridgely Fells's snow. He moved along to get warm, walked with storm-lamp in hand, which lit up into fairy beauty, delicate as things of dream, the frost-feathered rushes which rose through billows of snow, the speckled heather and ling beds where they had missed being covered. He saw moving, ghost-like shapes in the distance, passing as over grey, sheeted, shallow waters. He knew them for sheep, creeping over the misted snow.

He had come up to Ridgely Fells via Carbridge, to see the sunrise.

There was going to be no sunrise, such as they called sunrises around Rimton and Carbridge, such as he had once seen with Barbara on this very spot—a rapid change of colours which had been something to remember for a lifetime. Not a sunrise like that. He had never seen one like that before, and doubted if he would again. Ridgely had been slippery with rain and clouded with mist, and he and Barbara had had to climb up almost on hands and knees. Not a sunrise like that—no, and even if it had been, Barbara was not here, so it would have lacked something. They had walked almost half a mile through wet rushes in utter silence, and when they had got back Sarah had gone wild because Barbara's skirt was a dish-clout for wetness. But what a sunrise it had been!

His sensitiveness registered this slower, colder dawn with scarcely less pleasure. Barbara was not here, but he would tell her about it. The wild beauty of it all gripped his senses. The stars were going now. Charley's Wain had lost its "wagon".

Far down in the valley a pin-prick of light came through the mist and snow. They were getting up to milk at Ross Farm. Old Greeby had died last week of double pneumonia, caught through getting "canned up" on market-day and sleeping under a hedge. His horse had dragged the cart, with the pigs in it, back to Ross Farm, without him. This same snow which had fallen on the farm had fallen all the night on his grave. But the light was shining from the windows of Ross Farm, and Nelly Greeby would be jumping into her clothes, getting ready to go out and scratch the shippens free of dung before milking, the heavy, long-bristled brush going scrunch-scrunch-scrunch over the flagged dankness of the shippens. He pictured it as he looked across the valley at that point of light.

When Nelly had been a soft-eyed, rosy-cheeked child (he recalled her rolling her stocking down once to let teacher see the boils on her leg, to explain why she was late on a snowy morning) he had told her he would marry her when he grew up. But—her face had grown long and pale, her eyes hard, and she always scowled at him if ever they passed in the lanes as she was driving the cart, loaded, towards Ross. She walked like a cow and dressed like an Eskimo. How people changed, mused Dave, staring towards Ross. When he came to think of it, everybody seemed to change—but Barbara. And she—she was a creature the most variable he had ever encountered, and she had changed least of everyone he knew. She was like a tune, he mused, with infinite variation, but the melody always the same. Odd, how, when he was thinking, wherever his thoughts began, they always ended in Barbara.

He watched other lights appear in farms set on the hills across. They became winking planets set in that mist and snow that was looking now less like water, more like mist and snow. The light in the east was brightening. Dawn was not being poured' out of a golden jar this morning. Another of Barbara's definitions of a sunrise. Damn! It was odd how he could never escape from Barbara.

No, not out of a golden jar this morning—an endless golden jar which tippled out colours till they overran the sky. Rather, it was like a tide creeping in, wave by wave, very slowly, overflowing the shores of night. Clouds got thinner, lighter, drifted away like smoke. There were no streams of molten silver and gold, no rosy, floating flames, no bursting glimpses of radiance.

But he could distinctly see snow as snow now, not looking like grey water, as the sheep were sheep, not shadow-shapes. The trees that had looked like isles half an hour ago in the mist were trees, The valley was stretching cold and grey with its fields and hedgerows, and had lost its vastness. One could see the intersecting hedges which marked off "Thine" and Mine; even though being snow-covered they were not so distinct as when the bare trees made black lines along the fields. Already it was time to be getting back. He wavered about the way of return, and decided that straight down the face of Ridgely, across the valley, and through the Greebys' farmyard, was as near as any.

He put out his lantern, strung it through his leather waist-belt, and began the descent.

Snow, loosened by his steps, fell on him as he plunged downwards. He brushed it from his shoulders and went on and down. The soft, curved slopes—how beautiful they were, all lapped and lapped about with snow. Icicles, colourless, hung over the stream where he and Barbara had used to slake their thirst in summer-time, on school holidays. And there was a tuft of grass poked through the snow—dank, dark as the beard of some ancient wizard. How all this would have sparkled and glistened had there been the gorgeous sunrise he and Barbara had seen when she had come up to stand on Ridgely Fells for the last time before going to the city and to Crichie. Pagan gods, in robes of purple, had lolled on golden couches that morning, hurling flaming torches at each other, flinging rubied javelins, high above the world.

There was not enough of sunlight visible this, morning to make the trees in the valley fields cast blue shadows—the long, blue shadows on snow which Dave loved.

He stood at the bottom of Ridgely, snow-pads on his boots six inches high, kicked off the pads, and went through the rushes. They were snow fantasies this morning, not rushes; things for fairies this night to gather and dance with under the moon. But to-night he would be far away from all this silence, which was in itself music. He was glad to have this picture to take with him. Barbara would be sure to say: "Have you been up Ridgely lately? What was it like? Tell me."

He tramped on, and was soon on a field-path, kicked off fresh pads against an oak which must have stood there a hundred years. It cast a round, soft, filigreed grey shadow upon the snow under its spreading branches, through which the sky peeped wanly pale.

Ross Farm was plainly a farm now, a grey stone patch, not an opaque black box with a pin-point of light. The light was out. Daylight was cheaper than oil, and economy essential, in these farms with their rough lands.

It was smooth-going now.

He soon reached Ross, and set the dogs off barking. He passed through the gate and scattered its snow as he let the gate slip from his hand. It gave a bang that woke the echoes.

"Trying to knock the place down?" came Nelly Greeby's voice.

Nay, protested Dave. "Ross seems to be standing yet."

A muffled figure, bucket on arm, Nelly Greeby was crossing the yard from the hen-houses. He recalled that old Greeby had always believed in intensive poultry-keeping.

She scowled at him. He could feel rather than actually see the scowl. The high, overhanging eaves of Ross cast their shadows, and there were several great trees in the yard which added to its general gloominess.

"Morning, Nelly!"' Dave greeted the scowl.

"Mornin'," she mumbled back. Then, after a pause, "Oh, it's thee. I hadn't made out who it was in this leet."

"Ay. It's me," answered Dave.

He suddenly realized that though Nelly had lived long year on year at the foot of Ridgely she had probably never ascended it to see either sunrise, sunset, or moon-glory on its wide top that gave view to other hills beyond. Compassion, the compassion of the happy for the wretched, the comfortable for those who have hardships, touched him, ran through him quiveringly. It did not seem long since he and Nelly had got whacked for poor "joggroffy" in the old school-house where the map of Africa hung yellow and dusty over half the class-room wall. He was recalling her rolling down her stocking to explain why it had taken her longer than usual to reach school from Ross through the snow. And the hardships of childhood which had brought her four miles to school through drifts, with boils on her legs, had gone on and on and on, and Nelly Greeby had hardened under it. She stood before him now, scowling at life, a dark shawl crossed over her breast to form waistcoat as well as head-dress, her eyes looking oblique and dark, almost Mongolian—she had always had long eyes, he recalled—under the shadow of the peaked shawl, pulled down to screen her brow from this east wind. There was something almost Mongolian, too, in her aloofness.

"I was sorry to hear your father died so suddenly," Dave told her.

"He could ha' deed afore, an' no loss to us," spoke Nelly, with harsh, simple truth. "He weren't mich good."

Dave grew ever more conscious of a deep, surging pity.

"Eh, Nelly, you shouldn't talk so," he told her.

"It's true," Nelly said stubbornly.

"Well, it may be," he told her, "but I think it hurts folks to think them soart o' thoughts. I wasn't thinking o' your father, Nelly, but of you."

"Oh!"

Her tone told that she was considerably staggered. Then she went on again, as bent on revealing to him how hard she could be.

"I couldn't think naught too crool o' him," she told Dave, aggressively. "Just 'cause he's died doesn't alter th' truth, does it? He were crool, and crool folk make crool folk. He hawf-killed my mother afore he cocked his toes up, an' there's not one o' us childer but bears a mark fro' him, an' hate him though he's stiff an' cowed in the groun'. I could hit my mother for sittin' blitherin' in her chair. I was glad to see him stiff-toed, and I washed him when he was deyd, an' I said to him as I shut his e'en: ' Thear, old devil! There's a bit o' peace for thee at last, an' all as tha's kept fleyd o' thee.' "

Her outburst had taken Dave's breath, but not as she expected. Rather he was astounded that she had opened out to him.

"An' you'll feel very happy, hating him in his grave, Nelly?" he asked gently.

She started back as though he had dealt her a blow.

"That's why I said you shouldn't talk so, think so," he told her. "Hatred harms most those who nurse it. I'll lend you a book called 'Not Guilty', Nelly. Why, I believe I have it in my pocket."

"Tha doesn't need," said Nelly. "I've no time for reading. There's no time for owt here but work. An' I've no time for reading stuff as says you should forgive your enemies, for it'll be summat o' that make, I suppose."

"It doesn't say you should forgive them, Nelly," Dave told her. "It makes you understand that people who don't do right are not altogether to blame."

She hesitated, scowling at him for a moment.

"What's tha want to lend it to me for—really?" she asked suspiciously.

"Well—you see, if you could just stop hating your father, don't you think you'd be happier?" he asked.

She stared at him as he stood holding out the book.

"I don't know what tha means by happiness," she I said, "an' I don't know if I want to be happy. I'd be fleyd o' bein' happy. Once or twice when I've sin folk laughin' till tears run down their cheeks, or heard 'em singin' because they couldn't help it— I've known I'd be fleyd o' bein' happy. I've got used to being miserable. When you're miserable you can bide it an' you've naught to lose. But when you're happy it can be ta'en away. So if that book is to make me happy shove it back in thy pocket." She stood glowering at him.

Dave put the book back into his pocket as she had bidden him.

"Well, good morning to you, Nelly," he called, walking away.

He began to walk more rapidly.

Then—he heard her steps following, and turned.

"Reych it here," she said abruptly. "But tha'll know when tha gets it back. Oh, it's not so many pages in it. I thought it had happen a big lot o' pages."

She stood, the book in her hand.

"No. You'll read it in a few nights, Nelly," he told her encouragingly.

She stood staring at him, then down at the book.

"Does it mean as we haven't to blame folk for what they do?" she asked.

Dave nodded.

"Well," she hurled at him from over her shoulder as she moved away, "if I find I can't forgie yon owd devil after I've read it, I'll not be to blame either, will I?"

And she was gone with the book Dave had lent her, the book he had read over and over by the hearth after hard days at the forge—had read with beechen shadows falling on the sunlit pages on Sundays, and on the moors, lying full-length on the purple heather, with moor-winds cool when all the valleys were enervating with heat, not forgetting, as he read, to lift his head anon and note the silken beauty of a white moth's wings, shining in the sunshine; hearing also, as he read, the cries of the plover, the thin, sad callings of the curlews, wheeling round the heat-hazed skies. Would he get it back, he wondered, a little "moithered" lest he should not, for he had little money for books, "tipping all up" to his foster-mother, who gave him a shilling back out of his wages. With that shilling he had to get strings for his 'cello, new pieces of music, and—well, if he did not get it back, he consoled himself by thinking he knew it almost by heart, and then the turn of the road drove Nelly and the book right out of his thoughts.

For a full mile the road from Carbridge to Rimton was a reel of unfolding magic and beauty. Thick hawthorn hedges on each side were covered with snow, evenly fallen and wonderful. Almost like white coral, mused Dave. He strode down into a dyke and shook a hawthorn-bush above him. A flying snow-shower fell on him, head and shoulders, as he stood there, and he had the childishly delightful feeling of having been able to make a snow-shower. He shook several other little bushes, then desisted. Almost it felt as if he had robbed those little bushes of beauty just to feel like a demi-god who could make a shower of flying snow. How differently the holly and blackberry-bushes had taken the snowfall. There were fluffy, white balls on them, so that they looked like rose- or camellia- bushes. And the dog-rose-trees, which would be all red and white in a few months, had still a few berries left on—black-red against the brightening sky. They, the birds' cupboard-trees, had not held snow at all. There were frozen water-drops on them which were like big beads of colourless glass, like those Barbara had used to sit stringing, given to her by Sarah to keep her tongue from clapping away like a very magpie's, on fire-lit winter gloamings when they had come home from school and were waiting Dan's coming before they had tea, and running to the door every ten minutes to see if they could see his cart-lamp swinging like a yellow star through the mists that lay over everything like vapour.

He saw something dangling, and—palm! All in this world of whiteness, silver, silken grey palm! He broke a tiny sprig and fastened it in his coat and went along, drinking in the pictures of these northern, snow-filled dykes where faded winter grasses and rushes and leaves of the evergreens all8glinted as having been dipped in frost-boxes. The stone-heap by the road, there for road-mending when the weather was better, was turned into geometrical studies, as the projecting stones had caught the snow, whilst others had been thrown clear of it. He had once tried to study geometry. But life was too short. What things there were to learn if one had only time. But he loved the forge for all that, the forge with its dusky shadows and warm, rosy lights, and the flying sparks and the roar of the bellows. So, musing, he walked on.

He hurried at that thought of the forge, for Willie Barnes was a heavy sleeper and might not have arrived.

But when he reached the smithy, he found Willie had arrived, the fire going, the smithy in full working order. He went in, giving final directions to Willie, who kept saying: "Ay, ay, I shall manage, Dave; I'se sure manage," hands thrust deep in his pockets, and the strut showing in his very walk how proud he was to be left in charge of the forge, all on his own, whilst Dave went "playin' in Lunnon".

"Well, I'll soon be back," said Dave, but whether he was addressing Willie or the smithy, was not very plain.

"It's eight o' t'clock," said Willie. "I'se manage, Dave."

Dave felt as though Willie were pushing him out of the smithy. He felt a reluctance to leave it—a sudden passionate joy in everything in it, the sounds of it, the odours, the bird-songs that trickled in from the outdoor world, the sighings of the trees that stood close by it, the murmuring of the stream that clacked behind it when all was still, ere he quitted in the evenings. But—he pulled himself up for a very fool. He was only going to London for a week. In seven days he would be back in the glow and roar of the smithy. The snow would be melted by then. The stream would be brimful with snow-waters. The birds would be back, many of them. Nothing would stop just because he was away in London. And even in a week, spring would have begun to uncurl tree-buds into leaves. But it was odd how he lingered, how he felt reluctant to leave it, as though he might be leaving it for ever.

Barbara would have called it "something telling him", he mused. He thrust the thought off. What an idea! Short of being killed in a train-smash, he should certainly be back in a week. And—it seemed a long time since he had seen Barbara. Perhaps if it had not been for the thought of seeing Barbara he might not have gone, he pondered. Decidedly a long time since he had seen Barbara, and if he missed his train, she would be waiting at Euston.

"Be careful with Wilson's horse if he brings it," he told Willie. "It's mettlesome, an' has only been shoon once before."

Willie, hands in pockets, was strutting still about the forge.

"I'se manage," he said confidently.

Dave went out. He strode away to the cottage Sarah was standing in the doorway, her brow anxious, her eyes shaded with her hand as she looked up the road, for snow-glare always bothered her eyes.

She gave him an irate, affectionate glance, and eyed him from top to toe and then looked into his face.

"Tha's been up Ridgely?" she inquired.

Dave nodded assent.

"I guessed as mich. An' tha left the kettle on, an' there's a hole burnt in it. I've had that kettle twenty years."

"But, I—it hung a long way off th' fire," said Dave.

"Aye, tha fool. But two hours with a fire under it fit to roast a bull would boil a boiler dry, never mind a kettle. Never mind! It's done now, and it's just a good old has-been! Thy breakfast is ready, an' tha'rt not goin' to have too mich time to catch thi train, an' whilst tha'rt eatin' it, well, I've told a lot o' folk tha'rt goin' to stay with our Barbara—and there's a lot o' news to take."

Dave sat patiently down to breakfast, after taking off cap and coat.

Sarah pulled herself up in a very deluge of news which had to go to Barbara.

"Dave, there's tears in thy e'en," she said, perturbed. "What's up wi' thee?"

"I was only thinking," said Dave, and stopped.

"What?"

"If I feel havin' to leave this place for seven days, what Barbara must have felt leaving it for good," he said.

Sarah looked at him.

"Get out, tha goat!" she ejaculated. "Women leaves everything and goes anywhere to be with their fellahs. When she hasn't written mich, I've said: 'Barbary's all right. Barbary's happy.' "

Dave stared down at his plate.

He was thinking of Barbara—long ago—trudging with him from daylight to dark, and coming home with blistered, raw feet, blood on her stockings, and never a word, and when Sarah had railed at her she had said: "I only felt the pain—just now." She was a creature of slow reactions. He would rather, much rather, she had written a lot at first, and then gradually written less. He would have been surer she was happy. And he liked to think of the child with moon-fair tossed hair, threading glass beads, and the girl who had romped up Ridgely Fells with him, and the woman who had stood there bidding the Fells good-bye on that sunrise morning, wet to the waist with walking through dripping rushes, as happy. Only—what was happiness? Surely—just peace. Calm days that went by without any need for one to ask oneself "Am I happy?" Such days were Dave's now. He hoped such were Barbara's also.

Chapter Three

Rimton, such of it as was not engaged in the foundries and corduroy factories and dingy sewing-shops in the town (for the country must needs get its bread by leaving the country), waited at its little doors and windows to see Dave Reid go by on his way to the train that was to take him to Lunnon. More general information had been compiled in little houses and inns all along the valley about that "hub of the universe" during the past few weeks than the inhabitants had troubled to collect even when kings were being crowned. David Reid going to London meant that Rimton was going to London, represented by David Reid. Those millions in London would learn that Rimton had an existence, was alive and kicking, even if it was not on the big maps.

They had surmised all Dave could possibly have to eat when he got there, where he would go, and it was noised about that he was taking an evening suit. The consensus of opinion was that Dave would look rare and well in an evening suit, and this was based on the guess that a man who looks somebody in the rough dress of a blacksmith, with rolled-up shirt-sleeves and sweat pouring down his face, will certainly look somebody in an evening suit. Old Bodey, whose house stood near the pump, had stated that the Prince of Wales would not look a patch on Dave Reid in his evening suit, which had led to "barging" in the inn, where he had made the statement, as to what constituted treason. Whereupon old Bodey had banged his fist on the inn table, making the glasses rattle, and had declared that treason or no treason, Dave Reid would knock spots off royalty itself when he put on an evening suit, even if it was a borrowed one. And Josh Cranshaw, agreeing with him, had "filled 'em up" all round, and the subject had trailed off into a wrangle about the exact date on which the Great Fire had taken place in Lunnon, and then into a surmise as to how people could afford to live there, since there was really nothing doing there in the way of producing anything, whereas in places like Rimton the people were certainly adding to the world's wealth. And Josh Cranshaw had said that people had more sense in Lunnon—they spent wealth—and so in places like these they were helping to keep the whole show going. After which they had gone home to sleep, whilst Dave, troubled with the first restlessness of his life, had tossed about and gone off to stand at Ridgely Fells, as though he, too, were saying farewell to it as Barbara had done a year ago.

Now he was really off, walking through the village to the train.

Schoolchildren, on their way to school, gaped at him, Sarah walking on one side, Dan on the other side of him, with faces which told that they were proud and had the right of it. And little doors opened. Women looked out who recalled Sarah Farmer bringing both Dave Reid, Sarah's sister's boy, and Barbary Delling, child of a sailor friend of Dan's drowned at sea, through the village on such another morning as this, two parentless bairns, one with fair long hair hanging over a shabby red coat, and the other with brown curly hair and a cap too small. Not that it always turned out well to take other folk's children even when you could have none of your own. But here was the guerdon. Dave Reid was going playing to Lunnon. There was no disputing it. And Barbary had married well. Sarah certainly looked proud this morning.

"Mornin', Sarah," she was greeted.

"Mornin'," answered Sarah.

But she was a nipper, Sarah was, said a few over their brooms, when the procession had passed. They might have had a taxi take them down to the station on such an occasion. But there was Dave walking, carrying his 'cello, and Dan carrying Dave's box and changing it from one hand to the other, and mopping his forehead, and saying: "Go on, I'm comin'. I'll catch you up."

Once, when Sarah walked ahead and he and Dave were behind, Dan said in a whisper: "Don't stop over a week, lad, for I don't know what I'll do without thee. Shoo's terrible bad to get on wi', Sarah is."

And when Dan dropped behind and Dave and Sarah were walking ahead, Sarah said plaintively:

"Come back to t'day lad. Dan, he grows grumpier an grumpier, an I'll not ha' much comfort white tha'rt away."

And Dave, who was the confidant of both their little complainings of each other and who knew how fine they both were and how the light of life would go out for whichever one of the two was left behind the other, for all their little grumbles to him, heard them and smiled inwardly with genial humour even whilst listening to a blackbird who was fluting a roundelay on the topmost branch of a tree that was rooted amongst the hill-side bracken, standing sere and brown through the snow. There was a joyful, surprised note in the blackbird's song as it rang over the road. It was just as though the blackbird swinging on the bough of that tree had discovered that spring was really coming, the winter almost gone. Or so Dave heard it, lending his feelings to the blackbird.

"Aye, father, I'll get back in a week," Dave had told Dan, in the same whisper in which Dan had spoken to him.

"Aye, mother, I'll not stop over the time. I'll ha' to get back to the forge, you know," he had told Sarah.

And their hearts had grown warmer yet, fuller still that he was going away from them for seven long days, all that way, when they heard his rare "father" and mother". For Dave and Barbary had both been told to call them just "Dan" and "Sarah", since they were not really their parents. Barbary had said: "Good-bye, mother," when she was going away, despite Sarah's renunciation of the title, wishing the children to be true to whatever little memory they had of their own blood parents.

"An'—train-lunches is dear, Dave," Sarah warned him. "I've given thee ten shillings, so as tha'll not feel pinched, but there's no reason why tha should be extravagant an' spend it all in a week. I want thee to feel tha's plenty in thy pocket, but if tha brings any back, it'll not be amiss."

Dave nodded, carrying his 'cello, and smiling ahead, perhaps at the trees that he always loved, the two pines that seemed to lean together over the wall-top on the bank that went down to the valley on the left of them, as to the right rose the sheer hill-side where the heather had climbed down from the top. He had certainly never felt any penury. Food, shelter, clothes, his shilling a week for music and 'cello strings, the hills and moors and meadowlands had been enough. But if he was tickled at Sarah's sermons against his extravagance if he spent the whole of the ten shillings whilst in London, he gave no sign saving that smiling glance ahead at the trees. Sometimes they looked black, those pines, and without a hint of colour, when the sky loured grey, but this morning there was a faint blue in the sky, little curling sunlit clouds. The pines looked green, richly, duskily green, those pines of which Barbara had once said dreamily: "Dave, they are married, like Dan and Sarah. Can't

41

you hear them chunnering at one another?" It had been a windy day that day when Barbara had said that, and the pines had seemed to be "chunnering" at one another, when Dave had listened. And when next day they had passed, on a blue-and-white day and all was still, Barbara had said: "They're agreein' to-day, Dave, and Mrs. Pine has put her best bonnet and cloak on," and he had looked up to see the green attire of Mrs. Pine.

"For there's really no need o' train-lunches," added Sarah, much as though Dave had asked for a train-luncheon, "an' good home-made parkin in that box an' ham sandwiches, an'—drat, I've forgotten to put the biscuits in, after all."

"Well, never mind," said Dave.

He knew quite well what had happened. Sarah had made up her mind that sandwiches and parkin were enough for a train journey. She did not want to starve him, but she was certainly averse to bursting him. This nearness of Sarah's had been a rock on which she and Dan had often struck. Dave had early found out how to surmount it. He helped himself from the larder if ever he felt hungry, and knew Sarah would never ask who had taken this or that. Her logic always failed at that point—her logic that more people dug their graves with their teeth than perished of starvation.

"It'll be yeasier walkin' back than it is goin' " said Dan, lugging the box along. "The plough'll ha' been an' cleared th' snow away for the schoolchilder to walk hoam to their dinners."

"And it'll be easier without that box," agreed Dave. "Give it here, Dan. Carry this 'cello."

So Dan carried the 'cello, the 'cello that Dave was to play in London, and looked so proud that if Dave had not heard him say once that for his part he thought fitting a horse a good shoe that would not slip in frost or thaw was of more real value to the community than scraping a bow over some bits of catgut, no matter what noises a man could get out of the strings, he would not have been able to credit the fact that Dan could look so proud and yet have such an opinion. Dave looked at Dan as he carried the 'cello and minded where he set foot on the snowy road. Even Dan looked different this morning. Perhaps it was because Dave so seldom saw him "dressed up". And not since Barbara had been married had Dan worn a head-covering that showed his ears. Perhaps, mused Dave, that was why Dan looked different. One got used to seeing him in the cap with the tabs that went over his ears and which he wore even in the house often if the weather was particularly cold. All the world somehow did look different this morning, and there was a restless leap in his blood and yet a kind of sadness, too, as though things were changing, a sense that nothing was fixed, that unexpected new things could come into people's lives and lift them out of old ways and places, even when they had not sought any change. For here was he going to London, when he would really sooner have stayed home and been looking after the forge and playing in the evenings just to please himself and the old folk. Only, well, it had been the only way he could ever get to London. The fee he got would pay his fare there and back, and his earnings at the forge. It had been the only way he could afford to go up and see Barbara, since he could not do on less than a shilling a week for music and strings and books.

They saw a sweep of moorland where the snow had already melted under this almost spring sunshine as they took the bend of the road which brought the town in sight, the town where the sunlight struggled through smoke. Rust-red looked that bit of moorland, topping the landscape, as it stood in its dress of old bracken, and bents where the snow had melted and run into its pools, warmly glowing under the sunshine. When he came back the snows would be gone. They would start "sweeling" on the moors, burning away great patches of old heather and the bracken, to give the young stuff a chance to come up, and leaving big cleared places on the moor which a few years would see grown over, the new feeding-places of grouse, the new nesting-places of plovers, and dew would drip from the bell-heather and white moths glint in the sun as they went over the new ling, feathery green and bright over these fired places. Sweeling! A grand name that. Surely folk who had never seen the moors ablaze—long, quivering lines of flames that shone through the mists of the spring and burned all night sometimes and on into the next day, getting too much of a hold and having to be fought sometimes— surely anyone who did not know of these country things, if they just heard the word "sweeling" ought to know what it meant, mused Dave. Could not one hear the crackle and snap of the heather ablaze, in that word "sweeling"? He was glad he was not staying long, that he would be back when sweeling began, when he would lay his 'cello aside, even, and go out, and see on the moor-top the flickering, rosy flames, and catch, when the wind blew in that direction, the faint tang of the scent of the heather. Then he heard Sarah talking, and realized that if he did not wake up and answer her, instead of consoling himself for going away by the thought of all he would see when he came back, she would get aggrieved. Odd how he had got the feeling of reviewing how happy he had been here, just as those departing for ever do.

"I had thought there'd happen have been a family on the road by this," Sarah was saying. "But I expect if there had been she'd have let me know. But folk isn't like they were. They're more for pleasuring an' enjoying life, an' not struggling away wi' bairns. But the dolls that lass had, an' the way she talked to 'em, an' dressed 'em, an' nossed 'em, an' sung to 'em, like they were wick, but I expect she'd have tolled me if there'd been aught o' t'sort."

Dave realized that she was talking of Barbara. It gave him almost a shock.

Barbara had gone away, but until, this moment, engrossed with his own life and its interests, he had scarcely visualized her as a married woman, even whilst he knew she was one. There was Sarah talking of Barbara as a bearer of children, an idea which thrust on him the fact that Barbara was flesh and blood, and in the natural course of things would bring flesh and blood into the world. A bearer of children. He had merely thought of her as having gone away, of being moving about in some other place, whistling round it, lilting her sudden snatches of song, watching the rain on other windows, hearing the wind blow between houses instead of in these open places, setting Crichie's meals as she had used to set his, and had not fully grasped till this moment that marriage for Barbara would mean pain and care and the burdens other women bore, and the ageing and the sorrowing, and the passing of care-free youth. He had lived in the same house with her, from childhood to womanhood, and living near to her she had always been to him the companion of his walks, the one who exchanged thoughts with him, the one who could safely be sent to "talk our Dave round" when he was grieved by some misunderstanding, for the simple reason that she never troubled to talk him round, but merely said: "Dave, if you glump in that corner any longer, I'll cry—I will," which had dispensed with a lot of unnecessary argument.

"Doesn't ta hear what I'm saying?" asked Sarah, with asperity.

He nodded, staring at the white road which glistened in the sunshine now, shone ten thousand jewels in every stretch of it, and which had upon it the long blue shadows from the overhanging trees they were passing under—the long blue shadows on snow which he loved. But he scarcely noted them. A vague troubled jealousy was shooting him through. It had not stirred within him when Crichie Dennison had come and taken her away. It stirred in him now when Sarah had spoken of Barbara as a bearer of children. It worried him with the idea that his Barbara had been taken away—to grow into some other Barbara, who would forget all the hours they had had together on these wind-swept heights, watching the sunsets and the sunrises and seeing the stars swing into the big spaces. It was as though for the first time he saw Barbara's marriage as—a gulf—a wide, impassable gulf, with him on one side and her on the other, with him loving still all the things they had loved together, and with Barbara doomed, as a woman, to forget she had lived before she met Crichie Dennison, and live only in Crichie's life, in Crichie's house, in the memories she would string with Crichie till she was old and wrinkled and white-haired.

"I should have stopped it," was the tumult and cry in his heart. "I should not have let her go."

"Well, if tha hears me, tha might look like it," said Sarah. "Dave, when tha gets studying, tha looks daft."

Dave said nothing. He felt daft.

He was walking the last mile of his way to the station, on his way to the train to see Barbara, and he did not know now whether he wanted to go on and catch the train and see Barbara. Should he see Barbara? Even if he went, would he see Barbara? Would she be just the same Barbara, or would already some of the joy he had seen on her face, when the wind was blowing the cotton into moon-white loveliness, have passed?

Would he see Barbara, his Barbara or Crichie's Barbara? He felt like a man who had been robbed and had gone on eating and drinking and sleeping and playing his 'cello and toiling in the smithy a whole year without knowing it.

And the fact that she had written but rarely to them at home—of course, it was her home, he thought savagely—did not that bear out the bitter truth that Barbara had not only left them bodily but left them spiritually, that this place and all it had been to her was fading in her mind, -and that this gulf would grow wider and wider, and some day she would bring the children to see it and say to them: "I used to live here." Used to! It was the first time he had realized that for Barbara it must now be passing into what would seem a past existence—divided from her not by death, but marriage.

"I'll ha' the box now, Dave," said Dan. "Thee change back to th' 'cello."

"Nay."

He hitched the box on his shoulder stubbornly.

"But I'd sooner. This has cramped my hand an' it's nearly as heavy as the box, and a lot more cumbersome."

Agonized as he was, he did not fume about the interruption which meant an interruption in his thoughts—the thoughts he wanted to get clear before he reached the station and was actually speeding to the city.

He took the 'cello and Dan took the box, pleased with his adroitness in having pleaded a cramp to get the heavier load back again. Though it was quite true, he had a bit of cramp, Dan told himself. As he held the 'cello to him, for the first time Dave almost hated it. If he had not been absorbed in playing, he would have seen that Barbara was growing up. Why, he could have had her perhaps himself all his life,

47

by marrying her himself. She would always have remained the same Barbara then, and his Barbara.

"Dave, arta ill?" asked Sarah anxiously.

"Nay, nay."

She looked at him.

"Tha's ate too mich o' that sausage at breakfast," she told him. "And I got it at a fresh place, an' sausage is always a mystery-bag."

"Happen I did," said Dave.

If they would only stop talking, only leave him quiet, so that he could think.

"And there was a case o' ptomaine poisoning at Carbridge last week," said Sarah. "Tha'll look weel if tha'rt ta'en ill in Lunnon."

"I'm as right as a clock," said Dave.

"Why, tha'rt right sick-lookin'," avowed Sarah. "Tha wants to see thysel'. And' now I'se be wondering all the time, till I hear fro' thee, if them sausages was a' reight. Dan, doesn't he look sick?"

Dan looked at him anxiously.

"Tha looks a bit white round the gills," he told Dave. "Dave, lad, if tha art ill, best wait for the next train. There's no hurry. It'll only be another hour or two's delay an' tha'll get in by tea-time, an' have an hour before tha's to go to the theayter."

"I'm as right as can be," answered Dave.

"Well," said Sarah, after a little while, "tha' looks a bit better. Happen it'll pass off. The colour's comin' back to thy face a bit. It'd be better if tha can catch this train because tha'll ha' time for a rest afore tha goes to th' theayter."

Dan stopped suddenly and slapped Dave on the shoulder.

"It's just thinkin' o' a' those folk tha's to play to," he said. "Chuck it, lad! Just think: 'I'm playin' at hoam for you two owd fools'."

"Speyk for thysel'," chipped in Sarah, resenting being called a fool.

"'With the wind wurthering outside an' the fire blazin' on the hearth, and they're bearin' me two hundred miles away, an' watchin' the clock for when my turn's on.'"

"Well, I wish it was over," confessed Dave.

He saw with relief that they were near the town. Never had he been so glad to sec the roofs and chimneys of the smoke-grey town. To sit back in the train, with quietness, and get calmed down again from this shock he had received—the shock of realizing that Barbara was lost to him for ever, when by a simple thing like marriage he could have always had her, to journey with him to see sunrises on Ridgely Fells, to talk to her as he could talk to no one else in the world, to listen to her as no one else in the world would listen to her, to hear her whistle, almost like a flute for. sweetness, accompanying his 'cello, just as the fit took her, or to lift his head and see her, hand under cheek, silent, looking at him and the 'cello, as he had seen her looking so often, caressing him and the 'cello with her gaze as though they were indivisible in her thoughts of them.

"I wouldn't wait at the station. It's cold. You'll happen get cold," he told Dan and Sarah.

Their vociferous protests met him.

"Nay, we'll see the train off," they spoke together.

And then they linked fingers and wished and laughed at their own childish folly.

Well, Dave knew what they had wished. As they had spoken together, they had wished together, and their desire was for his success. With a little pang he realized that this was the goal he had told Barbara of when they sat in the heather, eating bread and cheese on Ridgely Fells in summer-time, as children. He was going to play a fiddle on a stage, and it did not matter very much, for she might have changed, and it might not matter much to her, who would be engrossed with other and weightier matters pertaining to her husband's success, to the house, to all this new life which had ended the old. And if it did not matter to Barbara it did not matter to him.

Fool, he called himself savagely. He had let her go, and had only now awakened to that fact. He ought to have married her himself. Then she would always have been there. He would always have been able to lift his head when playing by the hearth and see her there, listening, with that shining, still look in her eyes, to her favourite passages, or reading, feet on a stool, tired after the day's work, his playing not stopping her from reading when she felt like it, hearing it, as he had well known, when she had so wanted to hear it, as the wind blowing or the rain falling. And by the forge—why, even the forge would have been dearer. Every flying spark would have seemed merrier, brighter, and the vim of his hammer-strokes greater, because they would have been flying, have been struck for Barbara's bread as well as his own.

And if she had groaned for the bearing of one child —it would have been only one, for he could not have borne to have more come between them to take any of Barbara's affection away from him. But he had been slow, terribly slow. Barbara was gone. Already she might be changed, changing, since that which folk called life, meaning pain and sorrow and conflict, might have touched her spirit. She might not even ask him when he was last up Ridgely Fells and what they had looked like, as he had foolishly thought she would only that morning as he had stood watching the stars pale over a glimmering world.

"Thar't laggin', lad. That 'cello's heavy," said Dan.

Dave nodded.

"Just a bit. But we'll soon be there now," he told Dan.

He stared at the last bit of rust-gold and grey moorland before the wall shut it out, then the houses that were approaching. It still had the same beautiful colouring, but somehow it looked less fair than before he had thought of Barbara being lost to them, to him. He knew the change for one within him. Agony touched him. Things which had brought him unchanging delight were touched with change. Some milestone was left behind on life's road, which was altering, touched with human pain, human longing, human desire to have kept with him always one creature which would not have changed to him, and to whom he could have been for ever the same. And they would not have even "chunnered" at each other, as Barbara had said the pines did, like Sarah and Dan. Tune and harmonies they would have been, Barbara and he, whilst the world and its people had gone on being chopped and changed. But did such people ever marry? The thought crossed his mind vaguely whilst his heart was a wrack of emotions. Emotion answered: "Yes, sometimes, but not often." He wondered why, if it was so rare, why such people did not marry more often. Was it, could it be, that mere happiness was not the end of life, that there were in it bigger things than happiness? And, as Nelly Greeby had asked, what was happiness?

"Yesterday, when I never asked myself what happiness was," thought Dave. "Yes, that was happiness. When there was only joy in work, in the dawn, in the sunset, in all little sounds of the earth. Yesterday, when the thought of her was enough, whilst to-day I have realized that she is gone. Happiness, therefore, is a thing apart from deep emotions. I shall reason myself out of all this."

He set himself to keep the old folk in good humour, to make their faces crinkle with laughter, a jester who heard their laughter as from a long way off, jesting whilst his heart was torn with the thought that he was going all that way and might not see Barbara at all, even though he sat at her table and Crichie's and ate with them.

The scream of the train-whistle sounded from the tunnel half a mile away. Then the dull click of the signal going down.

When the train panted in Dave climbed up into the carriage, lugging the 'cello, the 'cello he almost hated now, for had he not been so taken up with it he would surely not have let Barbara go away, have seen that she was going away, and stopped it.

Dan was shaking his hand, and:

"Take it. Blow thyself out on the train, Dave. Have thy lunch on the train, like a gentleman. It's only once in a lifetime happen tha'll be goin' to Lunnon. Sarah, she's a poverty-stricken mind an' counts th' brass too mich. Nay, do take it, lad. An' don't bring a penny o' it back."

Dave took it, and Dan beamed and cleared his throat and stepped down on the platform, saying to Sarah, who was looking at them: "Aye, lass, I'm comin'. I was just telling him not to miss seein' the beaf-eaters."

Dave shot the window down and looked out at them until he could see them no more. They had grown less and less, faded, and were blocked out from his sight. Was that the way of life? he pondered. Did everything grow less and less and fade, blocked out? Was that why, in the ultimate end, people were glad to lie back on their pillows, bearing the last of life's pain, and say to those who stood round weeping: "Gie me up. I'm fain to go"? So it had been when the beloved master, who had taught him all he knew, had lain panting. Was all this life a fevered dream, restless, pursuant of happiness, and the spirit foiled of any happiness which remained with one? Was all life, therefore, but the proving to the passionate pilgrims after a joy that should remain, the transitory nature of man's existence, the smallness of his importance, the childlikeness of his wanting always to keep something so that at the ultimate end, tired and spent, he would loose his hold on life that had brought pang after pang of disappointment, and say: "Take it. Make me nothing, calm nothing at the centre of nothingness, void, where I can feel no more "?

Standing by the window, he looked out on the flying landscape.

He knew it was something he would not know until the end of things.

And perhaps—wild joy rushed up in him at the thought—Barbara would not have changed. Perhaps, well, he had got rather unsettled since this engagement had been proffered to him. Perhaps all this he was feeling was just nerves. And he had got a chill. It had been bitterly cold up on Ridgely. He was conscious of a feeling of rawness on the chest. Barbara would perhaps not have changed. If not, it meant that he had not lost her. There were only a few hours now before he saw her. He sat down and took a book from his pocket, but found he could not read.

Chapter Four

Dave realized that he was getting near London. Back views of its houses met his gaze. It looked dingy, smoke-engrained, straggling, nondescript. He saw dingy clothes hanging out in dingy yards, not like those that blew, bleaching in sunlight and wind, on Rimton tops against a blue sky, or with the wind roaring in them till it tore the pegs off the line and sometimes bits of the garments with the pegs on the wild winter days, or which hung out even in frost to come off the lines stiff as boards and go inside to be thawed and dried off. And not like those which hung out in Carbridge, which was bigger, but still hung its washing across the main street, carters going through it to the moorland villages having to knock on the doors and ask respectfully: "Missis, will you prop your washing higher till I've got this horse under?" There the washing was a triumphant bunting. Here it looked what it was—an evident misery. How could people live here, jammed in these boxes? How could they breathe? It stirred Dave's wonder. Little bits of the book he had read were jumbling in his mind even as he looked out on his first sights of London, vivid flashes from "The Martyrdom of Man", wherein, like a glowing fresco, fresh with the colours of life, the panorama of ancient life from Egypt to Carthage had stretched before him, to the chunk-chunk-chunk of train-wheels rattling on the rails, over valleys and through rocks, roaring as it went over the high places. He wanted to be unmoved when he met Barbara, so that it would not matter even if she were changed. It had been silly of him to think she ought not to change. He had read of eternal change, infinite progression, and how could there be progress without change? Why, change was Life as well as Death. Those calm days of his which had gone by, happy in work, ever the same, had been existence— calm, delightful existence. This restless pain which had touched him was Life, which changed people and developed them. They were born to be changed. They were born to suffer. Joy calmed one. Pain disturbed, changed, developed. He saw it now, after having read from this book. And if cities which had stood as though imperishable had passed away as though they had been bubbles on Time's river-flood, why should he have wanted to keep Barbara unchanged and ungrowing, just because he loved her? That was to wish her the impossible. Why, he had changed even as he had walked down the road and even as he now sat in the train reading a book new to him. He understood now what the old Greek had meant whose epigram had met his gaze in a paper Sarah had got wrapped round a cauliflower Dan had brought home. "Life is a becoming." Yes, it was an ever-changing thing in which, as one's skin was supposed to shed itself in the course of seven years, minds shed bits of the "I" away and became some other sort of "I".

The train was slowing now. His heart was beating faster. To calm himself he set himself deliberately to call up the series of impressions he had gathered from this wonderful book. But it was difficult. He managed it only brokenly. The train was going slower still. By a violent effort at concentration he was recalling the book's pictures. Priests chanting in dim temples, people feasting and merry-making under a sun (which had since set how many thousand thousand times?) to celebrate the rising of the Nile. Emperors in their pavilioned splendours; slaves in the market-places; captives of war building pyramids, whipped by cruel whips, the ropes that reined them together biting into their flesh as they pulled, the blood beating in their ears and surging, perhaps, in their hearts, in hatred and rebellion at the futility of it all as they dragged on, with bent heads, asking themselves: "Were we born for this only?" Generations, with their "high" and "low" swept away like sand and covered with the desert-sand, and over their passing the quivering sunlights of the sky that was also changing all the time, symbolic of Time's mosaic globe revolving against the vastness of Eternity. He called the pictures up as he had memorized them to the chunk-chunk-chunk of those wheels bearing him to London, this London which might pass as Babylon and Tyre had passed, leaving only, perchance, a few stones, just as the older civilizations had passed, the desert taking all but those pyramids—a pile of mocking stones to kings who had passed as inevitably as their slaves—or, if one chose to look at it that way, the monumental memorial obelisks to the agonies of wasted lives under a sun which was ever on the wane, and which would in time, however long, cease to warm the earth and its multitudes, all growing dark, cold, lifeless, the earth a piece of dark matter revolving peopleless in space, as though its joyous and sorrowing billions had never been.

Slower, ever slower, ran the train's wheels.

He believed; having philosophized all the earth into its ultimate end—Nothingness, that he would not be moved at all when he stepped down on the platform if Barbara greeted him with just the casual, pleased air one might expect of one who would naturally look importantly down at all petty past existence which had not held Crichie.

And, believing it, he stepped out when the train had stopped, first carrying the box labelled "Passenger from Rimton to London" and dumping it on the platform. After which he went back and lifted the 'cello from the rack.

She might not have come. He stood with the box and the 'cello, everybody pouring past him, hearing the echoes reverberating under the vastness of the glassed roof.

"Taxi?" inquired a porter.

Dave shook his head. People were still jostling past him and away. What a vast place it was.

And could some modern musician turn all these echoes of rushing humanity, as they floated up to this dim glass roof, into music, make a sonata of it or a fugue? Yes, he believed a fugue could be made of it. How much would a taxi cost to Barbara's? Perhaps he had better take one. It would save having to stop strange people and bother asking them how to get there by tube.

"Dave!"

She was there, by his side, with that still, shining look in her eyes, the emotion quivering in her voice as she spoke, the old impetuous rush in her movements, the old canna-like silken lightness in the shining hair puffed out a little each side of her hat.

"Barbara! I thought you'd perhaps not be able to come."

"I've been here half an hour helping the train along, feeling I was standing behind pushing it," she told him laughingly. "Oh, how handsome you've grown, Dave."

She made the observation with surprise.

"Why, you're heaps handsomer than Crichie," she said, her face expressing the inward gasp at this great discovery. "Now what shall we do with this luggage? You could have a porter carry it to the tube. It's only just across."

Dave followed the direction in which she pointed.

"But you'd be unhappy at the 'cello being carried," she added. "Afraid of its getting broken."

"I'll carry it myself," Dave told her.

"Do in Rome as the Romans do," Barbara chaffed him. "People in London don't carry anything if they can pay for it to be carried. I suppose it's seemed a long journey? Are you tired? You must be. Dave, we'll take a taxi. That'll be best. And I'll pay for it."

"Nay, Barbara—"

"Oh, Crichie gives me lots of pin-money," she told him cheerfully. "Oh, how good it is to see a face from home again. Yes, we'll taxi. Then you can tell me what Ridgely is looking like. I read there had been snow. But that was last night. You won't have been up. You'd be sleeping—"

"I was up there at six this mornin—"

Barbara flew away from him. She went over to a taxi and spoke to the driver. The box was lifted in with the driver. The 'cello and Barbara and he were together, and the taxi was moving.

It was only as Dave realized that it was moving that he realized also that they had met without shaking hands, without Barbara giving him one of her hugs, or the funny pat on his coat-sleeve, familiar to him I since their earliest days. Something had changed. But it was not the change he had feared.

They were rolling along in the taxi, the 'cello standing between them, and it was as though they were going through the silences of Ridgely Fells valley, each happy because the other was there, yet unobtrusive of each other's delights in it all. They had met without shaking hands, and had looked at each other like spirits who met after an absence, who had been quite content just to see each other. It was a change, but it was nothing strange. It was as though they had been so glad to see each other they had forgotten even the outward expression of the warmth of feeling each had felt, almost as though it was so secure, so eternal, there had been no need for the expression of it.

"Tell me about Ridgely," Barbara was saying.

Dave moved the 'cello to one side. In the dim taxi they were moving under a dim city sky, amidst other vehicles, which flew past them in a way that made Dave wonder. And, curiously watching the speedometer register the fares, he was yet far away on Ridgely Fells, describing it as he had seen it, and Barbara was leaning forward with shining eyes and yet was following him step by step, over the snow, watching the stars pale, seeing the lantern-rays light up the frosted, feathery rushes, hearing the crackle of the ice by the stream where they had used to drink.

"I can't properly grasp you're here yet," she said almost breathlessly.

He noticed the yellow blurs of lights through the greeny-grey atmosphere. And how the fog made the eyes smart. It felt to fill the taxi. Up on Ridgely this very moment there would be white mists, swooping the length and breadth of it, and under the mist the white snow, crystalline, untrodden saving only by his feet that dawn or the feet of the shepherd-farmers who had come up later to count the sheep, dogs barking at their sides.

"Well, I am," Dave told her.

And, contrary to being glad that he would be back in seven days, seven short days, as when he had stood in the red light of the forge that morning, he was thinking ruefully that in seven days he would have to return.

"That's Goffers's Emporium. Crichie works there," Barbara informed him.

He saw the yellow glare of a great, lighted, three-storied building—shops with blurred colours which ran into each other, the fog between the taxi and the windows.

And then they were talking of Ridgely again, and the lanes along which he had come all covered with snow that morning, and the larches that would soon be coming green, and of the blackbird that had sung as he and Sarah and Dan walked to the station.

"Yes. It's all the same," said Barbara in a tone that told of her relief that all was the same, that nothing had changed, that the grasses and rushes were still on Ridgely.

"Just the same," Dave told her. "Barbary, how do you manage to Eve away from it all? How do you breathe here?"

His gaze was on the great silver-fox fur round her throat, and, as he waited for her answer, which he imagined was long in coming, he recalled her in a rat-tailed rabbit fur which had used to get "sop-wet", as Sarah said, through their going out in all weathers, when Barbara had always refused to take an umbrella.

"Oh, there are parks and the commons," she told him, and he realized that the answer had been deliberately studied before being given, and that was not like Barbara.

"Barbary, you've been homesick," he said sorrowfully.

"Terribly, these past weeks," said Barbara. "Somehow I never felt it at first. It's sort of grown. But, you know, Dave, I always ended where other folks began. I ought to have felt it most at first, but I didn't. However, you can tell me all about everybody and all the old places, and I'll go on again satisfied—if nothing is changed."

"Stands the church clock at ten to three,
And is there honey still to tea?"

quoted Dave slowly.

Then silence fell on them, and Dave sat watching the speedometer go up and up, and Barbara had not even asked him why he had come.

She spoke out of the silence.

"Crichie gets home at eight," she told him. "They work late at Goffers's. Some of the others at other places leave by six. But he'll be home for supper."

He saw blurs that he knew for trees, now, lights of little houses; lights on the road, a suburban road; sensed space, withal fogged space; and was glad Barbara did not live right in the throng of the city.

"How's Sarah's cough?" she inquired.

"Much the same," Dave told her. "Are we nearly there, Barbary?"

She nodded.

"I got a cold on Ridgely," he told her, "but I'll take it up when I get back and leave it there."

"Oh, don't talk about going back almost before you've come!" exclaimed Barbara, almost a cry in the tones. Then: "I'll get some elderberry blossom at the chemist's and brew some."

It was Sarah's remedy for a chill. Barbara, Dan, Dave always had to take elderberry tea when suffering from chill.

"Do you give it to Crichie when he has a cold?" asked Dave.

She shook her head.

"I offered it once, but he laughed at the idea," she told Dave brightly. "Called it country nonsense."

"It s a darned good sensible remedy for a cold," said Dave, defending the country.

Barbara was looking at the 'cello.

"I'm glad you brought it," she said. "I wondered you would. I've not touched the piano for months. But I'll just make the notes scamper out of it now. It'll be like old times."

Dave was looking at Barbara. Not touched the piano for months, she had said. What could be the matter? And he had better not tell Sarah that, for on the top of the cost of that piano only three weeks before Barbara had met Crichie Dennison, there had been the cost of its carriage to Barbara's new home.

They were passing into a neighbourhood with the houses more closely packed now. The buildings loomed up in rock-like blackness and opaqueness through the fog, and the lights had a streamer-like effect, like tailed comets, in this density.

The taxi stopped. Barbara paid the fares, despite his remonstrance.

They were on a little flagged walk, which ran, with a tree here and there, railed round, and passing lighted houses, which seemed very high to him.

"Here we are," said Barbara blithely. "Dave, you can always find the house by the almond tree when you are over to see us, if ever I can't meet the train."

They stood within the gate staring up at a ghostlike tree, whose ghost-like branches appeared caught in a web of fog—grey-green trailing fog which clogged the air above their heads, went over the walk with its railed trees, and caught at the houses on the other side with their blurs of light which made them look like ghost-houses set in the midst of a wraith-like sea of spume.

"There's a bit of almond blossom on it, high up," said Barbara, pointing. "But the fog is too thick. I'll show it to you in the morning."

"There's palm out," Dave told her in return, "all among the snow. It looked bonnie, Barbary."

They went on and into the hall. Barbara took his hat. The hall was lighted. He saw electric switches.

And Barbara was stroking his hat just as she had always used to stroke his things before she hung them up. Nothing had changed. He did not mind. She could live here all her life and he would not mind.

He watched her hang the hat on the hat-rack.

"Let's get in to the fire," she said, the full Northern burr sounding in her speech. "I'm frozen."

And when she turned from putting his coat on the peg, he saw her eyes were full of tears.

"Barbary—"

She turned a smiling face, her lips curved in a smile whilst the tears yet trembled on her lashes.

"Oh, it was just your mentioning the palm out," she said. "Or else I'd almost forgotten what it was like to be called 'Barbary'. It's rather a time, a year, isn't it?"

Dave nodded.

It was. It had seemed a long time. But he was here now. It felt good. He was following Barbara to the room where she had told Mary to have a big fire.

On the threshold of the room Barbara turned and looked towards the hall. She could see the same gloomy, loud paper, the hat-rack, the little table where Crichie's evening newspapers were always left. A whim of his—morning papers by his plate, evening papers on the hall-table to pick up as he came through. It was the same hall which she had stood in, morning after morning, evening after evening, to bid Crichie good-bye as he went to work, to welcome him in when he came home. But it had ceased to have that air of commercialism—and the wall-paper did not look too bad. She could see Dave's thick coat on the peg and his hat hung just over it. It was the first time that hall had felt to her to be a part of the house. And as she stood pondering, the solution rushed upon her mind.

She had just been homesick and had only just found it out.

And what would Crichie say when she told him she had ordered new hall-paper?

The hall could always be part of the house now, she thought, for always she would be able, if things went a little difficult, to be quite nice with Crichie and not take him too seriously, but just look at the hat-rack and imagine Dave's hat and coat hanging there, thick, countrified, reminiscent of Ridgely and Carbridge and Rimton and the Tops, where men wore clothes to keep the cold out, and did not worry about the "cut". She almost flung at the hat-rack a look of triumph, as though she had conquered the sinister power it had sometimes conveyed to her when Crichie turned to leave the breakfast-table, the morning paper, and the marmalade jar, and sally forth to Goffers— Goffers, who had given him the hat-rack as a wedding-present, and where it had seemed to Barbara to stand every morning, saying to Crichie: "Come away. Business! Emporium! All things are small besides what I connote." And there they had always felt small to her, even she and Crichie had felt small to her, and as though they were only replicas of other people, just like all the other people who were standing saying: "Well, I must be off," and "Yes, dear, I know you must. Good-bye," and "Will you be late, dear, to-night?" and "I don't know. I'll perhaps get time to ring you up and let you know." But now she would hear Dave telling her that the palm was out, a most important fact, more important to them both than work and all the other things most folk did think all-important. The hat-rack from Goffers was defeated. The hall held a memory of Rimton, of Dave, of their talk of palm being out.

"Oh, I forgot to ask you," said Barbara as they went towards the glorious fire, "why you came."

He was just about to say: "Why, it seemed so long since I'd seen you," but what he did say was: "I've got an engagement to play at a music-hall. Oh, no need to look like that, it's nothing much. Old Jonathan had seen one of the managers two years since and had said I could fill a gap if ever they had one, that my playing wasn't too bad for a blacksmith. He must have remembered. It won't be much, Barbary, so don't feature me in your mind as a Kreisler. It's just, well, I'll get a week's holiday, and they say everybody should see the capital of their own country. What a grand fire, Barbary!"

Barbara pointed him to a chair. She sat down in the chair opposite. When Mary had brought in tea, she asked her to run round to the chemist for elderberry blossom.

There were sprays of mimosa in a jar on the tea-table. It was set out in London style, but on the plates were Northern pasties and Northern potato and onion cake. As Barbara handed Dave the cake, still warm from the electrically heated oven, her lace sleeve caught in the Swiss bell, and as she tried to loose it, it fell to the carpet with a ting-ting-ting that felt to go through the head. It irritated her. She removed it to a chair. The table was so small. There was not room for the Swiss bell on it. She leaned her chin on her hands and looked the joy she was feeling across at him, and said breathlessly: "Now tell me about everybody at home."

Chapter Five

Dave was waiting for the show to begin. He was sitting, bewildered in a world strange and incongruous, hearing beyond this room, beyond the curtain, the murmurs of a big crowd which was waiting to be entertained, and whilst waiting was talking of the weather, the programme, the foreign king's passage through the metropolis last week. The orchestra was tuning up its firsts and seconds and the 'cellos, and he heard the boom of a laugh. On the other side of him he heard doors opening and closing, the patter of light feet running, and before he had come to sit here had seen a man in a cloak and a sombrero, a very important-looking man, who had been standing in a doorway and who had glanced at Dave as though he were nothing. He felt nothing sitting here, all his own world far from him, saving Barbara, who had told him to look right in front, in the middle of the stalls, where he would see her. Dan and Sarah would be looking at the clock, as the cold winds hurtled about the cottage. Perhaps the hail which had rattled on the top of the taxi as he and Barbara had come, would still be beating a tattoo on those northern window, like the rattle of drum-sticks—tap-tap-tap. Sarah would have her spectacles on, so that she could look at the clock herself and need not trouble Dan. Willie Barnes would have locked up the smithy two hours since. The bellows would be silent. The forge would be dark, and all about the smithy would be sounding the murmur of the stream, evening mists upon it, drifting silver-grey over it.

And he was here, wondering why he should be here at all, wondering what all this world was to do with him, owing Sarah the tiniest bit of grudge for only having allowed him a shilling a week to spend, because but for that "nearness" of hers he would not have had to take this engagement to be able to come up and see Barbara. He was beginning to realize it would be an ordeal. He calmed himself as well as he could, thinking of his own world—the smithy; Ridgely Fells; the moors; that bit of palm out—and how, if there was more snow after his return, he would see the ruddy light of the smithy shining out across the white road, between the children who stood by the door, waiting to see the reek fill the smithy as he plunged white-hot iron into ice-cold water, the steam going quivering across the fire's fierce glare. Whether he played poorly or well, the smithy was always there. That was his world. This—a temporary holiday, a break in which he had to pay by this nervousness for the delight of seeing Barbara before his hair became grey and grizzled.

A boy in buttons opened the door and glanced at the obscure Northerner, his fingers nervously clutching and unclutching on the neck of the 'cello. Dave looked at him, this small boy, so at home in the theatre, and envied him. The boy closed the door and Dave felt that the young imp was sniggering. But old Jonathan had always said: "Dave, lad, tha can play," and old Jonathan had not been exactly a duffer where music was concerned. Still, if only someone had spoken to him, but they had all been too busy. A man with some boards under his arm had looked at him and said: "Reid, oh, the second turn," and had opened the door of this room and motioned with his head to show Dave that he was to go in and sit down. Then he had said, with his head pushed on one side with the board: "Cottage Scene, isn't it?" and Dave had said he did not know, and the man had said: "The boy will call you." If only it was over. Tomorrow night it would not feel so bad, perhaps. Or, he grinned inwardly, he might be like the chap he had heard Dan tell of, who had gone on the stage once and did not appear on the night after, and did not even need to walk off, for the audience had helped him off. It was worse, a thousand times worse, than when he had swung the hammer the first time. If only he had been the first on, not had to sit here waiting, growing ever more nervous. His hands were getting quite chill and damp. He stood up to see how his legs felt. They trembled under him. And there were six nights of it, with to-night. Oh, if he had never left the forge, if he were only back at Rimton hearing a cinder drop on the warm ashes as he drew his bow across the strings. He was going to play badly. He knew it. He was nobody here, just nobody. The man in the cloak and sombrero had known he was nobody. The boy in the buttons knew. The man with the boards had known. He was going to be so nervous, he would play so poorly, Barbara would be disappointed. And when Barbara was disappointed—he saw her, her hands holding the front of the stall, her eyes sad, her heart sick because he had failed, and sick for him, too, feeling every pang of nervousness along with him, and how she would say: "You did very well, Dave," understanding why he had not done better, allowing for it all.

The orchestra burst out. It was beginning. Offenbach! Better than Gluck, according to Dave. The great pulsing Movement opened, and he sat listening, swept away by it, yet with that under-current of nervousness still there, telling him that very soon the curtain would go up and he would be the turn after. He recalled that he had a programme in his pocket. Barbara had given it to him, and he had crumpled it up as he had stood talking to her, and he saw "Cottage Scene—David Reid, the Village Blacksmith". He was booked to play "Home, Sweet Home" and "The Hungarian Rhapsody" and "Kathleen Mavourneen". He tried his strings, drew the bow over them softly. The 'cello was in perfect tune, but one of the pegs, which held the D string, had a way of slipping. He tried it to see that it was all right, and to the clapping of hands which told that the audience was glad to see the curtain go up, he realized that the first turn was on. Who was No. 13? A Japanese Juggler. Soon, very soon now, he would be called. He took out his handkerchief and mopped a damp brow. Awful, this was. Why, oh, why, had he written that he would come? Why had he not thought it all out, seen that audience, thousands of them, in his mind's eye, recognized that he could not play for nuts, that old Jonathan had been partial to his playing, that Sarah and Dan were partial to hit playing? Why had he not written and told the manager that there was some mistake, that he could not play, only to please those he loved, and would drop dead if he looked at a big audience? Whereas, the letter had flung him into wild excitement. He had only felt it was a way of getting to see Barbara. He had never visualized this acute misery and commotion he would experience sitting here, waiting for his call. The thought of seeing Barbara had blocked it all out. And here he was, but tomorrow—well, he had his return ticket, and though he would lose his fee and Sarah would call him "too ill to turn", he was hopping it back. Not any more of this, not even for Barbara. He mopped his brow again. Faint clapping broke on his hearing. It had come. They would call him in a minute. He would be answering the call in a minute. There—the door was opening. He saw the impish face of the boy in buttons, just as he had told himself he would. With legs that felt wooden, apart from him, with chill hands clutching the 'cello, he moved as the boy spoke. The youthful imp winked. Dave felt that he was going without any volition of will.

"No, that way," said the boy in buttons, and winked again.

And he was on the boards, going along them towards the centre. He gave a despairing glance towards the middle of the stalls, but everything was swimming. He could not see Barbara, could not see anything but a jumbled collection of faces, and then the faces swam, and he could only see eyes—eyes— all looking in his direction, and the orchestra was starting. He looked away from the audience. Something about a Cottage Scene, was it not? He looked just at the space where he stood, and a ring of light appeared, and then the disc covered him and he was blinking in it, staring down on the board's to see the shadow of himself and the shadow of the 'cello.

"Chair. Sit down," came from one of the orchestra in a low voice.

And he saw there was an old-fashioned chair, done up in chintz, and he must be dreaming all this, or life was a marvellous series of coincidences, for it was chintz in the very same pattern Sarah had on her old chairs. If only the blood would stop beating in his ears. They would be watching the clock at home, saying proudly: "Our Dave's on now." And all he was desirous of was to have finished and to get off.

He sat down in the chair, feeling that he had wooden joints. And then the orchestra was playing the opening bars of "Home, Sweet Home".

It was a Cottage Scene, he recalled. Then, what I was he doing with his hat and coat on? He should have taken them off, left them in that room where I he had been sitting. What a muddle he was making of it. To the astonishment of the orchestra, he stood up, laid the 'cello on the table, and slowly began to take off hat and coat. But the orchestra filled in the gap and the movement had done him good. He sat down again, and now he did not look anywhere but at the 'cello. The dark, polished wood of it shone in the light that caught it. He swept his bow across the strings with a nerveless hand.

Crick!

The string had gone. It whipped his cheek as it broke. Through the silence of the theatre that little sound went echoing, echoing.

Great drops of sweat, cold as ice, were on his forehead. Eternities felt to roll. Silence—that silence which rolls up awful and intense—was battering at him. The damned string had broken and he had not another. Best get up and run. It became impossible to sit there in that awful silence and tie that string, though he had often soon fixed a string when he had one broken at home. What could he do? He must do something.

And then he recalled old Dan saying, as they had stood on the station: "If tha breaks down, Dave, make 'em laugh a bit."

The blood receded from his ears. Warmth came back to his fingers, and he was jesting about the broken string, talking now like Dan with his slow, cautious speech, now like Sarah, lamenting the cost of a new string, just whilst he got that string fixed up again. Then, as he had often imitated the wind as he had stood on Ridgely Fells, he imitated it now. It was a Cottage Scene, anyhow. Perhaps they would not think the string breaking anything but what had to be. Then, when the wind had died away, just whilst he tied the knot, turned the peg, he imitated Sarah again, moaning what a terrible upkeep music was, and then he talked like Dan, saying it was better, much better, to be able to shoe a hoss so as the shoe would stand frost and snow than to be able to make the finest din that had ever come out of a 'cello. Laughter was reaching his ears, fresh burst on burst, and now another bit o' that wind blowing and the thing was all right And a warm, rosy light was on him now—artificial fire-glow.

He looked at the orchestra, which was now an orchestra with faces and instruments which did not run all into one another. He nodded as he tried the string, and into that atmosphere and characterization of the North, he was playing "Home, Sweet Home" as calmly, as confidently as he had played by the hearth with Sarah and Dan and—Barbary there—before she had gone away. He felt that they were there, close to him. He heard the click of Sarah's knitting-needles, the wheeze of Dan's old pipe, and—what was this great noise that awakened him from his dream?

"Bow," came in a whisper from the orchestra.

He stood up and bowed. Then he sat down again, and played the other two pieces, wondering if the string would hold, ready to fill the gap if it broke again. But it held.

When he had finished, that thunderous sound broke again. Bewildered, he stood bowing and bowing and bowing, with only this conscious thought: "I can go now. Thank heavens, it's over."

He came back and bowed again. He had heard from behind the stage "No encore". Funny, that, be mused, as he walked off. The clapping had made him think he had done pretty well, but he was to give no encore. They had just been laughing at him, then. He was like the chap Dan had talked about. And he wondered if he would get his fee if he did not get to appear tomorrow night.

He stared into the face of the manager.

"Reid, you're a 'find'," said that individual.

Dave stared at him apologetically.

"I'm sorry the string gave," he said. "I'll see it doesn't tomorrow. I'm very sorry indeed."

A burst of laughter answered him. He was being slapped on the back, shaken by the hand.

"That string's got to break every night for a week," he was told. "They think it's part of your act, don't you see? You're a find, You've struck a new note. Your playing—"

Dave began to preen himself a little.

"I've been told I can play," he said.

"H'm! Not badly. I've heard as good down the East End half-drunk on Saturday nights," was the amazing answer. "What we want you for is—you're a born humorist and character-impersonator. The playing fits in. They don't criticize that from a high standard, because to play to a high standard from a cottage with the wind round it would spoil the effect. Fact is, you're made, Reid. Did you ever hear of Chevalier?"

Dave believed he had heard of him.

"He was the spirit of the coster. You—the village blacksmith will be your forte. We shall extend your line."

Dave stood staring. He heard the word "contract".

"But I've got to go back to the forge," he said.

"Forget it, Reid. You'll never see the forge again unless it's to say good-bye to it. Where are you staying? I'll come along some time tomorrow."

"I'm going back to the forge," Dave told him stubbornly. "I'm certainly going back. You'll see."

"I'll come along with my offer tomorrow," said the manager, folding up the address Dave had written.

"It won't be any use," Dave told him.

"Round about four, after the rehearsals," finished the manager imperturbably.

Dave found himself going out, behind the theatre, and Barbara was waiting.

"Oh, Dave, how wonderful!" she was saying, and she was kissing him and hugging him for sheer delight in his success, warm, impulsive kisses which she did not know were turning the scales, bumping them down against his return to the forge. For that matter, Dave did not know that they were doing so, either. He only knew that he felt rapturously happy, happier than he had ever felt in his life, that the stars in this bit of London sky he saw as they stepped into the taxi shone brighter even than he had ever seen them shine at home, and yet whilst he wondered why that should be, home felt quite near, too, almost as though "home" was Barbary.

"Let me hold the 'cello, Dave," she asked in the dimness of the taxi as they sped along.

He pushed it over to her.

She was leaning her face against the 'cello, caressing it with her cheek.

"It was queer my telling you you'd find the house by the almond-tree, wasn't it?" she remarked reflectively. "And, oh, how nice it will be to have you near us. You don't know!"

Dave gave no answer.

He was thinking of the forge, and as he pictured it, it seemed small, very small and far away, standing there by the little stream with the big oak near, and the little grey houses whose chimney smoke curled away into the air. There life would go on, unchanging. He could learn no more there, swing a hammer no better in forty years than now. There were no vistas, There was no development. It had been existence. This which was offered to him was opportunity. life, and perhaps it was better even to make people laugh than to put shoes on horses so that they would not lose them in frost or thaw. He was reasoning, to explain to himself his indecision, and from being very happy he became very unhappy. He had never dreamed he would have to decide whether he would go back to the forge again. Yesterday, these opening vistas were not. Today they were. He could not understand why he should consider longer than five minutes against going back to the forge. Barbara was happy. He had come up and had seen her. He knew she was not changed. Home was still home to her, he was still Dave to her. Why, then, hesitate at returning?

He could find no answer. It made him feel very restless trying to find an answer. So he leaned back in the taxi and rested under his laurels, and enjoyed himself looking at Barbara, who sat with her cheek against his 'cello, which had thus for evermore, he mused, another precious memory, perhaps the most precious of all, associated with it in his mind.

Book Two

Chapter One

"Crichie, we shall really have to have a little party," announced Barbara from the end of the breakfast-table.

Crichie looked up. His eyes over the top of the morning paper had that don't-bother-me-about-anything expression which generally abode in them when he was reading the morning paper. Barbara was so damnably irrelevant. She would keep tossing bits of irrelevant news out at him just when he was absorbed in seeing how the solid affairs of the world were wagging. Five minutes since she had been asking him if he had noticed in yesterday's paper that roses were out in some remote part of the country, the first to appear. Now she was bothering him about their having a party.

"Why do you want us to have a party?" he asked.

"Why—to celebrate Dave's success. It's wonderful, Crichie. You don't seem to realize how wonderful." She poured more hot water into the coffee-jug.

"The papers have made a splash about it," he told her loftily. "News for them. They are like to fill the columns up with something or other. What do you think, Barbara? Dinkermanns, the big bankers, have gone down."

He looked at her, eager for her inquiries into anything as exciting as Dinkermanns having gone down. Why, they had actually thought of opening an account there, but had decided on Parrs. Her uninterested look met him. She had almost tumbled the news on him of roses being out already, and he was sick of hearing of Dave Reid's wonderful act. Meant to see it soon, of course, all the same, but a thing as vital to the country as Dinkermanns, she was not interested in its collapse at all. And once more, they were looking across the table at each other with the puzzled look of people who unconsciously annoyed each other, but unlike strangers who had that effect on each other, must be very patient and forbearing, and pretend that they did not.

"You don't seem to realize, Barbara," he said, "that we almost put our money into Dinkermanns. You might try to look a little excited. It's a big concern, Dinkermanns. I wish you wouldn't tap your fingers on the table in that fashion."

The tapping stopped—stopped so immediately that it annoyed him equally, because he could not believe she had obeyed so swiftly because she wanted to obey. Everything had felt all right before that anniversary morning. Things had not run a bit smoothly since, and she was certainly looking thinner, paler, and more than a year older than the girl he had walked with through Chamounix, and with whom he had sung "Mont Blanc is the Monarch of Mountains". It hurt his conceit that she should be falling off. There was all the worry and suspense, too, of waiting to see if Goffers did become an amalgamation, in which case his partnership would go—a chimera—and he was doomed to a rut for the rest of his existence. She was not even deeply interested whether he got the partnership or not, though if he got it they could move into a better neighbourhood, run their own car, travel—oh, altogether a different sort of life and a different "set" to mix with, whereas now, well, old Goffers came to have tea with them occasionally, which was really to placate him, Crichie, whilst the amalgamation pended, and they were sometimes almost glad to see that bore, old Peachley. Even about Peachley they did not agree, he and Barbara. Barbara had actually said she considered old Peachley fine, and had asked him to bring the little boys with him sometimes—all three of them, and he knew she would be sure to let them run wild all on the lawn he had got looking smooth and nice, quite the nicest lawn in all the road, and she would have those harum-scarum boys running over it as he had seen them run over theirs at home, whilst Flora Peachley looked reproachfully at Peachley and said: "Fred, look what they're doing!"

"I'm sorry about Dinkermanns," Barbara startled him with. He gave her a look of pleased surprise.

"There'll be lots of people with all their bits of savings in it, won't there? Old people, who have worked all their lives, like Sarah and Dan," she said sorrowfully. "It seems a pity these speculations have to rob people of their life savings like this—"

He went back to the paper. He had really though she had seen the tragedy of Dinkermanns, as Dinkermanns, as one of the oldest banks in the country, with their immense powers reaching out to all corners of the world, with their vested interests extending front the rice-fields of China to the rubber of Africa, with their ability to give six per cent to their clients and bonuses twice yearly. But all she had been thinking of was the working-classes with their miserable little savings in Dinkermanns, and she had expostulated against speculation, which was the bed-rock of the financial world's greatness, which gave great chances, thrilling hazard of gain, if pulled off, and if not, an occasional melée, such as had come on Dinkermanns, Then, the irritation he had felt against her small outlook was forgotten.

"Another cup, Barbara," he told her. "Barbara, I've just remembered. The Peachleys are in the

Dinkermann smash. What a blow for Mrs. Peachley. Three thousand or so, that's all, but the interest has helped up Peachley's wages. They'll have to move from where they are now. They won't even have that scrubby little lawn."

He saw tears on Barbara's lashes, recalled that women had small outlooks, could not grasp the bigness of a thing like men, and his chagrin melted away.

"I must call in and sympathize," he said, after gulping the coffee. "You might call, too, some afternoon. Barbara, you are the oddest creature. You weren't in the least interested in Dinkermanns having gone down, and now—"

"Don't smile in that superior way," Barbara told him hotly. "I was thinking of little Henry with nowhere to run his railway on summer Sundays, of him always having to be poked inside, running it on the carpet, with Flora sitting there saying: 'Don't!' and Peachley trying to read in Greek, and the—the lawn gone. That lawn was all those children have of happiness."

He gave her a despairing look. One could not talk to her. No one could talk with any benefit to their intelligence to a woman who could only visualize the catastrophe of Dinkermanns going down by seeing all these sorry little straws-like old people with their pettifogging hundreds lost, and a little nuisance like Henry Peachley with nowhere to run his train.

"You are a child, Barbara," he said disappointedly.

She looked at him wistfully.

"Perhaps I am," she said, looking disappointed also.

The cloud on his spirits engulfed hers—as it always did.

Then she got an inspiration.

"Crichie, if you'll bring me some books on Banking," she told him, "I'll—I'll try to read them."

"Barbara! I wish you would. You'd find it awfully fascinating after you'd got past the first dryness of it, how they schedule and run things. It's marvellous, simply marvellous; I'll bring one back with me to-night. It's as wonderful, more wonderful than any romance. And if there's anything you don't understand—"

They were standing with fingers intertwined and a happy light in their eyes, and feeling very, very near to each other, when Mary came in with the tray and Barbara was saying, with an April face: "I'll try very hard to grasp it all. But I do think, Crichie, Plato and Marcus Aurelius and Maeterlinck, or even old Izaak Walton, and there are wide gulfs between them all, would have grasped my point of view and have seen how very real to me was Dinkermanns going down."

"Yes, my love, I'm sure they would," acquiesced Crichie buoyantly.

"Or—even Dave," said Barbara.

She was looking at the Wedgewood sugar-bowl with the lovely dancing nymphs flying through the blue enchantment of it, and realizing that Crichie had spoiled it for her by saying as he had unwrapped it: "New line. Two-two. Thought we'd best get one before the demand sends the price up. Two-two. Wonderful, dear, isn't it?" Always now on the sugar-bowl was Two-Two.

"Yes. Reid would probably see it as you saw it, agreed Crichie nonchalantly. "But, I say, Barbara—" He paused.

"Yes, dearest?"

Always after any little difference they were extremely polite to each other.

"Don't fall in love with Dave," he said, casually pulling on his glove. "Fine gloves, these. Six-eleven. Part of a bankrupt stock. Trust old Goffers for being the first on the scene."

"Oh, I always have been," said Barbara laughing. "It's too late to give such a warning. I think Dave's simply wonderful. I always did."

"And I?" inquired Crichie.

It was a long time since he had seen Barbara's eyes look like that—still and shining, like pools with sunlight touching brown-green depths.

"Oh—you—" said Barbara gently, looking at him as though she saw him a long way off. "You are the person with more power to make me unhappy than any other person in the world; Surely that is enough?"

And just for a moment it struck him that in Barbara's make-up there was the capacity for genial irony, for humour that could laugh at both their idiosyncrasies, and if there was anything he hated in a woman it was ironic humour. But when he looked at her, he saw that her chin was trembling, her lips held together, and her eyes had lost that still, shining look and were the troubled eyes of a woman who loved one man more than anything else in the world. They had certainly tiffed a lot latterly. It was good to see that look shining out of her eyes, troubled, perplexed, loving, but with the love which loved despite all differences and tiffing, and for a moment he felt like saying something foolish, something which she could remember whenever they had these little tiffs, so that she would know they were just little tiffs which altered nothing of all they felt for each other. Everybody had tiffs, and it never did alter anything. Still, he stood there, feeling that perhaps one might be able to say something, some great beautiful thing, which Barbara would keep for always and prize as she never prized all the other presents he gave her. Then—it seemed foolish to be standing there, pretending to button his glove whilst he thought of what to say. Damn! People did not say great beautiful things to each other when they were married.

"Well, train won't wait, Barbara," he said.

They went down the hall together. And as she reached his hat from the hat-rack he realized he was very ordinary, for he could not think of any great, beautiful thing to say, even whilst for a lightning moment, looking at Barbara with that sorrowful love shining clear and strong for him, her spirit had touched his so completely, just for a moment, that he had almost felt how she was looking at things, how Goffers's and partnerships and how the English Banking System was run, mattered nothing at all, but that it mattered a very great deal whether they forgot that vision they had seen together for a lightning moment as they had looked out on a wide sunlit valley and heard the cattle bells ringing up. No, he could not think of anything to say. But they had a wonderful new line of opera cloaks just come in that week, and Barbara was going to the theatre a great deal just now, and it was an advertisement for Goffers's as well, and a sort of peace-offering at the same time. They must try to avoid these quarrels. Perhaps they did take something away. But—things wore away for everybody. Could not expect to keep more than everybody kept. That sugar-bowl, now, how he had looked at it before finally deciding to have it. Had visioned it on the table, and now—well, it was just there. People were like that, and they were just like everybody else. And Barbara would realize it in time and not stand looking bewildered as at some strange phenomenon when she found they were quarrelling again, after all the vows not to.

"Awfully jolly, this new hall-paper, Barbara," he remarked.

"Yes, I think so, too."

It was something to find they could agree on hall-paper.

Her face had lit up in the eager, happy way that took away the year that had made her look more than a year older. And then, he recalled something he had read in a paper.

"Beautifullest," he said benignly, "if you laugh with your eyes like that, you'll have crow's-feet round your eyes by the time you're thirty."

"Dearest," answered Barbara calmly, "I don't care a damn whether I get crow's-feet round my eyes or not so that I don't lose the ability to laugh at you and myself. And now we've gone and quarrelled again and ruined the new hall-paper which cost five-five." She looked at him with rueful despair.

"Barbara!" he exclaimed.

For Mary's kitchen door was open, and Barbara's "Damn" had been vigorous and clear.

And from standing quite near together they felt to be standing miles apart. They had quarrelled again. But the unkindest cut of all was the way she had said "five-five" just because he had warned her against laughing with her eyes and getting crow's-feet by doing so.

She had gone from the hall. He reached his coat down himself and struggled into it.

Then, on an impulse, he followed after her.

She was standing by the fireplace in the drawing-room. All was dim, for the blinds had not been wound up there. They had ceased to have the fire lighted there, the weather being warm.

"Barbara!"

"Yes."

Her voice was very quiet—ominously quiet.

"I only thought—well, I don't want you to get crow's-feet."

She moved restlessly. Then she spoke.

"If I live long enough I shall get crow's-feet. I shall be old and wrinkled and grey. Crichie, did you only marry the shell I live in—not the *me*?"

She stopped.

"Of course, darlingest. But crow's-feet—I was looking at a woman the other day, and she had

crow's-feet, and then I read it came with laughing—
'contorting the face with one's emotions', the writer
called it. It was a very fine article. I cut it out for your
especial benefit. I'll let you read it."

Barbara turned from the fireless grate. To his
complete astonishment, she burst out laughing
almost hilariously. She stood staring at him, tears
of laughter on her lashes, her body shaken with it,
quivering with that burst of ringing laughter which
was so infectious he found himself smiling as she
stopped, stared at him again and burst out once
more.

"Crichie, you'll miss your train," she told him,
wiping her eyes. "More crow's-feet! But I couldn't
help laughing. You looked so droll. And I don't think
any other man in the world would have let me know
I couldn't even laugh to please him and then have
offered to let me read the article. But I'll read it,
Crichie. And I'll try to remember."

"Yes. You're not angry, Barbara?"

"Angry!"

She walked up to him and gave him a fierce kind
of hug.

"Dear solemn little boy," she said very tenderly.
"Dear solemn little boy!"

"Barbara, you said I was droll—" he said quickly.

"I said you looked droll, which is different," she told
him. "Yes, do go. I'll read the article; and don't forget
the book."

"And you're quite sure you're not angry, Barbara?'
He felt perplexed.

"No."

"'Onest Injun'?"

"No, not in the least, Crichie. Laughter may be bad
for crow's-feet, but it does the heart good."

"Yes, I'm sure it does," he agreed. "I didn't know
you could laugh like that, Barbara."

"I used to, dear, but never mind. You'll miss getting to Goffers's—"

"Oh, and you ought really to call on Mrs. Peachley and offer our condolences."

"Yes, dear, I'll go this afternoon. No, I forgot, I can't. Dave's bringing his 'cello round. We're going to play a great piece from *Cavalleria Rusticana*. It goes—oh, never mind, you'll miss your train. I'll go tomorrow to see Mrs. Peachley."

They had passed the hat-rack. They were standing on the mat.

"And we haven't spoiled the new hall-paper, dear, have we?" he inquired.

"No. I just thought we wouldn't quarrel there and spoil it," she said. "But I suppose we shall. I suppose it's the inevitable. But it doesn't matter. That laugh's done me a world of good."

She stood by the door, looking out at the almond-tree, watched him pass through the gate, go along the walk, past the second railed tree where the birds were twittering in the sunlight, amongst the green leaves which had already lost their first springtide green.

Crichie was trying to make up his mind whether a woman should think her husband looked droll. He could not make it up at all. Then he realized that they saw very few people, apart from apart from each other. Apart from old Goffers's rare visits, and Peachley's, and, latterly, Dave's, they practically saw no one, and Goffers's closed too late to allow of theatres, and, besides, one was too washed-out after grinding all day at Goffers's with a junior partnership in mind. Perhaps it would be rather a good idea to have a little party to celebrate Dave's success. And the Peachleys could come, both of them. And Dave could play and entertain them. Quite a good idea.

He swung along beyond the last tree on the walk. And then he put these domestic matters out of his head. He was walking to the station where the train waited to take him into the City, the City which to him was just—Goffers's. He stopped suddenly.

Wonderful posters artists did these days. He was staring at one which had caught the majesty of the Swiss Alps—felt it all gather about him as he stood looking, the clear wonderful air, the great spaces, the beauty of pines rooted on rocky ledges, the shining glory of the meadows over which the bees went, gathering such honey as could not be bought in London shops—honey such as he and Barbara had eaten, fresh from the comb, in that old guest-house inn backed by the solemn mountains, where the frescoes of mountain life panelled the polished timbers of the mellow walls.

Then he was hurrying on again.

Next year, if he had got that partnership, they would go there again, sit on that same great rock which seemed to look over the world's edge, which made one feel that such valleys as that, unspoiled by commerce, was all the world which made for happiness. Meantime, he hurried on, one of the hurrying throng which had so fascinated and puzzled Dave when he had first come to London, which had so reminded him of a lot of hurrying ants, hurrying their lives away.

He would approach old Goffers again about that partnership to-day. If he was not going to get it—well, he was going to take life a little easier, that was all. Take Barbara out at week-ends, enjoy life a little, for last week a man from Goffers's office had died, and he realized that the artist's poster of the Swiss mountains had disturbed him. It was possible that he was missing somewhat of life, and old Goffers's "Well, we'll see—before long," was beginning to irritate him. If there was not scope and the top of the tree, there were Swiss mountains and Barbara, and those were something. Certainly something. He whistled debonairly and ran to catch the train.

He was whistling an air which made him wonder where he had heard it. Then he recalled where. A Swiss peasant with wedding favours in his hat had been whistling it in that inn on the mountain slope, and they had sat listening, he and Barbara, and then had gone out to see the afterglow on the Alps, and he had tried to interest her in indexing. Yes. That was when he had heard it. He was relieved to find he had not forgotten where he had heard it. For to lose the capacity to recall such things was to become inefficient, and inefficiency was his bête noire.

He was still whistling that air as he hung up his hat and coat on the peg at Goffers's.

"Heard anything about the amalgamation?" he whispered to one of the oldest clerks.

The old clerk shook his head. Then his yellow, anxious-looking face bent over the ledger. The pathos of the back of his head, grey in the service of Goffers's, struck Crichie. This—this was his doom if an amalgamation came along. Superannuation at the end of life almost—and the rest a rut. It was an unbearable thought. Head clerk he would be, that was true, with his three hundred and fifty a year, but what was that? And Barbara was content with it. No spur came from her. She was content with it. Flora Peachley now—- Then he pulled himself up.

What—what the devil could he be thinking of to be thinking what he could have achieved with the spur of a woman like Flora Peachley?

Well, he supposed thoughts could wander like that sometimes. And at least she would never have thought he looked droll if he had warned her how to avoid getting crow's-feet round her eyes. He strode into his room, and, sitting down, switched up to the day's work. On Sunday he would take

Barbara over the commons. It was two months since they had been, and on that occasion Barbara had annoyed him by refusing to walk under an umbrella when it was raining. She had ruined a new hat at two-fourteen-four by obstinately refusing to come under the umbrella, had quoted him something about the "soft silver-grey rain", and when he had insisted that she should come under, had said she saw the sky so rarely she did not feel like having it shut out by an umbrella. But they could not quarrel about rain this Sunday. The barometer was going up. The meteorological office prophesied glorious weather, and Dave could go along with them, too. They never quarrelled when he was there. He had a soothing effect on Barbara. Yes, they would take the peacemaker with them, though he was rather dull and always shied away and changed the subject when he, Crichie, tried to get him interested in Goffers's. Why, was that perhaps the reason Barbara never got ratty when Dave was there? Just because Dave stopped him talking of Goffers's?

He sat back. Why, on Sunday he would not even mention Goffers's. Nor any time with Barbara would he talk business. And he felt that he had tumbled on the philosopher's stone which would give perfect domestic happiness.

Only—why, he would feel very lonely, with no one to talk to of Goffers's. Still, there was old Peachley. And once Flora Peachley had asked him quite a lot of questions, intelligent questions, too, about the Emporium. Good idea, that. He could always drop in and talk to the Peachleys. He would never worry Barbara any more about Goffers's. Work was work and home was home. He believed he and Barbara would get on very well in time.

He whistled the air they had heard in the old inn. And he must not forget one of those cloaks.

He bent over the ledger. The scratching of his pen was the only sound in the room, the room where the sunshine came through dark-blue gauze blinds. A bird flew past the window. But he did not lift his head. He was happy. He had solved a difficulty by perceiving it, and when he was working he was working. A mistake here, for they had not received five hundred pairs of grey suede gloves. Two hundred and fifty it had been. If Goffers had not him to spot these things, now. He had earned his partnership, earned it by looking at himself as a part of Goffers's, pouncing on things like these, putting his soul into his job, not just sitting like an automaton. And Goffers would have to give him that partnership. His pen scratched away busily, and the bird flew past the window again, the sunlight on its speckled breast and its song pulsing upon the air and melting into the multitudinous sounds of London, melting into that great discord and harmony of sounds, where all sorrows beat and all joys, and to which Dave had stood listening on the pavements, wondering if ever a man would be born great enough to create a Fugue which expressed the sounds of London, and even blend with its human motif the songs of the birds, so far his best friends, saving only—Barbara.

Chapter Two

The Peachleys lived in Hendon. Across the front windows were the fashionable lace and net curtains, At the back was the little lawn, where on sunny Sunday afternoons Peachley liked to laze in a white straw hat and tweeds and watch Henry running his mimic railway, lifting his head from the study of foreign languages (which Flora decried as a waste of time) to help Henry convey cargoes to all the important stations of the globe, which was one way of teaching Henry geography. There was a little tree at the far end of the lawn, and there every year the thrushes sang after being fed by Peachley when snow covered the ground.

The five rooms of the house were very small. The smallest room of the five was the dining-room. When Peachley cut the dinner bread there in the evening at seven, he had at first on several occasions banged his elbow on the wall against which his chair was jammed, until with the four other chairs, the meal being over, it was fitted back under the table. Now Peachley never banged his elbow against the wall as he sawed at the bread. They had lived there four years. He was always conscious of the wall. But he agreed with Flora that though the houses of the Avenue were small they were select. The three boys were always conscious of the walls also, but unlike the adult, had an inborn antagonism to them and frequently ran into them, particularly in winter time when Peachley could not take them out so much and they ran out of one small box-like room into another playing Indians, with feathered caps Peachley had got them from Gamages, which was, Flora told him, an encouragement to them to run about as they did. After much by-talk about it, Peachley had sent the Indian outfits to a children's hospital, and had substituted an Eskimo's outfit each for consolation, and they used the bath with the cork mat for roof as an Eskimo's hut, and when Henry, being youngest, objected to the cold and began to cry, they jeered at him with the superiority of more mature years and held before him as an example of heroism the story of the discoverers of the Pole.

When having pillow-fights in the tiny box-like bedroom, they missed the full excitement of the sport. The bed had just a narrow path between it and the wall. It was impossible to avoid being hit by the pillow when it was thrown, and equally impossible to miss hitting when throwing it. Once, in summertime, when Henry had thrown it at Eric, who had climbed over the bed-rail upon the window-sill, Eric having been hit with it every time it had been thrown, threw it through the open window. The pillow had burst and feathers had blown on every lawn down the Avenue. To placate Flora, who blamed Peachley for their high spirits, Peachley had punished them by refusing to take them to the Zoo on the following Saturday as he had promised. But as Flora had gone the same evening to an exhibition of futurist art, Peachley had taken them for a row on the Serpentine, having in that way satisfied both vague belief in parental authority and human sympathy with their disappointment at not going to see the sea-lions. They had come back along the Avenue like three young whirlwinds, and Henry had said as Peachley's yale turned in the lock: "Favver, we've liked it better than going to the Zoo." Then they had all crept into the little house like four conspirators, and Peachley had furiously hacked at the bread and burned the soup as he heated it for their suppers, and then had said: "Boys, not a word of our having been out to your mother. And I'm sorry the soup is burned, but eat it and hop it as fast as you can before your mother comes in." And they had all avowed the soup was not burned in the least, all but Eric, who had said it might be a little.

Very quiet and happy and tired for sleep they had heard Peachley scraping the burnt pan, and Eric had proudly observed to Bert: "He'd have forgotten to scrape it but for me, and then mother would have known he had given us supper, too, when she said we'd to have none for a week."

When Flora had rung at the bell ten minutes later, half-asleep they had heard her come in and had heard her ask "Are the boys asleep?"

"Ever so long," Peachley had answered.

And Flora had said: "You see! My methods are correct. You'd have taken them to the Zoo just the same, and they'd have been having pillow-fights just the same. Whereas, they are asleep and have learned a lesson."

Whereupon Bert, who was used to these dialogues, had spluttered under the bedclothes, and Eric, furious lest the laughter should awaken Henry, who might tell, being youngest, if awakened, had kicked Bert who had with difficulty suppressed a cry, only being able to keep it back by seeing in imagination his father's face if his mother came into the room and Henry got roused. For tomorrow it would not matter if Henry did blab and talk of the Zoo. After a night's sleep he would be vague as to where he had been; he would define the time as having been "the day after yesterday", which could just as easily be six months since or a year ago or the present.

It was this little box of a house, then, one amongst the multitudinous boxes of the city, with the three tow-headed boys—all like Peachley, according to Flora, and Peachley always heard it as though she grudged him the fact—this little box with its cheap reprints of the old masters in every little box of a room, with everything smallest scale to leave any space at all, saving the boys who seemed yearly to occupy more space and to make it grow smaller as they grew bigger, which the going down of Dinkermanns had affected and was to affect still further, since the changes it would make would be more deeply and crushingly felt.

Peachley had taken the lightning blow which had reduced them to absolute penury, as Peachley took everything—valiantly, quietly, from an outsider's impartial view. From Flora's standpoint—spiritlessly. For three evenings after the news had come through he had sat in his worn easy chair, staring into the fire, and never taking his books from the shelf in the corner. Then he had rallied, had told Flora she was looking ill over it, and had observed: "We shall have to make the best of it. We must not cloud the boys' spirits with it. It will mean leaving the Avenue. Supposing we go Hammersmith way? It's cheaper living—"

"We shall not move from here," had been Flora's reply, coupled with a gleam of her dark eyes. "Fred, I've brought myself to tolerate the idea of never getting beyond the Avenue, but I won't and can't move into a poorer part. Hammersmith is—raucous."

"But if we can't afford—" Peachley had appealed.

To which she had returned contemptuous silence. And, finding reasoning was of no avail, Peachley, who to an outsider's impartial gaze looked much more ill than Flora from the blow, had stretched his thin, fine hand towards the bookshelf and had gone on reading Montaigne in the original and had found that the writer's philosophic irony sustaining to the soul.

"Fred!"

He had come back from his quiet world of thought—to see Flora sitting bright and vital, her eyes aglow with hope.

"Yes?"

"I've never seen the use of your studying languages till now," she began.

"No?"

"It has seemed a sheer waste of time."

"I have found a deal of pleasure in it, and gain."

"Yes, but you know what I mean—you did not profit by it."

And Peachley, quiet-eyed, had given her a queer look, recalling the tranquil hours on the lawn with the boys, golden precious hours in which Henry ran his railway and the thrushes sang from the tree at the end of the lawn, and a passing cloud dimmed the golden sunlit page, or a burst of sun brought out the type, or a little wind fluttered the page, the exquisite page of Socrates in the original, or Montaigne in the original—recalled, in short, the one broadness of his life which walls could not narrow—his love of knowledge for the love of knowledge. A little smile had flickered about his mouth. She had said he had not profited because it had brought no grist to the mill in the accepted sense of the word. It had brought Greece to him, and France and Spain, the glory of the one, the valour of the other, the romance of the latter. It was the heaven which had no cloud—in Hendon—on a summer day, on a scrubby little lawn. It was the one essence of joy life had not adulterated.

"Yes, I know," said Peachley.

"But since we are reduced, could you not turn it to account?" asked Flora.

Peachley sat straight up in his chair, and stared at her.

"You could take up translating and copying, couldn't you? You've your evenings. In a year you'd make enough surely to pay the rent of this place? Fred, I don't want to move from here. I should be ill if we had to go Hammersmith way. You'll just have to make up for our loss, and you could quite easily."

So Flora—watching him to see the effect. As she watched, Peachley's worn face lit up.

"Why, I'd learn a tremendous lot!" he ejaculated. "I—I never thought of that, Flora. But won't we miss the quiet sitting by the fire? It will mean after the boys have gone to bed I shall have to swot right on into the mornings."

"Yes. We shall miss it, but think, we shall be able to stay here, and be little worse off," she told him, and laid her plump hand for a moment on his.

"All right, Flora," said Peachley.

Evenings, Saturdays, Sundays, they were all gone now. To cover the rent would mean week-end work. But there, he could still sit out on the lawn, as he translated, still lift his head and see Henry running his railway in the best of the weather, and perhaps occasionally get time to take the three of them out.

He left Flora sitting by the fire and came back ten minutes later.

"I've written the advert. I'll go out and post it," he told her.

His footsteps echoed through the little house. The door closed behind him. Peachley was trying to turn one pleasure of his life—languages—to account. It would save Flora from the heartache of writing to their friends from the address of some commonplace street in Hammersmith, though they might have had more room there, and on summer evenings the boys could have gone out with him to see the river under the sunset, to walk down the Mall, quiet and grey and echoing, and even have gone to the cheap seats in the theatre, since they would not have had to live up to the Avenue. He hurried along, scarcely noticing the shadows of the trees on the path by the little houses which criss-crossed it with light from the windows; It was a sacrifice. He felt it as such. But, anything for a quiet life, even toiling when the rest of the world slept for Flora's pride, when he would much rather have lived in Hammersmith, plebeian Hammersmith, and have had more room.

And whilst he walked to the post-box, Flora was sitting motionless just where he had left her. Fireglow gave a warm light kindly to worn brown velvet cushions, touched the few cheap copies of world-famous statues. Flora's feet, encased in Peachley's last birthday gift, slippers of bronze green, were sunk into the white sheepskin rug which looked life surf under sunset in the glow and leap of the fire. Her silhouette, splendidly proportioned, head and bust and sweep of her dress, just filled the little panel of wall. High over it in the shadow where the fire-glow did not reach were Peachley's books, the books from which he would read no more with the happy delight of standing near the souls of the great, hearing them speak, still alive, down the ages, for the edification of one Frederick Peachley, who, had he not made a sacrifice for a widowed mother long ago, would have been what he dreamed to be—a scholar—not the under-manager in business which jagged his very heart. He was again making sacrifices, the sacrifice of running the hazard of getting to detest Greek, weary in the early mornings when he should have been sleeping. And Flora, in the new dress from Pontings, sat full-bosomed and magnetic with energy—and discontent—murmuring with full curved lips of beauty and scorn: "Heavens! I've just mentioned it, and he has gone to do it! And the great "head-phones" of her black coiled hair made artistic curves on the little wall, as she noticed when turning her head, and under that high brow, eyes gleamed and glanced "Spain"—and told of fiery, adventurous blood which had travelled all the way from the Armada to this little Avenue in Hendon, to this day of futurist art, and "head-phones" in hair fashion, and of little lawns by select houses where there was no room to move, what time intrepid airmen looped the loop and Henry believed it to be for his special amusement as he sat on the lawn and watched them against the sky, or ran his railway and called out: "Favver, is Morocco in Africa or where?"

Flora realized that one of the children was out of bed.

She turned and saw Henry in sleeping-suit and tears—tears without noise—and his face, which irritated her by looking like Peachley's when she scolded him, puckered up.

"What's the matter?" she asked.

Henry came and stood before her.

"Go back to bed," she commanded.

"But I've toof-ache."

"You must go to the dentist tomorrow," she said, "but now go back to bed."

Henry looked at her.

Between the now and the tomorrow which held the dentist was—toof-ache, but there was no favver in the chair opposite his mother's. In a corner of the room was a little chest where favver kept something for toof-ache till they could get to the dentist. But he did not dare mention the hot stuff that took away toof-ache after one long look into her face.

"'Night," he said miserably, and flitted away, a little figure with his hanky pressed to his cheek.

It was no use telling muvver of the hot stuff in the cupboard which cured toof-ache, and perhaps made it you did not even need to go and sit in the dentist's chair, when she looked at you like that—as though you were some strange little boy she did not particularly care for, and not hers at all. And where was favver? And what a big pain toof-ache was as it went on and on, like something screwing round and round and just stopping to make you think it had gone, and then waking you up and screwing round again. Dolefully, and with tears that made no noise, Henry crept into bed and found he had less room than before, for Eric and Bert had almost taken up his place. He squeezed down between them somehow, and the night-light flickered its flame across his noiseless tears and danced in blurred fashion, and a world with toof-ache in it and that cold look of his mother's and favver gone out somewhere just when he wanted him, felt almost too much for him.

Ting!

It was the front-door bell. It was favver back. His heart leaped—leaped higher and beat faster than the screwing pain that went right up into his head—jump —jump—jump. In a little while he would call, and favver would come on tip-toe, and say sternly: "Be a good boy and go to sleep," just as though anybody could be good and go to sleep with toof-ache. And Henry knew quite as well as favver did that favver said that silly thing just because muvver was sitting there in the room beyond. Favver would scold. Favver would likewise wink, hear the whispered: "I've toof-ache," and go out and bring the little bottle out of the chest, and then the toof-ache would go, and favver would get scolded for taking any notice of their nonsense. And Henry was sorry to think favver would get scolded, but toof-ache was a dreadful pain.

So Henry—

Then he heard: "Oh, Mr. Dennison, come in."

The disappointment and another shoot of the tooth was too much for Henry. He gave a cry. Muvver came after a little while.

"Now, don't be a silly boy, Henry, and make all that noise about tooth-ache. Go to sleep. It will go away."

And she took away the night-light. And all was still, very still in the little box-like room.

Flora Peachley lit the shaded lamp.

"But Fred can't be long now," she told Crichie, standing by the lamp. "Couldn't you stay to supper? Yes. It felt rather a blow, Dinkermanns going."

"Barbara will be expecting me," Crichie told her.

But it was pleasant sitting there in the little room with the fire and the lamp, and the feeling that one was giving sympathy to another who also lacked scope, for who could think that Flora Peachley would be content with this small house and small life, or for that, matter with Peachley, whom one knew would never get anywhere?

And before he knew it, he was talking of Goffers's and was showing her the book he had got for Barbara.

"Oh, I've often thought I'd like to understand how banks were run," she told him. "It must be interesting. I wonder—"

"Yes, do read it," said Crichie warmly. "Barbara won't mind your having it first. As a matter of fact—"

He paused.

"She won't mind at all if you have it months", he blurted out. "She isn't frightfully interested."

"What a pity," Flora told him.

"Yes, I feel it a little sometimes," he granted.

And since Peachley was so long away, Flora, after putting the kettle on the stove in another box of a room, came back and whilst Crichie was reading the *Evening News*—just the main paragraphs, the events that really mattered, to-day's prices and the report of a new system of foreign exchange, and how quicker circulation of money would give new life to business houses—Flora was beginning the book which explained the banking system.

He realized with a thrill of astonishment and admiration that she had grasped the thing from the first chapter. And with flushed faces they were bending over the page, and Crichie was elucidating a point that puzzled her.

"Oh, yes, I see!" she exclaimed delightedly.

"Barbara would not have seen. I'd have spent weeks," he told her sorrowfully, "and then I'd have found she had not grasped it at all."

They got discussing another seat which Labour had won.

"Peachley thinks a little that way," said Flora. "For my part, I would dread the coming of democracy. I hate rowdyism, and democracy seems to be rowdyism. Don't you think so?"

"I do," said Crichie,

And then he was telling her of the great excitement which had prevailed in Wall Street last week over falling prices in wheat, the wonderful thrill and throb of the scene of the panic and fighting.

"I'd have liked to see it," said Flora with shining eyes. "You see, this is how I look at things, Mr. Dennison. In a sense the working classes have nothing to lose. But these men are staking fortunes all the time. Isn't that so?"

"Quite," said Crichie.

He felt quite excited. Here was a woman who understood greatness, the hazards of men playing with millions, who understood the principle of great men who led the benighted masses to accept their dictates without question, and saw that it was right that it should be so, since those who had nothing to lose, only bread and jam, were the mere automata dragged along by the great men who fought for more than existence, and staking a half-million might win two.

"Yes. That is where progress is made—in places like Wall Street," he told her. "'Men with their hands on the pulse of the world, fighting the battle of life,'" he quoted. "That would have been my world. As it is—I'm just head clerk at Goffers's."

"Oh, you won't stop at that," Flora told him.

"Think not?"

"Sure!"

"Well," he said, feeling very elated at such confidence in his powers, "I would not like to think I should. But about the working classes, where Barbara and I differ is this—if you have a class of people who will live without scope and without wanting it, it proves they have no initiative for anything beyond that life. Take the average person in working class districts like Hammersmith—"

He broke off. Flora had winced.

"Oh, I'm sorry."

She almost gulped.

"Fred—Fred actually suggested after Dinkermanns went down that we went to live down in Hammersmith," she said.

"Not really?"

"Re-ally!"

"Abominable!" ejaculated Crichie. Then he added swiftly: "But the bulk are content there."

"Quite so," agreed Flora firmly.

"Yes. It's the discontented people who make progress," he added.

"I think so, too," Flora agreed.

"And as for these petty Labour victories, they mean nothing," added Crichie. "Mere bubbles that have nothing to do with the undercurrents of the world's affairs."

Flora Peachley, in some mysterious way, made him feel quite a brilliant politician. He got up from the chair and stood back to the fire, feet planted firmly on the rug Peachley had bought Flora for her last but one birthday, having had to save for months to get it.

"Yes. Just a few people stirring the others up," agreed Flora mournfully. "They ought to be deported."

"They ought," said Crichie. "Not," he added magnanimously, "that I don't think things could be improved. They could with advantage to all. Do you believe in garden cities?"

"Absolutely," said Flora enthusiastically. "That is, I wouldn't like to live in one, personally."

"Oh, no, neither would I. No scope," agreed Crichie.

"No distinction," said Flora. "But I think they are a fine idea for checking social unrest. But for myself—"

She shook her head, and looked mournful again.

"And there I go," she said, "talking like that, and we are rapidly being driven down into the ranks of the working classes! Now that Dinkermanns have gone down, we are no more than working people. Don't shake your head. That's our position, and I wouldn't be a bit surprised if Fred voted Labour next time."

She conveyed to Crichie, who began to feel quite perturbed about it, the sorrowful fact that she, Flora Peachley, had joined those millions who must be content for the rest of their days to be satisfied to be dragged along, mere automata, tethered to the progressive splendour of men like those who fought with their hands "on the pulse of the world", and to which he, Crichie Dennison, belonged by magnetism of business ability, and where some day that ability would place him.

"But can't Peachley do something?" inquired Crichie. "Doesn't he feel the impetus? Surely he must, with a woman like you."

Very slowly and mournfully Flora shook her head from side to side. Her large pendent ear-rings, shaking also, cast a shadow on her white neck.

"Why, it's preposterous!" ejaculated Crichie.

Ting!

It was the door-bell, and Peachley.

But before letting him in, Flora recalled the kettle on the stove. It was almost molten as she lifted it off, and the odour of it filling the little house reminded Crichie of Dave, for once when over at Rimton, Barbara had insisted that he go and see the forge where Dave was working, and there had been the smell of hot metal, for Dave had been casting a "fire-back". As he stood, back to the fire, waiting for Peachley to come in, he recalled that he had come to ask the Peachleys to honour a house-party they were giving to celebrate the success of the "Village Blacksmith", whose wonderful act had now posters, and who had been asked to go across the Atlantic with it.

"Hello, Dennison. Glad to see you," said Peachley, coming into the little room. "Don't start commiserations about Dinkermanns. Had enough of it."

He was breathing quickly, and still blinking a little as he stepped into the lighted room after the dimness of the Avenue. And Flora, coming in, noted more than ever his absolutely insignificant appearance. His tie was awry, and his coat unbuttoned, and she knew that, despite the number of times she had remonstrated with him for it, he had run along the Avenue, trusting that no one would recognize him as he took what he called a bit of exercise to make up for having to sit in their little room and always mind lest one knocked something down if one moved, and even how one stretched one's legs on the rug, lest one damaged the pouffes Flora had insisted on possessing.

"Barbara and I were both sorry to hear of Dinker—"

"Don't, Dennison, don't!" appealed Peachley. "We've got over it. Bit of a knock, but we've got over it. Thousands worse placed than we are, poor devils! Wish it wasn't so, but when one picks up one's morning paper, it's appalling."

Crichie's gaze met Flora's, which was more mournful than ever. Crichie's gaze plainly said that he realized the despair a woman of spirit must feel tied to a man who was so obviously contented to see her thrust down into the working classes, and not content with being contented, even had the presumption to be expressing sympathy and his belief that there were untold numbers suffering worse conditions, associating himself with them in sympathy rather than trying to widen the gulf between them and himself. But Crichie had always told Barbara poor old Peachley would get nowhere. He was more convinced of it than ever in the face of way Peachley took Dinkermanns having gone down. And he was frightfully sorry for Flora—a splendid woman like Flora who knew how to put clothes on, as Barbara did not (those ear-rings, now, just gave the added touch to perfection), tied to a contented ignoramus like Peachley, who was blundering along, happy because they were not actually thrust down to starvation level. Here Crichie pulled himself up, and resolved not on any account to read any further exaggerated accounts of riotings for food. Newspapers had to have something in them, and these were most probably exaggerated. The Press would spoil your breakfast if you would let it.

"Well, I thought I ought to call to say how sorry we were," said Crichie. "Barbara was quite upset. She thought you'd have to leave here, and how Henry would miss having no lawn to play on!"

Peachley lost his off-hand manner. He was sitting down taking his boots off, and looked up, face aglow, its irritated expression quite gone.

"Well, I'm jiggered," he ejaculated. "That was the first thought that came into my head, too, on our getting the news. Tell Mrs. Dennison from me that Henry won't lose the lawn."

Crichie nodded. Peachley's snub nose and little twinkling eyes were again lost to sight as he struggle patiently with the obstinate knot in his bootlace.

"Translating and copying," grunted Peachley. "Just been out to post the advert., haven't I, Flora?"

Flora nodded.

"Poorly paid work, isn't it?" inquired Crichie.

"Oh, not bad. Spare time, you know," said Peachley, still struggling with the knot. "Hope I've not to go out to it, that's all. Hope I can do it at home. It'll save Flora from having to live in Hammersmith, though, for my part—well, we might have got a house with more room in it."

Crichie smiled at Flora. There was certainly no hope for a man who would think there might be more comfort and room living in a working class district like Hammersmith.

"Well, you can tell Mrs. Dennison Henry won't lose his lawn," said Peachley.

The knot was untied now, and his face, kindly and commonplace, was in view once more, and he was looking about for his slippers.

"They're in the slipper-bag, Fred," Flora told him. "And Mr. Dennison is staying to supper."

"Oh, yes, I'll get them. Yes. Stay to supper, Dennison. We don't get much company here. Everybody's so select, you know, in this Avenue, One nods in a morning coming out of a little gate at another man coming out of a little gate, and—where did you say my slippers were, Flora?"

"Slipper-bag," called Flora, who was attending to supper.

"Oh, yes. Well, as I was saying, Dennison, the first year one nods at the man and he nods back, and the second year one says 'Good morning', and the third year one ventures that it is a nice morning, and in the fourth year one looks at him as he sits on his lawn, and at the end of a quarter of a century I expect we'll be talking politics. That's the Avenue. It amuses me at times. Ever struck you that there's something—er—stultifying in this selectness we pride ourselves on? I can tell you it's a relief on a Sunday, after dinner, to read of Mrs. 'Arris. Sketch, you know. I sometimes feel I'd like to ask her to come and enliven the Avenue."

"Oh, Fred," came from the kitchen. "Don't try to be funny."

And then silence fell, broken only by the bubbling sound of the kettle, the moving of a pan. And out of the silence came a small voice, humble and appealing:

"Favver."

"Fred—don't take him the light."

Peachley, his feet in his slippers, listened to both.

"No. But doesn't he want something?"

"He's quite all right. Ought to be asleep."

"Certainly. I'll go and tell him so," said Peachley sternly.

His back, as Crichie looked at it, expressed the uttermost of parental authority, grim and indicative of the sentiment that there was no nonsense about him.

"You'll wake the others up," came from Flora.

"Can't. I've my slippers off," said Peachley.

"Fred, what are slippers for?" came from the kitchen.

"Oh, it's more comfortable in one's stockinged feet," said Peachley. "Don't you think so, Dennison?"

"Slippers for me," said Crichie. "We've some good lines at five and six ha'penny."

"Oh, yes. I'll just go and settle that little demon, Dennison. Children need a firm hand. No mistake about it."

And Peachley was gone—in his stockinged feet, and Crichie knew that a man so weak, so susceptible to a child's voice wanting something at nine o'clock, would, indeed, never get anywhere. He realized, also, that Flora's forebodings that Peachley might vote Labour next were not without grounds. Most of these Labour people were great sentimentalists. He could see, in his mind's eye, Peachley gravitating towards a working-class district, and mixing with working people and enjoying it, and getting worked up about people who were starving—if one believed the papers—arid eventually wearing red in his buttonhole as he went to the poll.

Flora came to put more coals on the fire with the tongs. He looked at her with sympathy.

"You see that he remains in his class," said Crichie in a low voice.

Flora nodded.

"I shall try. I'd rather commit suicide than live the lives the workers lead."

Then she stopped.

"Quite contentedly," added Crichie.

"Oh—quite—."

She flitted back to the kitchen.

Very odd, that, mused Crichie. When one got talking of the classes at all, and there always had been classes and would have to be, one was often led to be conscious of glaring inconsistencies and paradoxes just when one had said the strongest thing one could say. Flora had felt that. He had realized it as she had said she would sooner commit suicide than live the lives the workers led. Often when talking to Barbara about the working-classes she had made him feel quite a fool by making him conscious of these inconsistencies in his remarks, and he knew her intelligence was of such an order that she would never be able to see how great wisdom really made paradoxes. But he knew Flora would understand how one could be quite consistent even though contradicting one's self, as one did, he invariably found, when talking of the classes at all. And as Crichie sat pondering there, Peachley had struck a safety-match after having grunted after running into the bed-rail. Somewhere—now, where had he put it—was another night-light? He found it at length and lit it. Its feeble splutter came up into a dim light. And there was Henry, smiling, for all his tear-blotched face, as he saw—favver.

"Awful little nuisance you are," said Peachley loudly. "Why aren't you asleep?"

Henry smiled. The tooth was jumping awfully, but he smiled. He looked at favver and favver looked at him. And favver winked. And favver's face, with its smile now, and little, twinkling eyes, and favver's head, where the premature baldness was appearing, was unto Henry the face of a wonderful being.

"Toof-ache," explained Henry.

"You ought to be asleep," thundered Peachley. "Nine o'clock it is. You ought to be ashamed of yourself."

Peachley winked and Henry smiled again. And Peachley went back and to the chest, just over Dennison's chair, and took out a bottle and the dropper and a bit of cotton-wool, whilst Dennison stood up to let him get the things. And the anomaly of Peachley was suddenly revealed to Crichie. He had noted the same thing in the working-classes and in anyone tied to them by sympathy of outlook. And if anything ever made him fear that the structure of Society would ever be changed he found it in this attribute of Peachley's, which was also an attribute he had noted in such of the working-classes as were "Labour". Here was Peachley, quite inferior to himself in intellect and initiative and push, without ability to get on top, without ability to think a way out of the straits he was thrown into by the Dinkermanns smash, without ability to do anything more than plod and work till his hair was grey—till he was dead, in fact—and Peachley himself had no sense of that inferiority. As he stood with the tooth-ache remedy in his hand it was plain that old Peachley considered himself as much the equal of a man of business who would make a success of life as he would consider the man who emptied their dust-bins an equal with him. Was that, mused Crichie gloomily, the shadow of the forthcoming democracy? Supposing that spirit spread—the spirit which laughed at the qualities called forth by competition, which was assuredly the inspiration of all achievement? Suppose these little people who just worked and plodded on, and asked neither to dominate prices nor to run the thrilling hazard of great gain, grew more and more convinced that they were the equals of the captains of industry and commerce—what would happen? It was terrible to contemplate. Brains, as produced by competition) as they were assuredly, would be at a discount. The dustman would say "Good morning" to him, Crichie Dennison. And the dust-man would expect to be greeted back, or he might not empty the dust-bin! He gloomily pictured himself emptying his own dustbin. And it was people like Peachley who had the power to bring Labour into power—little, commonplace men like Peachley, who took Dinkermanns going down so calmly and went and advertised for copying and translating so that things would not be too pinched, and if he said more about Dinkermanns he quite expected Peachley would commence to rave against speculation—that bed-rock of the business life of the world. He knew he would. He decided to try it. Peachley would have no more sense.

"Supper is ready, Fred!" called Flora.

Peachley was coming along the passage. Crichie and he met on the threshold of the dining-room and turned into the little room.

"Start in, Dennison," urged Peachley, sitting down and tossing his serviette carelessly over his knees.

And then Peachley, with his little, twinkling eyes, was looking across at him and asking him if he had ever tried reading Greek or French or Spanish as a way of reaching out to the thought of other nations.

And—Flora looked bored.

With an inward gasp Crichie realized that, like most of these Labour cranks (he became more and more certain that Peachley would end as a Labour crank, and more and more sorry for Flora), Peachley was a student. Or perhaps Peachley was swanking. Some of these little minds did occasionally swank, try to make you feel they had brains, whereas the test was well, here was Peachley, who would have to grind away to the end of his days, and talking of languages.

"Never had time," said Crichie. "Goffers's taken all my energies."

Peachley actually looked surprised.

"Mastered three languages in six years," he said genially. "It's easy. Persian next, that is if this copying and translating leaves any time at all."

He helped himself from the salad. And from the room beyond came Henry's grateful voice:

"Nite, favver."

"Nite. Go to sleep, Henry "

"Yes. Going—"

"Wonderful to read in the original," said Peachley. "You try it, Dennison. Goffers's is making you look tired. When Dinkermanns went down I said to myself, well, Fred Peachley, you'll always be able to read Greek and French and Spanish if all the banks in the world go bust. There are things they can't take away, like the sun in the sky, though I suppose in time they may advertise across it."

Flora and Crichie regarded each other across the table. There was no mistake. Peachley was talking almost like a Socialist now. Crichie believed Peachley was himself not aware of it, but certainly Peachley would end by wearing red in his button-hole and walking to the poll, with those little eyes of his twinkling unconcern at all the criticism of opponents.

"And if Dinkermanns had not speculated, and 1 don't believe in speculation, I'd have been beginning

Persian this week," said Peachley wrathfully. It's a curse, Dennison, speculation."

"The business world could not go on without it, said Crichie.

Peachley grunted.

"I sometimes think it could very nicely," he said. Sometimes I think all this competition business is what causes people to have to starve, that we could have a happier life for everyone without it."

"Fred," said Flora, "if you don't mind you are going to turn into one of those horrid Socialists."

"Me!"

Peachley was plainly aghast.

"I'll lend you a few books against it," said Crichie.

"Oh, thanks," said Peachley. "I'd like to read them. Funny, isn't it? A man at our works said the same to me the other day. Always thought them rather—rabid people. But I'll borrow the books, Dennison. When I've read all that's to be read against Socialism, and that's an awfully good way of learning about a thing, to read the opposition, I shall get a few books on it. I suppose there'll be plenty. That's only fair, isn't it, when you've read all there is against it? What they call judgement by comparative methods. We had it in college. I'll find out if I am a Socialist."

"I'll bring the books along," almost gasped Crichie.

"Will you pass the dishes down, Fred?" asked Flora in an icy voice.

Peachley passed them and stared at the expression on her face.

"What have I said now?" he asked.

"Fred, if you turn Socialist that'll be the finish," said Flora. "I've put up with a great deal from you."

Peachley looked apologetic. Then his little eyes blinked.

"I shall certainly read the books against Socialism," he said, "and for it, since I read those against it. Only fair. What I call cricket. Here, Dennison, try some of this horse-radish. It's all right."

As Crichie went out he left them with the firm conviction that the Peachleys were nearing the rocks of domestic life. Why—they did not agree about anything. And then he pulled himself up. Did he and Barbara, for that matter? But, then, most people were like that, possibly, and still went on. And, after all there was always Goffers's, just as Peachley had said there was always Greek and French and Spanish. Good for a man to have something that remained static amidst all the changes and disappointments of life. He had Goffers's—Peachley had languages. But what had Flora? Nothing, those dark eyes of hers had said, then he recalled that he had left her the book he had got for Barbara. Good idea that. Give her some interest in life. He would take others when she had got through that—the latest out on the future mechanization of Society, showing how classes would always obtain. And he decided to drop in on them more frequently. And if Flora had had nothing till now to help her forget her conflict with Peachley, what about Barbara? The thought came to him as he sat in the tube. Barbara, he knew, would have liked youngsters. Most women did—but that was folly until he knew about the partnership. And possibly, since they quarrelled about everything, they would quarrel about the children. The Peachleys did. He wondered if he could persuade Barbara to put her hair in head-phone fashion like Flora. But, no, it would scarcely suit Barbara's face. And—he turned his paper over. "Is fair beauty insipid?" stared at him. Trivial sort of article. Still, he read it. Not bad on so flippant a subject. And there was something in it. He pictured Flora Peachley. There was attraction there—vivid, dominating. One felt it. But, then, fair women did not show grey hairs so soon. No, the head-phone fashion would not suit Barbara. But it suited that half-Spanish-looking face, with its mournful, dark, eyes, which could yet glance and gleam and scorn.

As he rang the bell outside the house where the almond blossom had long since fallen, but where the tree lifted its branches, all shadowy and touched with the gleam of the reflection of the street-lamp, he caught strains of Mozart's Overture to "Il Seraglio". He thought that modern music—jazz—had more "go" in it.

Then the door opened. Barbara had opened it. She had not even changed her dress, but wore her plain, afternoon attire. She saw his glance at this neglect.

"I hadn't time," she said happily. "Dave came at six, and we've been playing ever since. It's been simply gorgeous. Didn't you hear us?"

He followed her up the hall, where she waited to help him out of his coat.

Chapter Three

Crichie and Barbara passed into the room where Dave sat with the 'cello. Dave's gaze was turned towards them as they entered. Crichie saw it fall first on Barbara, and could have started. For in that look he had read an almost devouringly affectionate look, but, as it turned on himself, Crichie saw that Dave was unaware of the fact that his glance revealed intense love for Barbara, and for him tolerance as Barbara's husband. Just as well that he had noticed it, though. Barbara evidently had not, and, in any case, Dave was going to America soon. Meanwhile he would warn Barbara that Dave was twenty-five and evidently in love with her. That would stop any unhappy development. Forewarned was forearmed. Good proverb, that, very good. Lots of wisdom in those old saws. He would warn Barbara that very night after Dave had gone. That was the best way to save anything unpleasant happening. Always best to nip such things in the bud, and after he had put her on her guard, so that neither she nor Dave should be made unhappy by Dave saying anything of it, for example, or forgetting himself, as men could, particularly when Barbara was so warmly affectionate, as now, for instance, as she stood with her hand on Dave's shoulder, looking at the copy they were just going to start playing from, with both their faces lit up with the same enthusiastic glow—after he had put that matter right, so that Barbara would not torment Dave by these little marks of affection, he would show her the opera-cloak. Eight, eight and nine. Barbara would look wonderful in it with her fair hair. But, then, so would Flora Peachley with her dark hair. These shades, pastels, went well with blondes or brunettes. Wonderful line. Barbara would fly out at him when he told her of Dave, but certainly it was his duty. She must show a reserve towards Dave. That would save the situation.

"Isn't that a glorious sonata?" asked Barbara. "Isn't it, Crichie?"

Their faces were both turned towards him, hers from the piano, Dave's from the seat beside it as he sat with the bow silent across the strings.

"Quite nice," said Crichie.

Barbara's sigh travelled through the room.

"Quite nice!" she said, and shook her head. "What a platitude to describe Beethoven at his grandest."

And, looking at Dave, Crichie saw the same, large tolerance on Dave's face as was on Barbara's, the look of two people mad on music, and one of them mad on the other without the other knowing it, and both tolerating him good-naturedly because they had been enjoying a world he knew little or nothing of for hours and hours. Best warn Barbara, certainly. Heaps of marriages had gone mash on this common interests rock with some third party. And—she would perhaps see the common sense of him telling her. Only, did Barbara ever see the common sense of anything commonsensible? No. Distinctly no. She was like old Peachley, caring about things which did not matter, from his point of view. Still, even though she flew out at him, as she would be sure to do, she would perhaps see that Dave cared for her, and to save Dave pain would—well, she could be out sometimes when he called, or be going out, and treat him more coldly, and so it would be nipped in the bud. That was a common sense way of treating such a situation, according to Crichie Dennison. Barbara would surely quarrel with him. She would not see common sense in it. But there was the cloak, as a peace-offering for their quarrel that morning. If they quarrelled again to-night, well, it would cost no more to patch up two quarrels than one.

"Mozart at his best," said Barbara to Crichie.

"Oh, Crichie, it's Heavenly."

She left the piano; Dave stood his 'cello in the corner of the room by the oak table.

And Mary was bringing the supper-tray in. She brought on the tray the Swiss bell for them to ring for anything else they required. It fell off the tray as she set it on the table.

"What's the matter with that bell?" asked Barbara of Crichie. "It has gone flat-sounding, somehow. Haven't you noticed it?"

She looked at him with a worried look.

"It used to sound different. I'm sure it did," she urged."

Crichie smiled.

"It's us, Barbara. We're getting used to the sound of it," he told her.

She handed him his cup, and her face looked relieved.

"Oh, well, I expect it's that," she said. "But it has quite jarred on me sometimes lately, and there's not much room on the tray for it or on a small table. One has to hunt for it amongst the things, Crichie, Let's have a gong."

They were getting past the sentimental stage. Crichie realized it. That was good. A gong was better than that silly little bell which toppled over so often.

"Three, two and two, the brass ones," he told Barbara, munching.

"Get one," said Barbara.

It was the first time she had asked him to bring anything from Goffers's. There she was looking across at Dave to see if he wanted his cup filling up.

"Hasn't the time gone?" she asked, speaking to Dave. "It was just like old times, only this piano's better than the one I had before Sarah bought me this. You never seemed to care for us to play together after I'd got this new one. Why?"

"Barbara, fill my cup up," asked Crichie.

Dave had grown very pale.

"Oh, I don't know," he said.

Sarah had got that piano three weeks before Barbara met Dennison. Things had somehow altered then. And now the piano was here, in Dennison's house and latterly he had wondered whether he ought to come.

"Oh, Dave, bring Bach next time, and some of Mendelssohn—the grand old colossal. You'll be coming tomorrow? There's no rehearsal?"

"Shan't be able to get over tomorrow, Barbary," Dave told her slowly.

"Oh, well, the day after."

"Can't then."

She looked at him .

"You're glumping about something," she said. "Out with it."

Barbara had grown pale, too.

"I'm not——"

"You are, Dave. You shouldn't glump."

"Barbary, I'm not glumping."

"There's something. And you've always told me when there was something."

She got up from her chair and stood staring at him. She ended by looking very pale; indeed, and sitting down again.

"Dave, you're in love with someone," she said.

Dave nodded.

"Guessed right," he told her;

She sat quite still, staring at him.

"Is she very nice?" she asked.

"Oh, yes," stammered Dave.

She saw by Dave's countenance, which had changed from white to red, that it was true, that he was certainly in love.

"Well, I don't like the idea," said Barbara. "Somehow I don't like it a bit. But I shall expect you both to tea Sunday. Now don't go and glump. I expect you both."

Dave got up and departed hurriedly.

Barbara was still sitting by the fire when Crichie came in from seeing him to the gate. Crichie sat down and regarded her with amused eyes. Then he let out a roar of laughter;.

"Stop. Stop that idiotic laughter," said Barbara. "Stop it if you don't want to drive me mad."

Dave had just told her that he could not come tomorrow, nor the day after because someone else came first now.

"Barbara—"

"Oh, leave me alone!"

"But Dave was sure to fall in love with somebody."

"Why should he?"

"Barbara, you look fierce."

"I feel fierce."

"But why?"

"Oh, how do I know why? It's a world of whys. Why should Dave go and fall in love? Tell me that."

As she glared at him Crichie Dennison saw the full humour of the situation. And he knew that Dave would not come, could not and bring a sweetheart and that in all probability Barbara would go over and call at his hotel and have it out with him, as she would phrase it.

"Barbara, Dave is trying very nicely to avoid coming so often," Crichie told her. "He's in love, but it's with you, and he has got afraid of your finding out. Afraid, possibly, of coming."

Barbara turned her face from the fire.

"What on earth are you talking about?" she inquired.

Crichie stated his opinion. Barbara's silence perplexed him. At last she spoke.

"I—I can't believe it," she said to Crichie. "Are you quite sure?"

"Yes."

"You mean he likes me better than anyone else in the world?" she asked.

Crichie nodded. Her face lit up suddenly.

"Then he always will," she told Crichie. "So—he can get married if he likes. I think I'll be rather glad he quarrels with someone else and not me some day, only nobody'll ever get him out of his glumps like I could have done."

Crichie had got up. He was staring at her.

"Do you know what you are saying, Barbara?" he asked. "Do you know you're regretting not having married Dave?"

Barbara nodded.

"I said no one could have got him out of his dumps like me," she said. "It's quite a common-sense statement. Nobody could. So it would have been common sense to marry him. Only—you see, 1 didn't know. But if I had done it's possible you might have married someone interested in Goffers's. Then you'd have been happy, too."

Crichie nodded and yawned.

"So we shall just have to go for a walk on the commons ourselves," said he. "Unless we ask the Peachleys."

Barbara sat up in her chair.

"You mean Dave is not to go with us?" she asked.

"Don't you see, Barbara, he wishes not to go?" he told her. "It's becoming painful to him."

"I shall go to see him tomorrow," said Barbara stubbornly. "I shall find out if it's as you say, and, if it is, tell him how pleased I am. As for his staying away, I wouldn't really allow it. I should miss him too much. Not for the ten weeks he's in England. Possibly he'll bring a wife back from America—"

"But, Barbara, you can't tell a man you're glad he's in love with you when you're married!" gasped Crichie.

"Can't!"

"But people don't."

"If it makes Dave happier I shall."

"But it isn't as though you could marry him."

"Who wants to?"

"Then—"

"I can't possibly have him staying away," said Barbara. "There's heaps of things I wanted us to play together. She can have him afterwards."

"Who?"

"Oh, the unknown she—whoever she is—when he meets her."

"Barbara, you mustn't go to see Dave."

"I shall."

"But why?"

"Because Dave will have nowhere to go unless he comes here, and he'll be unhappy. He's homesick as it is. And I'd be unhappy because he doesn't come. So if he was trying to keep away for that—well, it's silly."

"Well—"

Crichie yawned again. Mary had put the other lights out and had gone to bed.

"You are going to ask Dave to come just the same?" asked Crichie.

"Yes."

"It's folly."

"It'll make him happier."

"It's folly."

"Just as I shall always be happier for knowing," said Barbara. "Oh, dear, I'm tired, Crichie; Good night."

Crichie switched on the electric light. They heard from afar the rumble of a train. Crichie yawned once more.

"Yes, good lines those brass gongs we've got," he said. "Good night."

He passed along the landing. Barbara was standing with her hands over her ears. Was she never, never to get away from the way he listed everything as though the house were part of the Emporium? Then she drew a deep breath. Why it was nothing, all this which frayed one so.

As for Dave staying away, it was absurd. There were only a few weeks before he went abroad. She felt unable to relinquish those weeks. She stood realizing they were all she would have. They would pass all too quickly. Then she would be without anyone to talk to, only Crichie, who would go on talking of business, of the things she considered mattered very little to people, just as he considered the things she was interested in mattered very little. She looked out on the stars. They swam a little as she looked at them. She realized that she was almost crying, and then in the modern way smiled at herself for being almost crying, like a big baby. Still, there were weeks and weeks yet, and she and Crichie had agreed about getting the gong. Weeks and weeks, and Dave would bring a big pile of new music, and they would play it together, very happy, why, more happy really than Crichie and herself had been even on their honeymoon, and much more near to each other, somehow. Life was certainly odd. Perhaps it was, she thought, that grasping a thing one lost it. She yawned, jumped into bed, and with Mendelssohn's "Spring Song" yet reiterating in her mind, dropped off to sleep.

Chapter Four

Wednesdays, in Rimton generally, were days on which women set their husbands' hash, the day following being the day when the: butcher's-van journeyed through from town, when small quantities of fresh meat were bought to "tide over" until the week-end's "buying-in". Sarah was no exception to this rule. Every Wednesday, as Dan led his horse along the roads, shouting "Hi-hi," or "Nay, come on," or "Gee up," as was his way, in a very mild tone, unless there was another horse behind, when he had no need to give that encouragement, he knew there would be on his return—just hash. As Wednesday was his second hardest day in the week, when he had to go as far as Greenshaw Hill, to a row of houses where sometimes they bought potatoes and naught besides, he always thought it very inappropriate on Sarah's part to set him hash at the close of that day.

He was jogging on now, thinking of it as he went along the hill-road, leading his horse, listening to the creak of the cart-wheels, and he was thinking of it disconsolately. Since Barbary had left them hash had always oppressed him more. Possibly, he pondered, he might not have thought so much about it if he had not this morning lost on a tub of apples. Grand they had looked on the top—rosy-cheeked snows— but when he had got a few pounds sold he had seen that he had been had. He consoled himself by holding debates with the man he had bought them from, and picturing their next meeting under the great shed of the town market. Then he reverted once more to the hash, then forgot all troubles, even his loss on the apples, as a great bush of wild roses came into sight. And all along the roads that day May-blossom had been out and honeysuckle was coming, mingling its sweetness with the scent of wild rose and "May". He had gathered a sprig of honeysuckle from a hedgerow at Greenshaw Hill, whilst waiting for a woman to bring her basket out. It was fastened in the tab of his cap. Hours had gone by since then. Sun had blazed down on Dan, and the honeysuckle and he were wilting. He felt very tired. Folk did not mend with keeping, he mused, and wondered with a faint surprise if he were growing old. The hill-roads felt a bigger pull certainly. The sun's glare tried his eyes more. He looked for the chimneys of his own little cottage more eagerly, was glad to sit in the ingle-nook, often without looking at the paper, and begin to write out, as the clock struck eight, the incomings and outgoings of the day's business. Aye, he must be getting older, he ruminated. Or was it that he had missed Dave a lot? Bit o' both maybe. Aye, most likely a bit o' both. That was the worst of taking aught young, watching it grow up, "marlocking" with it, knocking gumption into it, and then, just when you got you felt you could not live without it, off it went. Still, he was not grumbling, he told himself. Both of them, Barbary and Dave, had gone, but were happy. Sarah had got the whim to take the two of them, since they had been left orphans within a week of each other, and Sarah had said she could not bide that they should go to the workhouse, and, as they had no children, and never could have, they might as well take 'em. He saw them yet, as he thought of that March day when Sarah had brought them, standing by the cottage window, Dave crying his e'en blind, because he had lost father and mother, and Barbara staring at him in surprise, because she could not understand, having come to a better place than the one she had left, and having only the dimmest recollections of the father who had been drowned at sea and only too glad to get away from her mother, who had said to Sarah: "Take her, an' welcome. Barbary was an orphan in a way, and yet her mother was living, for all he and Sarah knew. They had expected Ruth Delling year after year to put in an appearance and try to take Barbary from them, and times they had discussed together whether they should tell her she had a mother. But Barbary was beyond her now, even if she did turn up. Married and well set up, with electric lights and stoves and all make o' things, as Dave had written about for Sarah's special benefit, and which glory Sarah had retailed to Rimton as she stood buying things at carts or went to tea finding therein a great consolation for the disappointment of Barbara's early marriage. They had certainly lost on Barbara, as Sarah had often said. Given her an eddication, passed her right through college, paid for lessons in music, an' all that make of thing, and then, so soon as she had got teaching, on her first holiday she had met Crichie Dennison— and was off. Still, she had done well, had Barbary. There she was, married and well set up, and not forgetting them for all that, writing them now almost every week and demanding letters back all about the countryside, and who was being married and who was being ligged low, and just what the meadows looked like. And he must write a letter to Barbary this night, for he had promised Sarah he would. Best part of an hour that would take. Then he'd have to go to the schoolmaster's house and ask the schoolmaster to address him an envelope, for, as Sarah had said, though it would be all right to Barbary his sending an envelope addressed in his uneddicated handwriting, there was Crichie to consider. No, not much time for a nap to-night. And he had thought to have a walk by the stream, to see the willows hanging over it, grey and ghostly in the moonshine, and hear the birds twittering their good nights and the stream singing its song that never changed whatever changes took place. Bonnie moon there had been last night. As he had come down the road from having an odd 'un it had shone full on the slates of the cottage, wet with a light shower It had looked a picture, and he had pondered how Dave must miss it, had known the lad did miss it, though he said so little. And Dave's forge, which he still looked on as Dave's forge, though Willie Barnes had it, standing silent and grey by the stream, had smote at him, and he had said to himself: "Never more. He's gone from it and us—for ever." Only, did one ever know? The lad might not go on "musicianing" all his life. But, no, he must not wish that the world would tire o' Dave's playing just to have him back, to walk on the bank-side with him by the stream, or smoke a pipe with him before they doffed their coats for bed, as in the old times. No. Dave was gone. By this time Dan was almost at the foot of the hill-road and could see the cottage, and the mournful thought that Dave was gone had made him remember once more that there was hash.

He could see the smoke curling up from the chimney-pot, which shone goldenly in the light of the setting sun; could see the lines of white paint between the stones of the chimney-stack, for he had newly- painted them last month at the risk of neck or limbs, with Sarah standing below and calling out: "Tha ought to kill thyself, Dan, for going up there, and I'd have no sympathy with thee." Aye, there was hash. The chimney-smoke testified to a good fire. The pan would be on the crow over it and Sarah standing by, giving it a stir occasionally, standing stirring, in Barbary's blue gingham apron, which was a mile too small for her. And if he snighed his nose up at hash she would remind him of the numbers who would be glad to eat hash. No. There was not much comfort these days with Dave and Barbary both gone, and unscrupulous villains in the world who sold you a tub of apples which you paid for in good faith, and found you'd lose a pound on.

He pulled his horse up and went up to the cottage, opened the door and shouted in: "I'll be home in a quarter of an hour."

"All right," called Sarah. See as tha does."

For Dan's quarter was sometimes a half when he went to take the horse to the stables and had an odd 'un.

The door closed and she heard the wheels of the cart pass up the road.

"Take thy hat off, Nelly," she urged to Nelly Greeby.

"Nay, I maun be goin'," Nelly told her.

"I've stalled thee, haven't I, talkin' so mich o' our Dave?" asked Sarah.

"Nay, I've noan been stalled," Nelly told her.

Nelly Greeby was certainly coming out these days. Sarah noticed it. A different look with her altogether from the one she had had before old Greeby died. And clothes did make a difference, too. But that, to Sarah, did not account for the altered look of Nelly Greeby. Three times now she had called at the cottage, and if it had been when Dave was over, Sarah told herself as she stirred away with the big spoon, she would have thought summat. But it had always been when Dave was not over. Not that he might not do worse. Nelly was a good, hard-working lass from his own district, and that was a lot.

"You don't think he'll ever come back an' work at the forge again?" asked Nelly.

She was taking her hat off, Sarah noted with pleasure. For now there was no one to tell how troublesome Dan could be, and all afternoon she had been telling Nelly, when she was not talking about Dave, and she did not feel so bad about Dan now.

"Eh, no, lass, he'll never come back to th' forge," said Sarah. "Why, he's goin' to America soon. They're makin' an awful stir about him."

Nelly sat silent. Sarah stole a look at her, and was convinced. Nelly was dropping in just to hear her talk about Dave. And she recalled that Barbary had once had a fight with Nelly Greeby because Nelly had told Barbary she, Nelly, was Dave's sweetheart. And Barbary had said he was nobody's and would not be ever, and had come home with a scratch across her forehead. But he might do worse than marry Nelly Greeby. There was Ross Farm, and that would come to Nelly, being the eldest. And it would be a link which brought Dave home oftener if he got courting with Nelly. And her ways would be his ways, the ways of the district where they had both been brought up.

Whilst they sat talking Dan came in.

"Well, Nelly, how's things?" he asked.

He hung up his coat and cap and looked around for any letter that might have come from Dave.

"It's there, on th' dresser," Sarah told him. "I left it till tha come. Open it whilst I serve thy tea."

Dan sat in his chair and read the letter by the fireglow.

"Aught fresh?" asked Sarah, referring to Dave's letter.

"Aye."

Dan's voice was tremulous with excitement.

"He's coming home for a ten days," he told her. "An' he says he may be here as soon as th' letter."

Sarah was ladling out the hash.

"But I thowt he'd to go on't stage every night till he went to America?" she said.

"Well, he's coming," Dan told her. "That's enough for me."

"I'd best be goin'," said Nelly Greeby. "I didn't intend to stay."

And she was putting her hat on again.

"Nay, just stop and have some tea," urged Sarah. "And if our Dave comes whilst tha'rt here he'll not eat thee."

There was nothing more to be said, as Sarah's attitude showed, for she set another cup and saucer and plate, and Nelly had to stay.

"Mightn't be here for hours yet," said Dan, eating hash with a better relish than he had eaten it with for a considerable time, Sarah served him a second lot.

Then she stood staring at him.

"I thowt tha didn't care for hash?" she told him.

"Well, it's gone down," Dan told her. "It doesn't allus go down wid sich speed. Tha sees—"

"Shut up!" urged Sarah.

Surely— Then she ran from the kitchen and was standing in the doorway of the cottage, and Dave was grinning and saying: "Aye, it's me." He was lugging in his box and the 'cello, which was now in a case, not in the old baize covering; And they heard the hoot of the taxi as it sped back to town. Dave did not journey on "shanks' pony" any longer. And he was taking off a coat that was very different from the one he had used to wear; after work was ended, to walk by the bank-side with Dan. He came over to the hearth, stood looking at the mantelshelf, with its coffee-grinder on one side and the tea-caddy on the other, and the alarm-clock in the middle, and he said, as they looked at him, warm pride in him in both their faces: "I'm chuckin' it." And they saw he had come home for ten days' "glumping".

"Chuckin' what?" asked Dan, looking across the table at Dave's figure, silhouetted against the fireglow.

"All of it. London. Saying the same thing night after night and having the laughs in the same places. I'm tir't of it. It isn't a man's life. I'm coming back to the forge."

Then looking at Dan, he saw Nelly Greeby sitting beside him.

"Oh, Nelly," he greeted her. Then: "I hadn't noticed there were anybody in."

"Come an' sit down thyself," urged Sarah. "I'll leet the lamp in a minute."

"Nay, it isn't time to leet up yet, is it?" asked Dan, waggishly.

"Thee shut up an' don't talk out o' thy turn," Sarah told him. She knew he would be suited if the lad did leave the city and come back to this place. And would she not be glad, too? Only it would be a silly thing to do after having left the forge and with all a wonderful life opening out for him. He was just glumping. He had always had these glumps. He had had them when he worked at the forge, and he would have them whatever he worked at. Only Barbary had been able to get him out o' glumps, and she wished she were here just this minute, for Sarah did not relish the idea of Dave coming to spend ten days and being glumping all the time.

"Aye. Come an' get thy legs under t'table, Dave," Dan told him. "Make thyself look a bit less. As for goin' back to t' forge—"

Then he caught Sarah's glance upon him and stopped. Dan coughed. He had almost forgotten that Nelly was there in the excitement of Dave's coming.

Nelly went soon afterwards. Sarah cleared the table and Dan and Dave sat smoking.

"Now what's this about chuckin' it?" asked Dan.

"Just what I said—I'm tir't, Dan. Put yourself in the same place. Every night the curtain goes up and you say the same words, an' folk laugh just in the same places, and you get tir't. You get weary o' it. You get thinking o' work that is man's work—swinging the

hammer, seeing the sparks fly, hearing the roaring o'
the bellows. Don't you see?"

They puffed away a little while together.

"I can understand it—a bit," said Dan. "But look at
the pay."

Dave got up and walked to and fro.

"And you've to live at an hotel. It's expected of you.
An' I sit there; knowing nobody, not wanting to know
anybody; and all my thoughts wander back here—
and I'm tir't."

"But tha can go to our Barbary's," said Dan. "Tha
can allus go there when tha'rt fed up. They make thee
welcome; don't they?"

"Oh, aye. They make me welcome; But I can't live
there, can I?"

This was certainly a bad fit of glumping.

"Well, I don't know—it'd be all right to 'em, 1 expect.
Couldn't tha live there and travel to the theatre fro'
there—"

"No, I couldn't," said Dave.

"Well, I don't see—" Dan told him.

"I do," said Dave.

"Why, are they fallin' out so mich or summat?"
inquired Dan anxiously,

"Nay. They're all right," said Dave. "But—well, let's
have a walk. There'll be some stars shining in the
sky an' the moon will be up soon, and I'm going up
Ridgely Fells tomorrow neet, an happen I'll be able to
think what to do.

Dan puffed at his pipe.

"There's no forge for thee to come back to," he told
Dave. "Has ta realized that?"

Dave nodded.

"There's others," he answered.

"Aye. A good way off. An' other men hammering in
'em," said Dan. "An' if tha got one, tha'll not be thy
own boss. Tha'd have the same shop as Willie had

before tha went. Tha'd be under another smith, and tha'd like that, wouldn't tha?"

Dave's face told that he knew all about how he would like working under another smith.

"An' lodgings," said Dan. "No, Dave. The forge is gone. Tha'll just ha' to go on."

When Sarah came in from the scullery from the washing-up, they had their coats on.

"That's it. Take him out as soon as he has landed," she told Dan. "I've been as long as thee without seeing him. Take him out, do."

"We'll soon be back," said Dan.

And when they had gone out, Dan turned back for a box of matches. Sarah was rocking herself wrathfully in her chair. Dan leaned down to her.

"None o' thy foolin'," she told him. I thowt we could ha' gathered round the fire, an tha'rt takin' him out."

"We're just goin' on t' bankside," he told her. "When he comes in, he'll happen be all right."

"An' encourage him to come back to t' forge," she said, irately.

"The forge is gone," said Dan. "Dave knows he can't come back. But tha knows, he allus walked on t' bankside when he was glumping. It'll do him all t' good in t' world."

"Well," Sarah told him, relenting. "I dare say tha'rt reight. Get off wi' you both. I'll get some supper ready against you come in."

Dave and Dan were soon walking on the narrow path that ran by the stream. This little bit of the north looked vast and grey in the gloaming. The moon had not yet come over the hills, but her light gave luminance to a few low-hanging clouds. The heat of the day was passed. Their feet brushed the grass that grew by the wall-side away from the stream, and so still was everything they could hear the grass blowing in the soft western wind. A thrush sang its last song, and as they walked on beyond the stream towards the dark sweep of the moors, the cry of a plover reached them from a field on which the moor rushes and couch grass had encroached. They sensed the beat of its wings as it went round the skyey greyness. And near the wall leaned bushes which had white roses which shook evening dew on them from their leaves, as they brushed past, and tossed towards them delicate fragrance.

"The moor-cotton will be out," said Dave.

In the hushed silence through which came the drip of the dew, the blowing of the soft wind, the neighing of a horse three or four fields away, his voice had dropped to a low note. Back again! He was back again, he told himself, with rapture keen as pain, walking under this soft grey sky with nothing to break its space but those walls, a wild rose-bush, which the moon would soon light up into a splendour of dim flowers set amidst grey leaves whose edges were touched with silver. They passed a hawthorn, heavy with scent, and paused simultaneously, sniffing it, and went on again.

"Aye. The moor-cotton will be out," Dan answered him. I saw some in a glass in a window up at Greensham. Tha'll happen go up Ridgely an' see it afore tha goes back?"

Dave nodded.

In his mind's eye he saw it all blowing, like dancing snow, its stems the colour of the bents, and invisible to sight, so that each nodding silken snow flower seemed to dance on air—cotton-grass, the summer glory of these northern hills, the canna of Ossian, who had sung it on his harp hundreds of years agone, sung it amongst the epics of red battle, whilst chieftains strove and fell, contending for their clans. Ossian slept. The chieftains slept. Ossian's harp was silent. But the canna was blowing still under the light of June moons, making these wild hillls wonderful before heather flushed them with purples and reds, and before the grouse went between sky and heather startled by the echoing crack of huntsman's gun. And all this world which changed from one beauty to another, from the brightening of the bents (over Greenshaw way the moors in spring, time were a wonder of hues, not being red, but ranging from brightest green to pale primrose and almost white), the calling of the sand-piper, the pale new heather which deepened to purple under the rays of sun and cloud, of white hazes of heat and grey wet winds and blazings of sunlight, that made the air seem to quiver. All this world he had left behind to wander in a city's thoroughfares, to breathe the stench of petfol, to view glaring advertisements, to stare through grey-green fog that made one gasp almost, for a wet wind blowing over northern fells, for white mists that stretched over the savannah of the moor hillocks. He had left the forge, and all his world, to see Barbary, and had stayed because of Barbary, and now he had lost her, too, because it was sometimes almost more than he could bear to be near Barbary, and realize that he could only look at her as across an impassable gulf.

He heard Dan observing that it would soon be midsummer-day, and that he had never seen the countryside look more grand. Dan said that every year.

"Aye. It's grand," answered Dave.

Tears were in his eyes.

"I thowt this would cure thy glumping," said Dan contentedly.

"Aye. It has done."

He had lost that bitter sense of rebellion against the fate which had taken him to the City. Bitterness was gone, fallen from him as he walked here under this sky where the big moon was now half-way up, climbing the sky behind Ridgely Fells, a long dark bulk which ran along before them. Under such a sky, and with all this about one, who could be bitter and "glump"? But a deeper sadness, to which the vast, almost melancholy, grandeur of the landscape contributed, was upon his heart. He recalled that feeling which had been his as he left the forge to go to the City. He had felt then that his life was drifting away, he knew not whither, that the smithy and the stream and old scenes might not be the same again, that going to the City might unsettle him. It bad worked out so. The City had kept him, claimed him, given him work there, and now—he wanted to be back, away from it, and there was no place to return to. Being near Barbara had become an agony. To get away from that agony he wanted to be back, but the smithy was no longer there to return to. He would have to stay. Loneliness had touched his heart and mind. He had seen that Dan and Sarah were growing older. They would pass away. At some time other people, strangers, would be in the cottage when he came over on brief holidays. They would lie in the churchyard. People walking about these roads would look, then smile, and say: "Why, it's Dave Reid." And that would be all that was left to him of Rimton. By the changes in thoughts and feeling which had come to him, as he walked the city's streets, he had recognized the transiency of life, its swift passing, and felt to be trying to find some great thing which would hold, be there to the end. Barbara might have journeyed with him through all changes. But he had been too slow. He pondered the littleness of all existence, and without knowing anything of Spinoza, he reached Spinoza's thought. "Did one exist? Or is all life a dream, and mankind creatures of dreams? Was reality—beyond— or was there nothing beyond?"

In this emptiness which had felt to come upon him and make his heart sore, he remembered Beethoven,

Handel, Mozart—even Purcell! No, life was real. Why, one could prove by its suffering that one existed. Just as one could prove by its creative splendours, by the great masterpieces men had beaten out from their hearts and minds—that life was real.

And Dan's hand was on the door-latch.

"Oh, you've found your way back?" came Sarah's voice. Then: "An' guess who's here?"

"Nay," said Dan.

He was wiping his feet on the mat. They went in. And there was Barbara sitting in the chair and smiling across at them.

"Crichie has gone to Eastbourne, partly on business, partly for a holiday." said Barbara, swinging her feet, and I couldn't resist the temptation to come and see the old places. The train felt to come very slowly."

Dave had hung his cap and coat up. The blood which had beaten a rapturous tattoo in his veins was calm again. He had forgotten that he had left the City to avoid this pain of being near her. He saw her sitting in the old grey woollen slippers she used to wear. And she had on the blue gingham pinafore ready to help Sarah serve supper. It was just his having felt too lonely in London, he mused, which had made him imagine that he could not live without her and that at some moment he might forget she was Crichie Dennison's wife. Why, tomorrow they could go up Ridgely Fells. The cotton-grass would be out. The moon foretold rain, but what matter? They would go up in their old clothes, drink from the little bubbling spring where they had slaked their thirst years ago, happy—happy as they would never be again, no, never again, because they were no longer children. If it was a grey day of rain and mist they would hear through the silence the drip, drip of rain from the rushes, the sound of their own steps following after, as their feet rose from the sopped bents, and the curlew's cry would make a mournful music and fade into the silences, and that also would answer this quiet, sad mood he felt of all things passing, changing, becoming some other life altogether. She was here for days and all the week-end, and after—

Before his vision rose the face and figure of Nelly Greeby, as she had sat eating, after flashing him one look.

He craved for some creature who would be there always with him, who would not pass away till he did, on whom he would have a claim as she would have on him. Above all, the thought of taking Nelly out of the life at the foot of Ridgely Fells—a life where joy was utterly swamped by the hard work of Ross, where she toiled from daylight till dark—appealed to him. That would be an action to prove that man was not nothingness, but capable of subduing his desires to the highest reasonings.

"Barbary," said Sarah.

Barbara jumped up and came towards the table.

"Thee set the table," said Sarah.

He watched her flit towards the cupboard. Dan was watching them both. A right, red-letter day, this, he was thinking. But surely Barbara was thinner, and—

"Bringt' chairs up, Dan," asked Sarah. Then to Barbara: "But couldn't ta ha' gone with Crichie? Tha looks like a bit o' sea air would ha' done thee good."

Barbara was laying knives and forks by each plate. "We both felt" she said, "that a rest would do us good."

"Oh!" said Sarah.

She gave Dan a look.

"Well, in my opinion," she observed, "you're startin' a bit soin on, takin' your holidays apart. An for all our fratchin'—" she pointed a spoon at Dan, "we're ne'er passed a neet away fro' one another," she added.

"Eh, lass," Dan told her. "We're back numbers. This generation isn't like us."

"Seems not," said Sarah. "So mich the waur for them!"

"Well, it's prophesied it'll be a wet week-end," said Dan. "So Crichie'll maybe not enjoy himsel'."

He did not like it. When folk went on their holidays separate, for a rest, well, it looked like things was a bit of a tow. Still, this generation was different. It would not stand as much, no, not by a long chalk. In Rimton, too, they were behind the times. Folks could not look at things as they did in a big city. Here, they stuck, aye, if hell stood in the gap—clashed and ding-donged, and even pitched things at one another, went on somehow, little short o' murder sometimes, but stuck. That was the old law of wedlock. Times changed. Outlooks altered. This generation was, as Sarah said, fonder o' pleasure than pain. It argy-barged about things. If it made a hard bed it did not lie on it for the best part of a lifetime and grin and bear it. It said: "Oh, hang to it," and left it, and made a new one, softer and easier, if it could. Happen it was a saner outlook. He did not know. What he did know was that it would break Sarah's heart if Barbara followed in the footsteps of this newer generation.

"Eh, there's the moin!" ejaculated Sarah dolefully. "First time I've seen it this month, through glass an' all. Dave, pull th' blind down. It were our Barbary comin' put me off pullin' it down afore."

She was very gloomy during supper, for, to her mind, to see the moon through glass augured ill luck of some make. And just as she was recovering her spirits a cock crowed. She turned quite pale and looked at Dan. He turned a smiling face on Dave, then back to Sarah.

"It's as leet as day nigh outside;" he told her. "The hens will be laying twice between now an' tomorrow at noon. Pass me the saut, Barbara."

Sarah snatched the salt-cellar from Barbara's hand.

"Nay. I'll give it him," she said.

Helping to salt was helping to sorrow. And she did not want Barbara to pass it to him, for in some vague manner she had arrived at the conclusion that the moon seen through glass, and the cock crowing at this time o' night, was something to do with Barbara's coming. She was trying to break the spell.

"Aye, thee help me to sorrow, lass," said Dan good-humouredly.

She snapped at that. And Dave was leaning back in his chair, one arm over it, whilst the firing went on, enjoying it, all the original northern repartee, the vigorous blow for blow, and then the softening of Sarah at some genial remark of Dan's. He looked at Barbara, and saw that all this battle was going on and she was quite aloof from it. Her face had a look he had never seen on it before, and her lips were compressed. As though she felt his gaze, she looked up, flashed a smile, and the next moment was talking away to him.

"Yes, we'll go up Ridgely Fells tomorrow," he answered her. "Rain or shine, we'll go up the Fells. They are always the same, Barbary. They never change."

The by-play between Sarah and Dan was still going on, but Sarah's tongue was losing its sharpness.

"Oh," said Barbara, "don't places look different to us as we change?"

"Do they heck!" ejaculated Dan, breaking in. "Nary a bit, Barbary."

And Dave saw, as he looked at Dan, that Dan had never changed, that his life had been too quiet, too away from the forces that bring change, to have felt places grow different. No great emotions had beaten across his life, no changes of thought. He had never groped for solutions to life, nor wished to alter anything in the cosmos, either for himself or others. Dan had lived with Sarah as happily, too, as he would have lived with any other woman. Short of a virago, Dan would have got on with any one of the species. He did not ask for any understanding. If he had he would not have got it. Dan had the cottage and his business, and Sarah. If Sarah died before him he would go on without Sarah, regret it, but jog on. Without her. It came upon Dave, like a flash, why people struck against sorrow. They were people who felt deeply, loved too profoundly, asked too much. The little people were satisfied with even the remnant of all they had dreamed life would be, together. It did not hurt. They let dreams go soon and said: "Well, it'll do, this that is left." And' so it was much better to marry Nelly Greeby, caring less for her, than it would have been to have married Barbara. Certainly he would have to have someone to care for and to care for him, someone all his, and dependent on him for love as well as bread. He decided to talk it over with Barbara on Ridgely tomorrow. The world was so big. One felt lost in it.

From outside came the soft soughing of a moorland wind, blowing from the west. Then they heard the patter of the rain oil the window-panes. He looked at the dock. The hotel, as it would be just now, noisy, glaring, with a syncopated band pouring out jazz music, came before his mind's eye.

"Aye. It's goin' to rain, Dave; tomorrow," Dan told him.

"Let it," said Sarah. "More rain, more rest. You'll not be going up Ridgely if it rains, will yo'?"

"Course we shall," said Dave.

Sarah looked at him. Folk talked so in these places. And Barbara coming over without her husband would make 'em talk a lot as it was, and they sometimes made two and two into more than four. And now she came to think of it, there was a different look in both of their e'en than she had ever seen before, as if they were a bit scared of one another, or else seeing that moon through glass had upset her.

"Well," said Sarah, "if it rains an' you go up Ridgely you'll be fools."

Dan said something comical. She snapped at him in a way that made him look at her. What was the matter with her? He usually knew why she snapped, but now could not make it out.

Later, when they went to bed, she told him her fears. It set Dan off chuckling.

"Well," said Sarah, "that's a fine way to take it if there's aught in it. Dan, couldn't tha go wi' 'em?"

"What! An' miss goin' my rounds?" asked Dan, staggered. "Sarah, tha grows owder and sillier."

"Well—happen," said Sarah. "Dan, it'd break my heart."

Why, mine, too, said Dan. "But there's naught in it. They were allus tarrable fond o' one another, an' they allus will be. Don't be a fool. If Dave had wanted her he'd have asked her afore Crichie came. An' if he foun' out too late he'd say nowt."

"Not if she were content," Sarah told him. "But I don't like Crichie goin' to one place and her coming home for a rest."

"They look on it as absence makes the heart grow fonder," said Dan soothingly, "these days."

"Oh, do they?" she rapped out. "An' out o' sight is out o' mind, too, Dan. Take thy feet further up thear. They're like snowballs."

To which directions Dan gave heed and, leaning over the bedside, blew out the candle. Sarah was soon asleep. He lay listening to her breathing, the soughing of the wind all round the cottage. She must be going wrong in her head, thought Dan. Still, folk would talk, happen, if Barbary and Dave went up Ridgely together now. He half-decided to go with them. But it would be a tow, climbing Ridgely at his age, and there would be the day after, when he had to work. Still, he decided to go, even whilst his decision felt to implicate him in doubt against those two sleeping in the little rooms beyond. Still, best be on the safe side. He would go up with them. Better backache, however severe, than heartbreak for him and Sarah. But it would certainly be a tow getting up Ridgely. He drifted off to sleep to that soft soughing of the wind, whose wings were rain-laden and sweeping across the moors, vague as a cloud almost, where through the darkness the rushes were dripping in the rain, and the pools gave back little pattering sounds as the rain from the rushes fell into them.

Chapter Five

The same rain which fell over Rimton cast long, shining slashes on the carriage window of a train speeding Eastbournewards. In die darkness beyond were reflected the lights of die compartment—the rack with luggage on it, Crichie Dennison's new hat, and below he and Flora Peachley sitting opposite each other,

"How did you get away?" inquired Crichie.

Flora laughed scornfully.

"Fred advised me to come, gave me the money, said I looked ill. I left him working twice as hard to make up for the expense."

Her heartlessness appalled him for one flashing moment Then he saw her face, untroubled, calm, not even a little pale, and realized that she had not made this leap from any foolish emotionalism. And, as he looked at her, whatever he had of conscience perished.

"Yes, read," she told him as he glanced at the paper he had bought at the bookstall.

She took up a copy of a fashion journal. The action, casual and careless, almost awed him. She was just riding away from Peachley and those three little boys and the little house. That was all it was to her.

She had told him she would see if the more easy life he could offer weighed against Peachley and the boys. She was riding to sample it, and going to decide afterwards. Emotion was quite apart from all this. That she would decide afterwards was another surprising factor. He was glad, rather than sorry, that she looked at it from this standpoint. Had emotionalism been a factor he might have been afraid she would leave him also. But, for her, the deciding factor was whether Peachley and the three boys were worth a life in Hendon, Struggling between lower middle-class life and the possibility of being ultimately driven down into the working-classes. And, as she had told him, she could not decide without trying the life he had to offer for a short time. Even if he only kept on as head clerk the difference between him and Peachley meant to her the difference between what they had lost in Dinkermanns. Barbara was a pigmy beside her. He knew it. Why, even the book he had bought for Barbara she had fallen asleep over. The train ran on, and he heard the pages of the fashion journal being turned over. Flora's bright eyes glanced over them with interest. Then she laid the journal on the seat beside her and yawned.

"He'll just be putting them to bed," she told Crichie, glancing at her wrist-watch. "He promised them they could stay up till ten if they were good. It's a minute past."

Her amused laughter rippled above the rattle of the wheels. Crichie joined in.

"It's raining still," Flora told him as they sat back after the laughter at Peachley, who was fastening buttons and strings and marshalling the boys off away in Hendon. So it was. The rain was coming down the windows of the Rimton cottage, on the windows of the little house where the scrubby patch of lawn held a few daisies and one of Henry's little train carriages, under the trees where the thrushes had sung, Henry having forgotten to take it in. It was falling also on the train in which Flora rode to make her decision.

It was falling soft and slow on hamlets, towns and dries, and people, with their little dramas going on, were saying: "It is raining."

As they stepped out on the platform, umbrellas being unfolded, Crichie put his own over Flora as they went towards a taxi-stand. They stepped into the taxi after he had seen the luggage in.

The same June moon that was trying to shine through rain-clouds over the dancing canna, over the little lawn with its few daisies, was trying to shine on the sea here in Eastbourne. They did not note any of the glamour of rain, lights and clouds. Crichie was smoking a fine cigar, whose aroma was very different from that of those Peachley smoked, and he was saying: "We'll go there. It's the best hotel in Eastbourne. The lounge-room must have cost at the very least—"

She sat awed at the stupendous cost, pulling about her the fur Crichie had got at Goffers's', and which she had told Fred had cost only thirty-five shillings at a sale. It had cost as many pounds. When she had shown it to Fred he had lifted his head up from a book of Cervantes in the original and had grunted, as he saw the sheen of it under the lamp when she held it up: "H'm! Quite cheap. Glad you got it. What d'you call it?" And she had told him: "Oh, it's just a good imitation of Russian squirrel."

He had grunted again, and said something apropos of women having to array themselves in the skins of happy little creatures who probably lived nearer to the Almighty's idea of perfection than humans could, and had bent over his book again. Then, without lifting his head, he had deplored Dinkermanns having gone down, adding: "I'd have loved to study Russian. But that's off now. I can only allow myself a quarter of an hour's more reading. Tell Henry when the time's up to come and tell me. I'll have to get into that translating."

Chapter Six

"Going, Barbary?"

Dave stood outside the little bedroom door, after having knocked on it until he had received a sleepy reply which told that Barbary was awake.

"What kind of morning is it?" she asked.

"Dull."

There was silence, through which he heard from outside the song of a lark, a happy lark, greeting the morning light, diffused, as it was, through mist and cloud.

"Best not go if you mind a wetting, Barbary," added Dave. "Or, if you like, we'll wait till ten or eleven, see how the day turns out. But I thought we would go round by Rilsden and back by Greenshaw. And that's a long way."

"Oh, we'll go, whatever it's like," Barbara told him. "Is the fire lit?"

"I'm just going down," Dave told her. You'll hear it roaring in a few minutes."

They heard Sarah coughing, and then her foot set to the floor. She was getting up, an hour sooner than her wont. Dave had planned to have fire good, breakfast ready, when the old folk came down. But Dan was stirring, too, now. They heard him inquiring where in thunder had he put his braces. Dave felt that his coming had flung the old folk out of their usual routine. Almost he wished he had not come.

What purpose had it fulfilled beyond temporarily appeasing that desire in his heart to be back again where he could not remain, where each day as it dawned was one less of the few in which he could abide here? To see the forge, which was no longer an environment, no longer the busy scene of his working life, but a scene of the past? And he had come to make the old folk miss him more when he had gone, just when they were getting used to his being away, and to make himself more homesick when he had returned to the City by having revivified these memories of hills and moors, streams and valleys, country roads and wide spaces; above all, revivified his recollections of freshness in the day-dawns, of silences in scented evenings that closed to a thrush's song on a swinging bough amongst leaves that held silver gloamings of a moon that came up behind the Fells. Well, when he went back he would remain, stick the home-sickness, conquer it, as others had to do. For going back it would be worse. Walking lonely through the City's highways and by-ways, held to them irrevocably by the necessity to live there now to the end of life, if not in one city then in another—this glimpse of home again would float before his eyes, make it a thousand times harder.

As he went down to light the fire these thoughts ran through his mind, but less coherently. Why have returned to one spot to recall it more keenly, since he was now for ever a bird of passage?

"I'll soon be down," called Barbara. "And we'll come back round by Spen Wood."

"Right." answered Dave.

Barbara was wide awake. He could tell by her voice she would soon be down. Unusually wide awake she sounded, she whose waking had always been leisurely. Had she also been awake, listening to the soughing of the wind, the tap-tap of the blind against the window, the pitter-patter of the rain, and, morning side, the blowing of what was almost a gale for summer-time?

He went out into the wood-shed. No firing. He realized what had happened. Sarah had let the shops close in the excitement of his arrival, then Barbara's. They would not open for an hour. But wood was not a difficulty in the country. In the hedge, just up the road, was an old stump of a tree.

"Sarah," he called.

"Aye, lad."

"'I'm going to bring a tree back."

"Eh—I plump forgot to get wood," she called.

He opened the door and looked out into the misty morning world. And the City, as it would yet be sleeping under greyness, the tiers of roofs, the haze over the parks and gardens, came before his mind. Was it possible, he mused, that despite the way his heart clung to this place, to the road's and family faces and ways, the City was weaning him away from it, imperceptibly, and that in years to core, as others had done who had gone away, he would just run down for a holiday, and, before the time was up, find it dull, be glad to get back, because be had become rooted in another life, another world, and other work? After his walk with Dan last night, and the sense of inevitability he had felt, he knew it was quite possible. As people in trains looked out of the windows and saw the landscape passing them, flying, hurrying away, so—it was not that old scenes became different and passed. People passed them. New ones encroached. Life had to be lived. The Present swallowed the Past. The Future became Present and swallowed that, in its turn, the Past. All was kaleidoscope. There was no standing still. On, on and on, called the forces of the world. Time, like the policeman, moved everyone on, hurrying them along, past childhood, youth and manhood, always away and on, from what one had loved. Yes. All the people in the world were sitting in a non-stop train whose junction was—the City of Nothingness, called Death. There alone Change ended.

There Progress ended also, unless it did not. And that was always the unsolved question, would be still in thousands of years, when men's speculative attributes would be just the same, only keener, because they would have more time.

He walked along, feet on the grass, country grass with white, sleeping daisies speckling its greyness, the greyness that would flash into lively emerald-green sparkling with a thousand dew-drops and the gold of awakened daisies when the sun came out. Foolish to ruminate like this, to brood on life's temporary and swift rush into nothingness, on the loneliness of the human, the puniness of the human, swept along by the forces of change, a puppet who wished to mould life to his desire and was swept away by even such things as a change of work, a new environment, people one met—all that interplay which was life, and who, humanwise, cried pathetically to loved scenes, "Remain", and, so crying, passed on, and in time forgot them, or recalled them as the past.

He looked up at the straggling rows of houses with the gaps between them in which meadow and hill was glimpsed, or the dusky foliage of a tree—faint as shadows of meadow, hill and tree, veiled in the morning's heavy mist. Little blinds were yet unwound. They slept, content with their lives, these people, for the main part. They would get up, work, eat, grow weary, sleep again, living here all their lives. One would think they stood still. Last night he had thought Dan had stood still. Now, with a deeper perception, he knew they did not, that Dan had not, stood still. Sorrows touched all, changed all, life's odds wearied them more. As time went on the hillroads did not fill them with hope and joy and courage. From saying with delight: "A bonnie morning, this morning," in the hey-day of youth, in the end they stood with bent backs, tired eyes, worn faces, blood that soon chilled in the winter's severity, and nodded with dulled senses, glad only of the sunshine because they could keep warmer, and glad in the end to lie back on their pillows and give up, almost easily, life, friends, kin, earth, with its starlit nights, morning, when the thrush sung at seven, blaze of the sunset's pomp, whispering leaves of the summer trees, taste of food. They also were in a non-stop train, though they journeyed slowly. The pathos of it touched him almost to tears. And to this end was man born? No more, surely no more in Natures plan than the creatures that lived on the moors, the bright-eyed hares that scampered away, the curlews that circled the sky. No more, indeed, than a patch of moss on some old wall, under sun and rain, at last falling and making an infinitesimal speck of dust which was blown on the wind or sunk into earth.

But, unlike curlew, or hare, or moss, man, imbued with a sense of his own importance, went on as though his day would be endless, until at some moment he thought—thought deeply, only to feel bewildered by the forces that brought him hither unasked and scurried him away unasked. And then, against this sense of being of little importance in the cosmos, winch would go on very well without him, which had, indeed, got on very well without even the greatest, to feel the great longing for a mate to grow old with him, whose affection would be some shield against this sense of being a bird of passage through one brief age, whose passing wings would leave no vibration on the air—eddies of eternity. And his mate was gone. Well, did a bird go mateless because one bird was gone? No, some other bird did equally as well. The nest, the young, and another breast to warm them, another mate to sing to. They were not afflicted, these birds, with the poignant depths of feelings, the constancy of humans; therefore they had not tragedies. The sky, the nest in the bough, the search for food, and other birds left to sing when they sung not, that was their cycle. And was man wiser or more of a fool for forgetting less easily? He walked on brooding.

There, from a dim bough of a tree whose moisture fell on him from leaves whose edges held rain and dew, came the song of a thrush, happy and unthinking in its joy, greeting another day. His heart leaped up. This day he and Barbara were going up Ridgely. This day held hours, long hours, of wind, rain, blowing rushes, tumbling streams—or, if they were favoured, sun, blue sky, silver-white clouds that changed each moment, clouds in shape unlike to any which had swept the sky since eternity began, since no two days were ever alike, since even clouds changed, too. And they would see the canna, either grey and wet or sun-dried, dancing hill-side of snow-flowers, amongst the bright green of sheeny rushes and the reds and browns and bronzes of the bents. To-day, hurling into eternity as though it were, was yet to-day. And on such days one gathered memories, and these remained.

The thrush was singing still. Warm gratitude to the little warbler touched him. He stood still and I stared up at it where it poised, with its throbbing, speckled breast, in its world of trees, which, to it, no doubt, overlooked the whole world. Dim leaves and their shadows hid from him its colouring, but, though it was a tiny spot amongst the leaves, he saw well in his mind's eye that tawny, speckled breast, that bright eye, that upward, pulsing throat. And, as he stood, its wisdom, its joy, in each clear drop of flowing melody enfolded him. There was only to-day, and surely the sun was coming out a little.

From every bush and tree as he walked along fell raindrops. He looked towards the hills. Grey mist obscured them from sight. They were one with the sky's greyness.

A colourless, grey, English morning, which could open, one knew, into all miracles of colour before the last bird sang its last song. The sun was there, though lost in cloud and mist, and if he burst through what splendours would break on bush and brier, on meadow and hill, on these roads grey with the rain. And surely over there that tree held a touch of green, green breaking like an oasis in this grey and dewy morning. A beech! Of all the trees of the world was there a green like beechen green? Spen Wood came into his mind. Spen Wood was almost all beech, birch and larch, the feather-airy larch that went up in spires of fineness that finally melted into blue and white sky. He grew more and more certain that the day was going to be one of sun and blue. A rift appeared in the mists, and he saw a little space of meadow over the wall-top. It was going to be a fine day for going up Ridgely. They would bring cotton-grass back for Sarah, who would stroke the silken beauty of one and wish she could have seen them blowing in their thousands. At Rilsden they would call at the inn and get Dan an ounce or two of his favourite tobacco, sold only there for miles around. And in the evening they would gather round the fire, and perhaps, if she were in the mood, Barbary would whistle as he played the 'cello, whistle in that clear, flute-like whistle which came as from a bird's throat.

He made for the hedge where he had expected to find the old tree-stump to take for firing. It was gone. Some other country-dweller had seen in it good firing. He turned round and retraced his steps. Sarah might have found some bits of wood or something that would get the fire going.

He walked in, and the roaring of the fire, as he opened the door, told that Sarah had solved the difficulty. And Dan was saying: "No, I can't go, Sarah, and I can't even get out in't cart. My back's bad. I can't go."

Dave was in the kitchen as Dan finished his sentence, and realized that Dan, being overheard, was looking sheepish.

"Can't go where?" inquired Dave.

"Eh," said Dan, "I'd thought o' goin' up Ridgely wi' you two young 'uns. But I were just telling Sarah I couldn't."

"I didn't think you could have got up Ridgely," Dave told him. "Which was why you weren't asked."

"Aye, lad, I know. But it seems a wet, dull sort o' day. Couldn't you go to morn?"

Dave looked at him. Sarah was blowing at the fire with the bellows, though it did not need it, as the roaring testified. The sound felt to fill the small cottage.

"You don't mean to say," inquired Dave with painful slowness, "that you thought Barbary and me needed company up Ridgely lest we couldn't take care o' ourselves?"

He looked at Sarah and he looked at Dan. Through the silence went the puff-puff-puff of the bellows, the roaring of the fire.

Dan coughed and cleared his throat and looked tentatively at Dave, with that reproach in his eyes, looking at them both.

"Nay, lad," he said feebly.

Sarah swung round, the bellows slid from the bars.

"Tha knows, Dave, she's come here without Crichie, and folk soon talk, an' you're not lad and lass any more. You're grown folk. Tha'rt twenty-five an' not walkin' out.

She fronted him with the bellows, and met that irate and scornful look with shrewd, common-sense glance.

"Well, we're goin'," said Dave. "We're goin', hail, rain, or shine, just as we've gone lots o' times, an' if Rimton doesn't like it, it can lump it." And Dan saw that go they would.

"What's all the to-do about going and not going?" called Barbara from the top of the stairs, and she came running down at such a speed that Dan trembled as he sat in his chair lest she break her neck.

She stood looking from one to the other.

"We can take an umbrella, but I hate umbrellas," she said, thinking Sarah objected to their going because the day might turn out rainy.

Nobody spoke.

"What's it about?" she asked.

Still nobody spoke. She turned on Dave.

"If you don't want to go, say so," she said. "Don't stand there glumpin'. I'll go by mysel'."

"Nay, I'm goin', too," Dave told her.

"Aye, it'll no doubt turn out a fine day," Dan said from his chair. "T' clouds looks to be leetenin'."

Sarah laid the bellows on the fender.

"It's just, Barbary, that it might set folk a-talkin'", she said, ignoring the fierce looks both Dave and Dan threw at her. "I know tha's never thowt o' it, but tha's come 'bout Crichie, an' Dave's none a bit o' a lad now. And though you're both grown up and just come home for a holiday, an' 'll go away, not livin' here any longer, well, me and Dan does. This is our bit o' th' yeth. An' we live here. An' you ought to consider us."

She faced them, sitting on the fender, looking at them, from one pale face to the other, from one fierce pair of eyes to the other's, and saw the red leap into both their cheeks at once.

Barbara, without a word, went and sat down in the chair by the dresser-end.

Dave sat glum.

"All right. We'll not go," said Barbara. "I suppose we can walk along the roads and look at the cows?"

"Barbary, we're goin'," said Dave irately. "We've both come home to see Ridgely and Spen Wood and Rilsden and Greenshaw, an' to hell wi' gossip. We're goin'. We're grown up, we'll act like grown-up folk."

156

"That's a'reight for you two," said Sarah, "but Dan and me have to live here."

"Now, Sarah," said Dan diplomatically.

She was going the very way to drive Dave up Ridgely, and if he went Barbary would go with him, and, also, they would go under the most dangerous of conditions, with hearts pulsing against silly village conventions, with a new sense of being something contrary to Rimton, with the sense of being not just companions, but man and woman who had to have fences between them, and he wished Sarah had not spoken. It would have been better, far better. Dave would not be driven. And Barbara, Barbara sat looking at them from her chair at the end of the dresser as though she were not at home but was just over on a visit.

"Well, we're going," said Dave decisively. "Don't see why we should sit in on a day like this is going to be just to suit Rimton. If it doesn't like it, it can lump it."

That ended the matter. But breakfast was a poor sort of meal. Dan did his best by talking of Greenshaw and asking them to bring eye-bright back for Sarah to make an eye-wash of, to make easy conversation take the place of the strained silence winch had fallen on the little kitchen, but the ticking of the clock sounded very loud and the song of a bird outside, a happy song, which intensified the strife winch had fallen oh them all after the unusual "fratch" which was caused by Sarah's jealous regard for Rimton opinion.

They departed at eleven o'clock, along a road which looked as though no drop of rain had fallen in the night—a road all sunshine on white limestone—a glistening, winding road which ran towards moors and hills.

Passing through a stile, waving meadows were on each side of them, meadows where buttercups and daisies, clover and vetch, were lifting their heads, from which the sun was fast drinking the dew. Beyond a green flame on the hill-side, was Spen Wood. A lark went up and sang. They stood still, watching him become a speck against a big white cloud, then drop down, down to a last sweet burst of joy, to his nest on the ground.

"Too fine a day to spend inside," said Dave as they went on again.

Barbara nodded her head. Her eyes were glancing at all this world of morning gladness—now at the sky, now at the grass, now ahead at Spen Wood, and then over towards that little patch of brown with green slashed across it which was the wild moors with the new bracken uncurling.

"'We shall be at Rilsden by three if we do three miles an hour," said Dave. "You'll be able to manage three miles an hour, Barbary?"

"Four, if you like," she answered.

"Oh, nay, four's too much for a woman," said Dave.

"There!" said Barbara, grievously.

"What?" asked Dave.

"You've never made distinctions between what I could do and what you could do before," she told him.

"Why, no—" he said, "but you look tir't, Barbary. Are you?"

She turned her face towards him.

"Not a bit," she said emphaticaliy. "Not here, where there's air to breathe, and—no, I'm not tir't. Let's do the four miles an hour, Dave. We'll be at Rilsden by two."

They swung along, along the little paths that ran by the stone walls and rough hedges dividing the wood from them. They could look down on the beginnings the wood now, all blowing grass slopes and bluebells and tangle of bush and whin—whin that had somehow wandered from the moor, its leaves turning flush-pink here and there, and with already a few little pink beads that were the flowers to the purple fruit for which Rimton children would later scramble with tin cans to get enough to make a few big plate-pies and eat most of them as they gathered them, and return home with juice-stained mouths and hours of sun and haze and gipsy-joy in their blood. The breath of all this wild, fresh beauty swept up to them from the wood. They heard the rush and roar of a torrent that went down a rock-side and splashed silver rain, a ceaseless baptism on tossed ferns and trailing greenery.

A larch laughed, wind in its spires, every one of them like green, iridescent, feathered foam, light as though blown and suspended in the radiant air. They passed the three birches with pale, sun-glistening barks. A bird flew from one of the birches as they disturbed it. Its wings, as it beat across the wood, glinted silver.

"A rabbit!" ejaculated Dave.

They leaned on the rough wall-top and watched it scamper away, hind feet flying and its little bob of a tail.

The voice of the tumbling water was behind now, just a murmur which chorded in with blowing leaves, grass, and the silence which was occasionally punctuated by the sound of blasting from a gun away beyond sight.

"And next week I shall be back," said Dave.

"And I," sighed Barbara.

"And all the weeks," added Dave.

"Yes, all of them. For me, too. We shall be back for always. I don't think I shall come again for a long time," said Barbara.

"Nor I," said Dave.

They moved along, and on along the path which gave them at every turn glimpses of sun-bright daisies, of blown "wind-flowers", of anemones, with the purple-veined petals, of celandines, sun-splashed celandines, wide open and yellow, and across between the trees they saw blue sky, with the trees of the opposite height making a green, wavy edge, occasionally breaking to show a high, ribbon-like road along which motors ran, lighting up the sky like great, golden torches each night—torches which flashed into the vast darkness and flared out. Returning this evening, they would see those motor-lights like comets.

There was so much to see and delight in, they were not going two miles an hour, as Dave noted when they had gone two miles. They climbed the wall-top and dropped into the wood and there, with the sky a glinting loveliness through green boughs, with feet on the wood's brown path and a carpet of wood-grass littered with wood-flowers each side them, with the cool, pleasant flow of a stream accompanying them as it wound through fern and early foxgloves, time became a thing of no moment.

Barbara took off her tweed hat, folded it and thrust it into her pocket. The wind blew her moon-fair hair into a radiant halo around her happy face. Hands in pockets, she followed Dave down the brown path with the twisted tree-roots across it and the stones that were almost always grey-green in places, saving for these few bright, sunshiny weeks in midsummer. But the stones were dry already after these two blazing hours of sunshine.

At times she paused and gave a swift glance along the way they had come, afraid lest she should have missed any of its beauty, then went swiftly on again, catching up to Dave, and just when the trees opened and gave a full glimpse of the moors ahead, simultaneously they burst into song, the same song which went rolling away through the wood, over the wood-grass, the wind-flowers, the sun-bright celandines, the bluebells, and the little beaded buds of whin.

"I'm glad I came, too," said Dave.

They were sitting down after the climb up from the wood to the heights—the heights which brought again into full view the white, winding roads, the rough, grey walls, with their strips of wayside grass, the hills rising against the sky, a wide, spacious, summer glory unbroken by tree. The moors near enough now for them to see the spaces between the ranks of new bracken, each stalk of which crowned by its green cockade, row upon row of the like sentinels, all moving in the wind, and among them the tiny creatures of the moors, to whom they were forest-high.

Dave took out his watch.

"One o'clock," he told Barbara, surprised.

"Well, we shall get into Rilsden by three," she said.

"Might, if we went straight up the hill," he told her.

"Yes. We'll go up," she agreed.

They moved across the road, climbed the wall, and were ascending the hill-side that ran up to the moor.

"Look, cotton-grass!" cried Barbara.

A few specks of white dotted the moor as they topped the hill with the joy hill-climbers feel, that feeling of climbing up nearer the sky.

"Oh, just a bit," Dave said. "We'll come back by Ridgely. It'll be showered there. You can gather some for Sarah then, and remind me to gather some eye-bright."

They were now on the moor. Grouse went up as they intruded—a whirr of brown wings against the sky, and—

"A sand-piper," said Dave in a hushed voice.

They heard that sweet, thin thread of sound, woven through the silences.

"Yes. Glad I came, though I've to leave it again," said Dave.

"Pee-wit, pee-wit," came down to them from the sky's wide and glorious space as they stood still, drinking it all in—all this quiet, peaceful silence, of which, amidst the city's restless movement and stir, they had often longed for just one breath.

They watched the tufted plover, with her little jerky movements, as she alighted probably not far from her nest, outlined half against the blue sky, half against the moor. She moved, as they watched, sighting them moved, as they knew, to lead them away from finding that nest which held brown, feathery balls with big, bright eyes, the next generation of the moor's plovers.

"Doesn't she look like some old Methodist in a new bonnet?" asked Barbara.

Then they moved on again. The night rain had made the bents soppy, and over against the horizon arose smoke, the smoke of a moor-fire, which hazed the village beyond it.

With the ease of moor-rovers they passed over the rough earth-bobs, stepping from one to the other, as from stone to stone, not between them, as did the city-dwellers who came to holiday and found moor-tramping hard work, as hard as they had found walking the city's thoroughfares.

They crossed soft, quaky mud and peat beds, and saw, on reaching the high moor again, the great crag of Rilsden clearly outlined against the sky and the great valley below, with its gleaming river. Sea had once covered that crag. It stood now, pinnacled above a world of heather and gorse, of roaring river, brown with peat in the winter, clear and green and sun-rippled in the summer.

"We'll go by the valley and climb up again past the crag," said Dave.

So they went, walking for half a mile on the slope of the hill, passing through the young, fresh bracken, which swished as they touched it in passing. The scent of the brown, warm earth beat up to their nostrils. Dave turned round once, missing Barbara. She was away behind him, holding a tuft of heather, moorland on its roots, sniffing it as though she would hold that beloved fragrance in her heart and soul for ever, beyond Time's taking; He waited, watching sky and the moor where light and shadow touched it into brightness or left it sombre and grand. She caught him up.

"Shall we go slower? Half-past three won't be too late," inquired Dave. "There's no need to hurry that I see of."

Barbara shook her head.

For half an hour, as they had walked through the bracken, she had not spoken, too happy to speak, as Dave knew well, Crichie forgotten, the little house with the electric stove and quarrels forgotten—all forgotten but this rolling space and glory and beauty and silence broken only by voice of bird or sound of running water, and ever this incense of earth-fragrance flung up from bracken and earth touched by rain and sun.

"No. Let's get there by three."

The sun was beating down now. Acting on Dave's advice, she tied his big handkerchief on her head. When he looked round whenever she got behind, forgetting that she had said they would reach Rilsden by three, he saw that white head-covering against the sky's blue, and the sun catching that pale, silvery-glinting hair, and the lithe figure, and then, having hurried, she would arrive beside him, her eyes mirroring that deep delight she was feeling in all this world of freshness and joy.

As they descended into the valley it was warmer still, but the water, as they followed it, flung off coolness, which came to them gratefully. They carried their coats now. The rhythm of walking had seized them.

They had that feeling of being able to go for hours yet at this steady, swinging pace which carried them along. And deep in the heart of each was the regret that this might, could be, their last walk together in a world of sky and heather, amongst this solemn grandeur of hill and moor, this delight of green valley and ever-changing loveliness of riverside. They had come. They had defied Sarah's opinion, which was ever the opinion of Rimton, but, because they loved her and owed her duty, each realized that they would be influenced by her. They were grown up and had not even kinship of blood.

Barbara was married, and Dave, in Rimton's opinion, ought to be "looking round". It would be their last day together of all the days that would follow, and dawn for them, on these wild hills and rolling moon. It was another farewell amongst life's endless farewells, as they now perceived life to be—that life which had stood still and happy for so long—uneventful—each day as happy and care-free as the last, but which, even whilst standing still, had been leading to this newer life, where they were hurried along as by a maelstrom of change amongst the rest of the world's changing humanity, for life was now an eventful thing which brought new people, new ideas, new thoughts, new scenes. And, out of all this, what in exchange for the lost world of sky and heather and care-free freedom, where they had been happy as the birds that went round these heights? Dave pondered and could find no answer. Growth, possibly. A becoming, as the old Greek had said all life was. But the irony of it was that he had not wanted to move. Barbara was behind again, gathering flowering whin, singing now, as she plucked the pink beads of it, the richly-coloured leaves of it, to take back with her when she went citywards.

The church clock struck three as they came into Rilsden. The notes sounded mellowly from amongst the trees, floated out to them as they stood on the old bridge Romans had built ages ago, where moss, green and golden, clung between the stones on the riverside of it, as they stood leaning over it, watching the tumbling, sunny ripples in the clear-green water which held tree-reflections almost from bank to bank, with just a narrow strip of sky between, blue and white with afternoon's full radiance, a world of sky held by the world of river, and fish aleap, as circles on its surface told, in this river that ran on to the sea—to be lost in it—as their fives now flowing beyond their desire, as all lives were flowing, changing all the long way. So Dave, standing looking over the old bridge. But Barbara was pondering nothing. She was drinking to the full the splendour of the day, knowing all the time it was going.

"Do you remember, Dave, falling off this bridge?" she asked.

He nodded assent.

"How long it seemed before we got home!" she remarked. "And how Sarah scolded all the time as she bandaged your head. And how I came up and gave you the little cart pulled by ostriches?"

He nodded again.

Let's go down and have some food," he answered; They moved from the bridge along the village road, past the church amongst its elms, and with the cawing of rooks making a ceaseless murmur. They could see the inn, square and grey, at the turn of the road, which was going up between hedgerows gay with wild rose and hawthorn at its fullest bloom, but where already the rains of the past night had brought down petals.

Barbara clutched Dave's sleeve suddenly.

"Look!" she ejaculated.

He followed the direction of her gaze. Then he smiled, without speech.

"But a magpie, Dave!" she said. "One magpie!"

"Well, there are sorrows, aren't there?" he asked.

"And folk seem born for 'em. But I don't see why a magpie should have anything to do with human destinies."

They stood watching it, saw it alight on a tree, then the beating of its wings again and its poise upon another tree.

"Queer how these superstitions linger in us, Barbary," he said. "There can't be anything in them. Magpies fly in ones betimes. People see them and say 'Ill-luck'. Since they're alive, life is like to hold ill-luck as well as good for 'em. An' they blame the magpie which they have happened to see as it flies engrossed with its own struggle, in a world of its own."

"Yes. That's reasoning," admitted Barbara, "but, all the same, I wish we hadn't seen the magpie."

They walked on towards the inn.

As the road turned a funeral cortège came into sight. On the brightness of the white road the nodding, old-fashioned, black plumes on the hearse, the black horses, the black attire of the mourners, who were walking, struck upon their sights and gave them that keen sense of pity for those who have drunk their last cup, which the young and life-loving feel. They almost experienced, too, a sense of resentment to be reminded of death, of the end of skies and earth and of laughter, tears and affection, as they stood still by the houses to let the cortège go past.

A woman, white-aproned, was standing in the doorway of a little cottage. She was wiping a tear away. She stood watching until the black line on the road's brightness was gone round the bend towards the old churchyard.

"Who is it that's dead?" inquired Barbara pitifully.

To be dead—dead on a day like this, of wind and sun and fragrance of wild rose and hawthorn. How very dreadful. So Barbara, looking into the face of the woman wiping a tear away.

"Susan Graham she was called," said the woman. "But she's where she has wanted to be for a long time now. She has suffered so mich. She got fain to go. They do when they suffer a lot."

They walked on. The tolling of the bell sounded to them as they went along the narrow flagstones that made a path up to the inn door.

Barbara could hear the bell saying: "Gone! Gone! Gone!" with every dolorous stroke.

She looked at Dave. They had not only seen a magpie—they had met a funeral. She looked at the inn. The blinds were down even there.

"Dave," she appealed, "let's go farther on to the next village. I'm not going to have a meal here— all the blinds down. It's dismal.

"All right," agreed Dave.

They turned back when almost at the door of the inn and swung out of the village by the high-road.

"But it's thrown us five miles out of our road," said Dave. "And, Barbary, it's bad luck, too, to turn back."

"Well, I couldn't really enjoy food in that darkened inn," said Barbara. "Dave, it'd take an awful lot of suffering to make me glad to die. There's so much to lose. Fancy having to give up the joy of wild roses, to be going one knows not where, not knowing if one will see anyone one loves ever again, or to feel the sun warm on one's back as it is now. No, I should fight for life to the last bit. I know I should. It's so sweet."

They were passing along the high-road.

Dave had lit his pipe and was puffing away at it.

"When it gets too bitter, Barbary," he said, "I expect folk want to shuffle off then."

"Not however bitter it was, Dave," she said suddenly, "would I wish to shuffle off."

She stood still suddenly, looking at the bright world about them. The whin flowers in her hand were trembling.

"I'd like to live for ever if I could," she said, passionate joy in life in her tones. "I can't see how I'd ever be resigned to shuffling off, nor that an' pain could be big enough to make me forget the beauty and wonder of life, however it changes. I just can't. To leave the warm sun—".

She stared along the road, all radiant with summer.

"Let's hope you won't ever find bitterness nor pain big enough to blot out life's joy," said Dave.

He had felt some bitterness and pain himself. But it was buried deep in his heart.

As the heather and ling and rushes waved in the brightness of this wind and sunshine, so his heart rejoiced in this day's beauty, but it was passing. Half the day was almost gone, and it was the last day when he and Barbara would walk here. They were saying good-bye to it, even in this joyous last day of it, as they would see it together. Sarah had reminded them that folk might talk. Deep in his heart was the bitterness and pain of the buried knowledge that had he not been too engrossed with music, too slow to catch cold, as Rimton would have expressed it, she would never have gone away had he asked her to stay. Barbara never going would have meant he should never have gone. All their lives they would have lived here, with the right to walk together under the sun, moon and stars, till they slept together in some little old churchyard where moorland encroached on the very walls, where heather and harebells might have blown over their dust.

The last mournful tolling of the bell was blown to them from the church whose spire they saw on the opposite hill, sun-fired against a white cloud.

It sounded to be tolling their farewell to companionship which had to be left behind no more a part of their lives. His look turned to Barbara's, filled with deep regret. Hers met it, quiet, tranquil and understanding. There was no need to say a word. And he had let her go away when he could have had her there, kept her with him always in a world which was full of changes and chances, but where that affection would have shone in him steadfastly through all life's hazards. Still—there were hours yet, six or seven happy hours before they reached Rimton and Sarah's reproachful looks. They would pass over Ridgely before that—all its rushes a-blow in wind and a-sheen under the moon, and the canna's snowflowers, too, aglow under the moon, and every little rushed pool a silver mirror on the moon's dark breast.

"Let's go back by the reservoir," said Barbara. "I'd like to see the heron which used to stand on one leg."

"No use," said Dave.

"Why?"

"Dan told me it died last summer."

"Oh!"

They passed on, over the hill-top road, and saw below them the village where they could get tea. They were ready for it. Sarah had only put them up two small sandwiches each, which they had eaten walking on the slope of the hill amongst the bracken's uncurling stalks, which Dave had said would grow so swiftly now under this sun that if one stayed there one would be able to see it grow. They were feeling a little tired, too, healthily tired with sun and wind and walking. Tea in an inn-parlour was something to look forward to. They would sit there an hour, see those little grey clouds which were tingeing the sky spreading, the greyness of evening which would finally overspread the sky, after the sun's going down. The day was almost gone.

Chapter Seven

Crossing Ridgely Fells, they saw across the valley the burn of sunset fires behind the semi-circle of the sweep of hills. Longden Pike was glowing, plum-bloomed purple, with a tinge of yellow flame where the setting sun caught the brown of last year's bracken. Ingletop Heights were green and amethyst. One hill on which the last blue of the dying day and the crimson blaze of evening fell, was palest lavender. Swift as from the magic shuttle of some magic weaver, colours were woven over sky and landscape, and passed into other colours whilst the hills grew darker. The wind that had blown fresh and bracing all day, making the sun s heat bearable, had sunk to a hushed whisper which the rushes gave back at intervals. The voices of a few moor-fowls yet sounded, but their sounds only felt to make the silence deeper, on ceasing. It was almost chill up on Ridgely, now the sun was sinking. They had put their coats on half-way up before reaching the top. Barbara's hands were full of canna, and Dave's pockets held eye-bright gathered from a little knoll half a mile from the inn where they had had tea.

They stood on a rise of heather, springy under the feet, and watched little pool after little pool catch the colours of the dying day. Pink, emerald-green and blue, purple or dim grey with a star rippling its reflection, tremulous as the wind shook the rushes around it, the pools lit up the moors. One was like a great amber shield.

How long they stood they did not note, watching that flare of day's passing. Then, when the moors were looking sombre, the moon was rising on the other side of Ridgely. She came up round and full, and the moor-pools were gently rippling silver against the dark rushes, and out of the sky came the last curlew's last cry—and all was silence, hushed, mysterious, through which sounded the spring of the heather beating back after their feet passed, the shake of the whin, and the murmur of a little stream flowing through the evening.

"We shall never come up here together again," Dave remarked out of a long silence.

"Probably not," Barbara told him.

"But we could have done often if you'd not been in such a hurry to wed Crichie—"

"Hush," Barbara said imploringly.

"Well, one might as well," Dave answered her. "And if it had been a good thing, a happy thing, for you to have wed him, I wouldn't have minded."

"Oh, hush," Barbara appealed.

They walked on, hearing the wind going over the bents and through the rushes behind them. Then all was still again. A few drops of rain fell.'

"It's raining, Dave," she told him.

"Nothing much," Dave told her. "Might be a shower or two if this wind drops altogether. But Barbara—"

"You're a big glumper, Dave," Barbara told him softly. "The beginning of wisdom is not to glump over things that can't be altered. And Crichie and I are very fond of each other. I don't want to talk of how it would have been if we hadn't met, because we did. We had to, I think. And—it feels treachery even to be talking of if we hadn't met. And the best thing you could do, Dave——"

She paused.

"Well?"

"Is to get wed yourself," she advised. "You'll be kept so busy then, wondering why she does this or that, you'll not have time to worry about Crichie and me."

"Doesn't sound very encouraging," said Dave.

"No, but joking apart—"

"Didn't know we were jesting," Dave told her.

"You'd find it—at the very least—interesting," Barbara informed him.

"Thanks," said Dave. "One marries, then, to be interested?"

"Yes. And to interest—"

"Just that?" he inquired. "Why, life is full of interest now. There's so much—books, music, walks. No, Barbara, that's not why people marry. Why do they? Looked at from a rational standpoint, it's idiotic. Look at it—two people meet, grow wild about each other, feel they can't go on without each other, take a house, live there all their lives, and seem to spend quite a big lot of their lives wondering why they did such a thing."

They walked on.

"Why?" asked Dave.

"Most women marry to have children," Barbara told him. "There'd be such a fuss if they had them without."

"Barbara!"

"Yes. Just as birds marry to have baby birds—"

"But lots o' folk don't have them."

"Oh, not lots."

"You think that people just come together to leave their kind?" asked Dave.

"Yes."

"For nothing more?"

"Oh, that's quite a big lot. Yes, I think it's quite enough to come together to leave one's kind."

"Doesn't seem so," Dave answered. "And so, if they have children, the whole end of their coming together is fulfilled, from your point of view?"

Barbara laughed.

"I—you see, Dave, people lose their point of view in marriage. They try so hard to see each other's, try so furiously to adopt each other's—they lose their own. The most successful marriage, as far as I can gauge, appears to be when both individuals have blotted out each other's individuality. They call it merging. But I think they do come together just to add to the race. They don't think so, but they do. And—how they affect each other, Nature doesn't care. No, not the least. Her end is achieved."

"And that end justifies their living together all their lives, however they affect each other?" inquired Dave.

"Oh, look at the cotton-grass!" exclaimed Barbara. "Why waste time talking and pondering? 'Make game of that which makes as much of thee.' "

"But, Barbara—"

"I'm tired of pondering on life's preposterousness" said Barbara. "One must take it as a joke. What you think of it—what I think of it, doesn't weigh. Nature's end is the race. It's a big end. Without it there would be no people on the earth. And for those who pay dearer than others, to justify that end—the race—well, they do, and so—let them. The race goes on."

They were walking side by side over the hill.

"Then happiness is not an end?" inquired Dave tenaciously.

"Yes. Happiness is seeing the new race—

"And seeing that new race—pitched into conflict of individual with individual—and a new race beyond them—the end?" asked Dave.

"Oh, Dave, I'm weary," said Barbara. "Besides, it isn't all conflict."

"Shouldn't be any," affirmed Dave

"That's idealism, Dave, but life's real. Besides if one or the other gives up self entirely—becomes the other—conflict ends. In most cases, I should think, it's so. The one who loves most ceases to contend," she told him.

"Becomes nothing?" queried Dave bitterly.

"No, becomes the most—surmounting self," she answered.

Vaguely, he grasped that this was Barbara's plan for life for herself and Crichie.

He laughed jerkily. Barbara, sitting and listening enthusiastically and entering into Crichie's enthusiasm for business till her hair grew white, appeared to him a ludicrous and impossible achievement.

"I can't see it, Barbary," he told her. "You could only pretend."

"It's valiant to pretend," she said, her tone dogged.

"Then, all life's a masquerade?" he asked with passionate intensity.

"Yes, when I play Chopin, Crichie yawns, and says: Very nice, Barbara,'" she said, "and goes to sleep. And when I listen about Goffers's without saying anything till all the furniture gets tickets on it whenever I look at it, that's pretence, but I shan't yawn. I've realized now that one or other has to pretend and pretend, and I shall till I care more about Crichie's ideas on systematized business than I do about Chopin. I fell asleep over a book Crichie brought me, but I'm going to read it again and astonish him by the way I've got the hang of it."

"And this will make you happy? interrogated Dave.

"Oh, no, it will make Crichie happy," she said.

And staring into the evening's blue and silver and upon the wide top of the Fells, where now every little rush was plainly distinguishable, where the bents were pale or dark under the moon, where the shadows of the moving sheep fell over a land drenched in pale, silvery light which made their newly-washed wool look snowy, the doctrinaire of reaching happiness through the misery of utterly subjugating the ego, faced Dave with his sceptical, wondering gaze.

Silence, and the wind blowing softly in the rushes, was all about them.

"You see, Crichie will be happy," she explained.

They had come to the edge of the Fells. Steep below them went the path, through bracken, fresh uncurling bracken, a dream of beauty as it stood touched by moonlight.

Dave went first and stretched out his hand to help her down the first steep yard or two until the path was reached. They were leaving for ever this world of sky and heather. With others they would come, or alone, all the years that lay before—the unknown years which stretched to Dave vague, infinite. And she liked Crichie so well—if he were happy, she would be. Fierce, unreasoning jealousy stung him through and through, rebellion against the ludicrousness of life which pitched people together who must blot their personalities out, to exist together. But, above all, the sadness that never again would they roam Ridgely together, to find Heaven in its silences and winds, rushes, pools and the wide sky over it all, was like a scourge of unbearable agony.

"Dave," sobbed Barbara aghast.

He had pulled her near him, so near that warm, human hearts beating were like a rhythm to which the pulse of life went for all creatures but humans who philosophized! how to make unhappiness—happiness—some religious, fanatical, sacrificial happiness. The warm, young mouth that had talked the doctrine of pain, talked of nullifying personality—that electrical force which created all art and music and sculpture and poetry—was near his own.

He kissed her whilst her eyes stared upwards, tear-filled, unbelievingly.

"Oh, Dave!" she almost sobbed.

Their faces were tremulous in the moonlight.

"I believe folk come together to be happy, and to make happy, or else they're best asunder," Dave declared. Don't look like that, Barbary. I've only kissed you—farewell."

They were walking now with the memory of that warm, passionate kiss between them. The bracken waved its green cockades in the moonshine. The silence was deep, so deep they grew afraid of it, and talked of tomorrow's weather, the hay-time coming, and hoped Dan's back would be better when they got back.

"You're not mad with me, are you, Barbary?" he asked as they reached the foot of the Fells.

"No."

They walked on again on the flat stretches that I ran by the stone walls.

"Oh, I thought you might be—"

"No. But I'd rather—"

"Well, I just couldn't help it. He'll have you all his life. I thought perhaps—"

"Well, it won't make me happier. I shall just forget—you kissed me like that," she avowed.

"Do. Forget quickly," said Dave.

His mood had changed. Bitterness was in his voice. His face was pale and almost satirical as it turned towards her.

"Do you see that light?" he asked, pointing away across the valley.

"Why, it's Ross, isn't it?" she inquired.

He nodded.

"The future Mrs. David Reid lives there," he told Barbara. "So you needn't be afraid of me."

"I'm not."

"But I shall always remember," he said in a voice from which bitterness had fallen, "and I shall hold that memory as the difference between one kind of loving and another—between the feeling those have who are akin in spirit and those who marry that the race may go on."

Their feet were on the land that was becoming interspersed with grass. The lights of Ross Farm were coming nearer.

"Shall we call?" inquired Barbara.

"Nay, not to-night. I don't want to spoil it," Dave told her.

They walked on in silence, stars overhead, grass underfoot. As they passed through the farmyard of Ross they saw Nelly Greeby's figure silhouetted on the white blind—fine, well-proportioned, the figure of a woman superb in animal physique. She was reaching some garment from the strings that ran along the ceiling.

"I shall make her happy," said Dave to Barbara. "She will want so little—wages, kindness—to worship me and be a nurse to my children. She will never know that I married her because I just got appalled at the loneliness of being one amongst all earth's twos. I shall still be lonely, but she'll never know. So—don't grudge me—that kiss, Barbara."

"I don't—so long as you just forget it,"

"But I told you I shan't."

"Well—let me."

They moved along between a sky and earth which had somehow changed—which felt to hold a menace— the menace of blood held in check by thought and will. They were more glad to see the cottage-chimneys pouring pale smoke against the white of the moon than they could have believed possible when they had set out that morning. And Barbara, after supper, wanted to write to Crichie a warm, passionate letter of appeal, expressing the hope that would not quarrel anymore—that silly hope wished so often and which would look so ridiculous and tragic in life—on paper.

But he had said he was not sure where he was staying in Eastbourne. She could not write. And if she went home on the morrow—she had left a house with the furniture covered in brown, holland coverings, and waiting for Crichie there would seem longer than here. He had told her he would wire when he was coming home, but had warned her that he might be detained by business over the week-end. She decided to ask him all about the new business Goffers's were trying to get in Eastbourne. That would please him. She would inquire into every detail of all he had been doing in Eastbourne, and sit interested in every detail whilst he told her all about it. Then next time he would not say: "You wouldn't enjoy going with me at all, Barbara. It's just business—every minute of the time I have to be away."

Chapter Eight

Barbara sat in the train which was speeding Citywards—homewards. She was glad she had been back to Rimton whilst Crichie was away in Eastbourne. Like Dave, she had perceived that whilst its hills and dales, moors and valleys, were the same, life had gone on and taken her with it. At moments, in the pauses of the new life and interests, she knew she would look back, see the sunshine streaming over miles of blowing heather, hear the curlew's cry and the plovers calling, and seeing the snow on their garden as she opened, the door and watched Crichie depart for Goffers's, would know it was drifted in great, dazzling drifts up on Ridgely—would see that picture of a world left behind float before her eyes, and an exile's sigh would beat up from heart to lips. Years would go by, and the exile's sorrow, recalling that world of heather, sky, and of water running through fern and rushes, would dim. She knew it. Already she was glad to return to her own place. It seemed ages since she had opened the dining-room window to let air in and had sat down and run her fingers over the keys of the piano, watching the new curtains blow in the breeze. Had Crichie missed her very much? She realized that she had missed him very much— seeing his face over the newspaper in the morning waiting to hear him ask for the second cup of coffee, yes, even his talk of new lines in at Goffers's. She was glad to be going back. Rimton was the Innisfree of peaceful life where nothing happened, an idyll from which she had torn herself for life, in its reality with Crichie.

Mary would be back from visiting her people in Shropshire. The holland covers would be gone from the furniture, the blinds wound up, fires lit, and, one amongst the million little houses, their house would be alive again with movement, conversation, and everything would go smoothly now she had laid self entirely away, now that she could sink herself in Crichie, no more a creature beating restlessly to find in him some answer to her delight in music, to her cry that she could have done more than spend aimless days just going about with a feather-duster or filling vases with flowers. Other middle-class women did not find life empty. She mused how they filled their days. She, also, would have to fill hers the same way. Shop-gazing, concerts, lectures, circulating libraries, visiting, talking inanities, living inanities. She would study how they got time over and pass it likewise. Only—they had children, mostly. But that was denied her unless Crichie got the junior partnership. Everything depended on that. To her, also, it had become the pivot of a destiny where she would have to fritter time away or having the satisfaction of realizing that their marriage had produced life—new life—added something to the world's enrichment, and where she herself would find a vocation.

At Derby she had a cup of tea, tasting of tea-urn. Yes, it would be delightful to be home, to sit by the tea-table pouring out tea from the teapot which was one of Goffers's most expensive lines, to look out of the windows and see the sunset blazing in the little strip of City sky, and to ask Crichie all the details of the business that had taken him to Eastbourne. Little bits of the house came up before her mind's eye, its comfort and beauty—a comfort and beauty which vast multitudes had not and fretted after amidst ugliness and privations. She felt humbled at the thought. And—it looked eternities since she had seen Crichie. And she would have to wait hours for his return from Goffers's that evening. Then she got the happy thought of going straight to Goffers's, haying tea in the tea-rooms there, and going back home with Crichie. She would walk through all the showrooms of the Emporium, notice everything, talk of it, and how happy that would make him.

She sat, wrapped round with the glow of one who has discovered how easy it is to be happy, to think no more of one's self, but just to be happy in the happiness of another. The world over, individuals were sinking themselves thus. One or the other in every couple—the one who loved most—surrendered what he or she wanted, that the other, for whom they cared more than for self, might be happy. She saw that in that way both were happy, one in surrendering, the other in taking.

The sun came warmly through the glass of the carriage-window. She scarcely noticed the flying landscape as she sat glowing in the ecstasy of the devotee for whom for hencemore there was no self— only the self that would find its Heaven in the expansion and joy that would be Crichie's. She realized that it was quite commonplace, too, this surrendering of the ego in marriage. She had realized it, and in lots of ways given up self. But she had not been thorough enough, she thought. Self must be swept utterly away. Crichie liked jazz music. She did not. She would buy a copy of jazz music in the music department at Goffers's. It would not always be easy, she knew. Still, was anything worth while easy? Bits of Barbara Delling would crop up, she knew. Barbara Dennison, ego-less, would beat them down. Why, that in itself was a vocation. And it would be a lifetime's work.

"Euston," called a porter.

She stepped out. The City looked like a study in pencil-smudge and sunshine. She breathed density—

air that was twice-breathed, that had no freshness in it. Petrol-stench greeted her nostrils. But joy flushed her cheeks, joy that beat up from the heart self-conquering.

"City", she said, hailing a taxi. Then: "Goffer's".

The taxi moved, one amongst a sea of taxis. The flight shone on the silver-grey stone of the, City's monumental public buildings. Barbara looked through the taxi-window, after cleaning it with the tips of her gloves, then realized that she had soiled a pair of Goffers's suede at six-eleven. She looked down at them ruefully. How difficult it was to stop being one's self. Yet she had expected Crichie to be something which answered her. How unfair that had been of her. But she—she would accomplish the changing of herself to what he required. She would become one of those model wives who thought exactly as their husbands did, who had no interests outside their husband's interests.

"Heavens! I've forgotten to powder my nose. It will be all shiny," mused Barbara. "And if I see Goffers he may tell Crichie I'm here, and Crichie will be annoyed at my having forgotten. Why, oh, why did not Nature make noses dull, so that they would not need powdering?"

The taxi was standing before Goffers's. Hurriedly she was dabbing her nose with the powder-puff, looking critically at the reflection in the little mirror from the bag which had been one from Goffers's. The taxi-man waited. Barbara stepped out.

She caught the taxi-man's smile. She, also, had often smiled at the idiocy of powdering one's nose. But—

One had to do all kinds of idiotic things in this world. One got used to it. She was getting used to it. And the great achievement of the struggle to lose one's own point of view and see someone else's, all the time, was to bring success in that hazardous speculation, marriage. It seemed a little weird that in order to succeed in it one had to proceed to become some other person than the one the lover had said he could not live without. Still—this was to endeavour to make the emotion which brought people together— logical and consistent, thought rather than emotion.

She realized as she went through the doorway of the Emporium that Crichie sank all his individuality here. The price he got for it was success. She realized marriage now as a business also. As he sank himself in Goffers's, she, to achieve success, was to sink herself in Crichie.

"Why, Mrs. Dennison!" exclaimed old Goffers, as he was parading the first floor. "And how well you are looking."

"Just stepped off the taxi from the station," Barbara told him. "Been in the country."

They stood talking, amidst the throng that eddied about them.

Old Goffers was teasing Barbara.

"You can always know that a man is in love with his wife," he told her, "when he gives an order for a Russian squirrel fur at thirty-five guineas. I hope you liked it, Mrs. Dennison? Excellent line. Wish we could have got more. You were lucky to get that one three weeks ago. The supply was quite inadequate for the demand. Having tea?"

"Yes," said Barbara.

She put out her hand to steady herself. She saw old Goffers's face, smiling, genial, moving away, and a jazz band was blaring away from the tea-room. She had got no Russian squirrel fur three weeks ago. And when Crichie brought anything from Goffers's he always unwrapped it immediately, so it was not put away. Still, this was silly—this—this idea that he could have bought one for anyone else.

She moved away towards the tea-room. There was some mistake on Old Goffers's part, she told herself. Then she turned round from her walk towards the tearoom. She was walking towards the lift for the fur department. The note of the purchase would be kept. It would require diplomacy to see it. Her limbs felt to be about to let her fall. She hated herself violently for this feeling of suspicious jealousy. Could this be she—Barbara Dennison, who was feeling this chill rush of suspicion—suspicion that made the heart feel dreadfully cold—then blazingly fierce, then sick, sick at having believed, even for a moment, that Crichie could be deceiving her so grossly. And to feel one's self moving upwards in the lift towards the fur department, and to be feeling all this, and yet debating how to get to see the note of the purchase. The lift stopped. Barbara stepped out. She was in the fur department, and the manageress, smart and businesslike, was coming towards her. She felt sick and faint. The counters, filled with furs, the walls round which stood waxen models of women with inane, foolish and self-conscious smiles, were all swimming.

She saw the manageress come ever nearer and rallied her strength. They stood chatting for a few moments.

"Yes," she said nonchalantly, "you will find I got it here. I suppose I could have it altered? I don't care for the style."

"Certainly, madam."

They stood looking at the carboned duplicates of purchases.

"There it is," Barbara told the manageress. "It wouldn't be very expensive to have it altered, would it?"

"Oh, no, madam." Barbara lifted her head.

The place was yet feeling to move round her. The faces of the wax models, the waxen throats rising out of furs, the dresses in the new season's colourings, were all swimming, and the lights of the room. She was swallowing hard. The effort to smile felt to be twisting her face. But the manageress had noticed nothing, was smiling in the deferential way Goffers's employees must smile at moneyed customers.

"Thanks very much," she said, nodding to the manageress. "I'll send it back before very long. There's no immediate hurry."

The lift took her down. Jazz was still blaring from the tea-room. She was walking out of Goffers's Emporium—stunned. The unbelievable was true.

Crichie had paid for a fur—a Russian squirrel at thirty-five guineas, and it had not been for her.

"Excuse me, but are you ill?" inquired a kindly voice.

She stared into the face of an elderly woman, and realized that she was still standing on the kerb outside Goffers's.

"Oh, thanks—no," said Barbara.

She moved on and away, amidst people, jostling people. There was a mirror in one of the shop-windows. She caught sight of her own reflection. Best have tea somewhere. One could not go about looking like that. But the cafés were noisy.

She hailed a taxi.

Hendon, she told the taxi-driver.

Flora would give her some tea. She would recover somewhat there. Perhaps there was some mistake. She clung to the hope. She sat back in the taxi. There were some hours yet before Crichie would be home. She must feel fitter than this, much fitter, to find out if he had bought that fur for someone else. No. He could not have bought it for anyone else. Still, where was the fur, then? Goffers's had been busy three weeks ago. He might have laid it away and have forgotten to tell her about it. Or, why, he might have got it and kept it aside for her birthday. Yes, that would be it. And she came back from stunned misery to vigorous scourging of herself for an utter little beast to have been thinking Crichie could have deceived her.

The taxi was speeding down the Avenue. It stopped. She got out, paid the fare, and rang the door-bell of the Peachleys' little house.

The door opened. Flora, who had evidently been out herself and had not had time to take her outdoor things off, had opened it, and now stood smiling at her. Barbara's gaze fell on the fur Flora was wearing, Her head was spinning again. It was Russian grey squirrel.

They had tea and discussed the events of the day. Peachley came in when they had finished, The children were out playing on the lawn. Their voices drifted to their elders across the twilight that made the lawn look so much larger, obscure and dusty.

"That new fur of yours is dinky," said Barbara, looking at Flora. "I must get Crichie to get me one, Was it very expensive?"

"Expensive?" chipped in Peachley, "Yes, it was for us, you know. Thirty-five shillings, at a sale, too. So what the real thing costs—"

"I should have said that was real Russian squirrel," said Barbara, looking at Flora. "They had a lot come to Goffers's three weeks ago. But they were thirty-five guineas."

"Oh, I can't get things like those," said Flora.

Barbara looked at the little timepiece over the fireplace. She rose from her chair,

*Well, I'll have to get home,'" she told them.

"Shall I get you—" began Peachley.

"No. I'll walk to the end of the Avenue and go by bus," she told them.

Flora took her to the door.

"Must you really go by bus?" asked Flora. "It will be packed and stuffy."

"Yes, I think I must," Barbara told her. "Crichie must have spent enormously at Eastbourne. I shall have to begin and cut out taxis."

"Oh, when he gets the partnership—" began Flora.

Barbara laughed suddenly, shakily.

"Do you think it's going to make any difference to me?" she asked.

Then Flora was standing by the door watching her pass along the Avenue. Her face was a little pale in the dusk of the Avenue. She went in and closed the door, walked back into the little room where Peachley had lit the lamp and was bending over the copying and translating which was to pay the rent next year. And next years—

From outside came the laughter and voices of Eric and Bert and Henry. A little wind had at last caught the kite father had brought home with him that evening. It was going up against the Hendon sky.

Chapter Nine

They had talked all night, talked whilst realizing that no amount of talk would alter anything, talked in the curiously calm voices of those whose emotions are bludgeoned, who can feel no more. They had realized that every hour from their meeting had led up to this impasse.

"You had better go to bed, Barbara," Crichie told her.

He sat in the big lounge-chair.

"I am not tired,," she answered him.

"You must be. It's four o'clock. See, there's dawn."

She stared out at the light coming—a blue streak under the blind.'

"You must look me up an early train to the north," she said.

"You don't look fit to travel; You had better get a few hours' sleep," he advised. "Besides, need you rush off like that? Do a few days more or less matter absolutely? We have not yet discussed what I shall allow you—"

"No. It is quite unimportant."

"I consider it very important."

"I don't. It's sheer waste of time to discuss it."

"But you will need money, until you can get teaching or something.

"What I shall do is my concern," she reminded him.

"Certainly, but I must see that you have sufficient until you find a post. You will see my outlook on it if you think of it."

"I see it," she told him. "But I don't agree with it."

"I must insist—" he began.

"You can't say more and be logical," she told him.

She was staring into the mirror over the fireplace, straightening her hair. The little ornaments on the shelves of the overmantel looked just the same. The fire was flickering in the grate. From time to time, as they had sat, Crichie had replenished it from the coal-scuttle.

"I think I will make a cup of coffee," she remarked.

"Yes, do. I should be glad of one also."

"Or—should we have breakfast?" she asked.

"It's early, but if you can eat—"

"1 can. We missed supper, you know."

"Yes. We'll have breakfast."

The birds were awakening. Their chirpings came upon the morning's stillness. Barbara moved from the sitting-room into the kitchen. Its blue- and white-tiled brightness, the shining pans and kettles, were touched with dawn-light coming in through the little beaded curtain. She wound the blind higher, and turned on the tap, filled a kettle and set it on the stove.

People were sleeping yet. She saw the houses across, dim in the dawn, their blinds drawn. They were sleeping in Rimton. Dave was sleeping in the hotel he detested, with its glare and the jazz band. The Peachleys were sleeping. It was queer to think of it—all those people, and all these millions calmly sleeping whilst they had been talking of their impasse, pale, tired face looking across at pale, tired face, their voices quite calm and quiet as they reached the end of life together, knew that they had reached the end irrevocably. The creeper round the kitchen window was already brightening in the dawn. The leaves waved in the breeze. They tapped the window and made faint sounds. The kettle was singing already. She moved mechanically away from the window, turned from watching the leaves of the creeper tapping the window. She looked around for the casserole, and found herself staring at it without recognizing for a little while that it was the casserole. She broke the eggs into the fat she had melted, and set the light going to keep things warm whilst she laid table and made toast and placed it in the rack, whilst the coffee boiled.

"Breakfast is ready," she told Crichie, ten minutes later, from the dining-room.

They sat down opposite each other.

"I've been looking up a train," he told her. "There's one at eleven-ten. You'll get to the North by three-thirty. It's quite the best. Only one change. That is, if you insist on going today."

"I must."

"I don't see it—"

"Oh, I must."

"You'd do better to sleep."

"Pass me the toast."

He passed it.

"Really, Barbara, I don't see—"

"I do."

"Very well, then, if you must. There's just the one change at Derby, and not a long wait. Yes, I'll take another cup of coffee."

He passed his cup. The cup rattled on the saucer just a little. Barbara filled it. She filled it quite steadily, and he recalled reading that temperamental, emotional people were always calmest in a crisis.

"You'll allow me to see you to the train?" he queried.

"Certainly. And later—I should like the piano sent on," she remarked.

"I'll send it."

"But—you'll be late at Goffers's if you see me to the train," she said.

"Yes. But I'll go."

"Thanks."

He looked swiftly at her to see if it was meant sarcastically. The pale light of dawn from the window had caught her hair and lit it up, as Barbara's hair always lit up in any light, catching it and throwing a radiance around her face. Her eyes looked shadowy and tired. Her whole being looked tired. But she had not spoken sarcastically. Still, she ought to be sensible and sleep before travelling. He was relieved to see that she was eating.

"Mind there are no bits of shell in the omelette," she told him. "A few pieces fell in. I couldn't be bothered to fish them out. They say one can get appendicitis—"

"But that would not matter—" he said briskly.

"Oh, certainly not—to me," she told him. "Pass me the sugar." Then: "I'll take the big box. I'll have to. I've quite a lot of things. I'll send it back."

"Need you?"

"I'd rather."

"Very well."

At the close of the meal Barbara switched off the electric light and wound up the blind. It was a gorgeous sunrise. Morning was being poured out of a golden jar this morning. The light felt to hurt her eyes. She was glad to sit down again after crossing the floor to wind up the blind. She almost felt too tired and weak to reach the chair again, There was a dragging pain across the top of her head. They heard Mary getting up.

"What shall we say—about being up so early?"

"Say?"

"Yes. Mary will be surprised to find us finished breakfast," he told her.

"Oh, nothing," Barbara told him. "After all what is there to say?"'

Book Three

Chapter One

The light of the afternoon sun streamed through fast-moving, stormy clouds—streamed like the rays of some great lantern, illumining here a late-mown field, there a heathery hill, or the sweep of bleak, rust-brown fells, topped by half-waste fields taken back from the moor, and with lonely farms, like grey boxes against the wide, cloud-trailed sky. Morning had been rainy. The grass of those fields which had been mown early in the season looked almost as bright as though it were spring, not autumn. So good had the weather been for farmers, with its alternate rain and then long days of sunshine, that many were thinking of getting in a second light crop of hay—a rare thing in this wind-swept corner of England, with its long winters, its early-closing summers. At Ross they were expecting a second crop. If the grass continued to grow as it was doing, another fortnight would have it ready. As half its fields sloped almost sheer, they would have to mow those with scythes.

Barbara, her hair blown by the wet wind, sat on a bed of heather. Occasionally she reached forward to a great patch of whinberry, pulled a berry and ate it but without losing the expression of abstraction which during these past weeks had become more and more a fixed look. She watched the valley below, sheep moving over the fields with their dividing hedgerows, where wild rose and hawthorn and honeysuckle had given place to elderberry, to trailing blackberry bushes, and where the dykes below held richness of wild mignonette, yellow hawkslit, purple scabrius, wandering vetch. Mountain ash would soon be out Heather would be fading. Harebells would blow, heavenly blue, on the moors in some places, on the bank-sides by the loose stone walls, on the field knolls. The year was going. Already a leaf or two was touched with the red of "Autumn's fiery finger". She had seen, whilst sitting here these two hours, the cart go from Ross Farm towards the moor, and knew they were gone to cut cattle-bedding. The bracken, which had waved its green cockades on a day that seemed divided from her by an eternity of suffering, would soon rustle, all yellow and drying if one walked there, giving at every footstep which passed amongst it a ghostly, echoing whisper. And over the red heather, before then, the blood from the moor's happy birds would drip as the guns rang out their sharp shots.

The past two months had been an agonized waiting, every day almost too long to get through. Now the pain had passed, leaving her numbed, unhoping, undespairing in that state of mind where she realized dully that even keenness of emotion would be a relief, even the ability to quiver with pain. She could feel nothing, saving the consciousness that dull blankness had fallen on her spirit, that in some way she saw all things as a spectator, noting them chilllily and without feeling, with no response leaping to these scenes which had once stirred joy and wonder and made her feel part of them. She no longer felt to belong here. In the house with Sarah and Dan she no longer felt to belong there, either. And when she thought of the house left behind, the mauve room with the powder-bowl, the Devon fireplaces, the little, tiled kitchen with its electric stove and shining, aluminium utensils, and of Crichie, and the hall, from that also she was utterly sundered. She could think of it without a quiver of emotion. From the moment when she had stood in Goffers's Emporium and had left the fur-room with the knowledge that there could possibly be no mistake, this odd feeling of being apart from everything and everybody had been creeping round her. It utterly surrounded her now. Crichie had left her no possible chance of believing there was any mistake. She had followed his advice that she should return to Rimton, and await—changes. She was waiting still. Taut nerves had now ceased to vibrate with any emotion.

It was queer, she mused, that since suffering itself was dead, she could not sleep.

She sat quite still on the red heather, watching the clouds move by. The grey rocks high above her were scarce more still. For two hours she had sat thus, motionless save for the picking of a berry to quench her thirst, since she had forgotten the flask Sarah had put ready for her to take.

Clouds had changed overhead. Sheep had moved across the fields and back again. Birds had flown on swift wings across the wide sky. Like one in the thrall of a dream, she had noticed the movement, the stir, the changing sky, feeling utterly cut off from it all, with no pain but the weary ache that she could no more respond to the beauty, the magic, the fair freshness of these once-beloved scenes. Even the wind blowing in her hair gave her no sense of joy. Thunder had vibrated on the air and died away again. She had lost her old terror at the approach of thunder, that deep-rooted terror which had once used to make her flee homewards with all possible speed when thunder was in the air. But now—she had no home. Perhaps that was it, she mused wearily. She sat on, hearing the voices of the birds filter upon the silence, float up from the hills, recognized a meadow-pippit's faint, sweet twitter carried upwards to her on the wet wind's wings, heard the more sombre cries of grouse and plover float down, over heather and ling and whin and bents a-hundred feet down, to her where she was sitting, listening to the faint tinkle of a stream which yesterday had been dry, but which the night rain and this morning's had made a silver thread amidst the bracken and fern. She had been listening to it while realizing dully that she was thirsty, but it had felt too great an effort to get up and from it. She thought she would get up and drink from it now. It would be cool and fresh. Then she changed her mind and sat on, staring at the sky. The cloud that had been like horses and riders a few minutes since was now like an Alpine peak with the glow of sunrise upon it. It reminded her of Crichie and herself, coming down the mountain path and hearing the little stones roll in the silences of the glimmering dawn, and saying they would love for ever. And they had got to the end of things in just over a year. And Crichie was quite right. It was best to end it all, not go on all their lives trying to make failure appear success. But what a long time she was kept waiting. He would choose the best possible moment, she knew, to wind up the bankruptcy and start again. But it felt very long waiting.

The intense cruelty the wholly unimaginative and wholly practical person can inflict became apparent to her. She knew quite well the meaning of this long suspense. Day after day, as the postman had passed, she had said to herself: "He has not got the partnership at Goffers's. She will not leave Peachley till then. They are both practical people." Life had seemed at times during this strain, a titanic joke. Only here, where the winds blew over ling and grass, where the heather, red under a grey sky, or purple under sun and blue, waved its million, million bells, where the curlew gave its thin, sad music to the vast, deep silences, or the plover called, had she been able to find calm. Now nothing hurt her. A stoney apathy had seized her.

She could hear Sarah's voice, hours on end, rasping out arguments that she go home, without the least distress. It was queer, she mused, that she could not sleep, that all through the nights she must lie awake, hearing the blowing of the wind, the rain pattering, see the windowed sky, with its night and stars, change to morning's dawn and sun, and then, utterly exhausted, sleep for a couple of hours, to hear Sarah's voice calling: "Breakfast, Barbara."

She rose from the heather and looked in the direction of home. The clouds hung heavy and dark over the hill which hid Rimton from sight. Their edges were brassy. The storm might burst before she got home, and with it rain, thunder-rain, and she had brought no mack. Getting wet, Sarah would scold at the additional work wet clothes drying made. She must get back for supper, too. Walking along, she visualized the meal. Dan on one side the table, eating in heavy silence, Sarah on the other, and from them both to her the perception of what they were feeling, the heart-break of two old folk who have laboured to bring up a child, and that not their own, watched it grow, hoped for it, dreamed for it, and find their own life's work tumbled down, since all they had dreamed for it was gone down. She walked along. It must be very hard for Sarah to be having to answer questions as to why she was here so long.

From springing heather, to bents, from bents to the path that ran by the wall-side.

If only there would be answer to her application the post of teacher at Rilsden. Perhaps there might be. A fluttering of hope stirred her. It died away, leaving her lethargic once more. Nothing would have come which would take her away from Rimton, away from the oppressive realization that Sarah would gladly have her away in order to cease being asked questions as to why she was here.

No. Nothing would have come to take her away from the sight of the sadness this had brought to old Dan, the bitter thought of all they had spent on her, just to have her eddicated to attract a man like Dennison, who now wanted a new arrangement. No, nothing would have come. Dave would be home this week-end. He, also, would torment her with his view of the matter, that since Crichie preferred Flora, that left her free left him free, also, since he was single. She walked on, visualizing again a letter propped against the clock, visualized herself opening it and reading: Dear madam, we have accepted your application for the post of teacher—" A wild burst of hope—a vision of herself walking along the little roads of Rilsden, away from all these bond's of affection that kept her in an atmosphere of confusion, radiated her spirit for a moment. To be packing her box. To journey, find herself in lodgings, away from it all for a time, to hear herself saying in a quiet school-room, where the sun came through plants the children had reared: "Can anyone tell me who invented the steam engine?" To get back to a place in the world with work to do away from Dan and Sarah and Dave, away even from watching the postman for Crichie's letter, which would bring Sarah grief but to herself release and relief. She marvelled dully at a world which did not liberate at once those who had no desire to be bound, which said they belonged to each other when all was dead between them, which encouraged in its rigorous sanctifying of a paper bond actual immorality as a desperation to break that bond when it meaninglessly festered in the flesh and had no joy for the spirit. Then she fell to thinking of Rilsden again. How freshly the winds had blown that day when she and Dave walked on the tops there. How long ago it seemed, yet it was only a few months. And how should she feel when the little stock of money she had placed in the town bank was done, and she had to begin living on Dan and Sarah, failing to find a post? Perhaps no worse. Possibly she would not feel anything even when that came.

Over the bents, past the rushes which grew in such profusion where the water ran in the hollows—rushes, green, shining rushes when the wind sang still, reminding her of summer days when she and Dave had used to gather great armfuls, one against the other as to which could get most to take back and make toy furniture of, and long, green, plaited whips, or to try and get the white pith free to twine into shapes of rose and daisy and star to place under Sarah's glass globes on the dresser. How far back it all seemed She was going back to the house where Dan and Sarah quarrelled about her, Dan saying she had done right to come, Sarah saying that women should all stick to their homes, sohowbeit, and if there was another woman the best way to do was to go and rive the hair off her head, but that stick to their homes and a living they should.

Always now, if the days were fine, she set out early in the morning with sandwiches, and carrying a book, which she never read, to avoid Sarah's bothering arguments, irate and disappointed that she had come home. Returning at sunset mostly, sometimes later, when stars were out, she found it ever more difficult to make herself return, since to open the door was the sign of the recontinuation of the battle, either Sarah contending with her, or Dan and Sarah contending about her. Outside, under the sky, there was stillness. She had walked two pairs of shoes away since her return, walking joyously along, but hearing water run, a peaceful sound, or the voices of birds. At first these bird-sounds had sounded a mockery. Now she heard that they were singing, saw there was a sun in the sky, moved along the day through, tiring herself out so as to be able to sleep at all. Always she awoke in the morning with the dull, oppressive weight of another day to be got through. Always she came home glad it was got through, wondering if she should sleep a little, if blessed oblivion would fall a little before that weight of another day's dawning came to her consciousness again. Dan had suggested one morning that she should stay in bed and sleep in the day if she could not catch hold of sleep at nights. Sarah had protested that she could not do with folks coming down all hours, that it kept one "agait", that it was bad enough having 'em go in and out all times, like a dog at a fair, without adding that to it. She heard them with a dull sense of irritation. With frayed nerves she often heard them, herself the bone of contention, after she had gone to bed. She was going back once more. The sun would soon be setting. A dull, orange and red glow in the west told that it would soon dip. She would open the door and find Dan returned, and that deep silence would hang over the kitchen until some attempt at conversation would lead inevitably to some discussion which would end in "fratching" at the best, or quarrelling at the worst, she herself set outside it, hearing it dully, wishing she had not come in, but having nowhere else to go. These last nights she had lost even the least capacity to sleep. How long they had seemed. And to-night she knew it would be the same. And Dave, back this fortnight from a six-weeks' tour in America, would be home this week-end pending new arrangements in England. The battle would begin to rage once more between them—the battle which Sarah seemed' conscious of, for if she could help it she never left them alone together for a moment, but watched them with suspicion and hostility, all the deeper for its being unexpressed verbally. Dave would say: "Come out, Barbary. Do you good," trying with all his force to get her out, and Sarah would say: "She can't. There's something to do besides gad. Besides, you'll have folk talking," which was as near as she dared to go. Or Dave stood, hands behind his back, the fireplace looking at her. She was walking back to this. Tomorrow was Saturday. Dave would arrive. If only there had been somewhere to go, to escape to, to stay for a couple of weeks, quite undisturbed, and not dully pained and affected by all these differing and antagonistic points of view. She tried to think, but there was no place to which one could go without money, and to go about to stay with people was to fill Rimton's mouth, as Sarah had pointed out to her, for they would wonder why she was over.

She was coming down the lane which led to the cottage. Oh, to be able to sleep. Perhaps, she thought, she would. She felt very tired, almost too tired to drag her limbs along. She looked away right along the road, and caught the gleam of white headstones over the grey churchyard wall. The quiet and peaceful dead. They slept always. And one had to die some time at the end of life—decrepit, bending, deaf, half-blind—

Then, with a sense of horror, she realized that for a moment she had been wishing herself there—quiet, beyond pain, on the other side of that wall.

She stood stood still, still in that shock of surprise that she was so unhappy she had been wishing for death. For really, she had told herself lately, she had been feeling nothing at all, only an absence of feeling which somehow was worse than any suffering. And now she had been wishing herself dead. It was the waiting, the day after day flitting past waiting for news that she was liberated.

Someone was coming along the road. She looked and looked again.

"Barbary," said Dave, reaching her. "Why, whatever's the matter? You—you look awful! Here, this won't do. It won't, really. It shan't. See, I've chucked the whole tarnation stage-business over. Willie Barnes has got another place. I've got the forge back, bought it back. There's a cottage at Rilsden. We're going to live there. Let 'em talk. That'll finish it. Let 'em. Does it stop the sun from shinin', the birds from singin', or make a man shoe horses any waur, their talkin'? Let 'em talk. In fifty years we'll be dead. Why waste life?

He was walking by her side, having turned round with her.

"You—you are staying here, then, all the time?" she inquired.

"Yes. Till we go to the cottage," he said doggedly.

"But, don't you see, we can't both stay here?" she said.

"Why not?"

"We can't."

"Oh, well."

Too tired to talk to resume contention against what felt to be overwhelming force, the force of one who was unwearied by having waited, just waited as she had, who could decide, act, reason, as she could not, tangled ever with perceptions of the views and feelings of others, the sense that one did belong to all whose lives one was associated with, and could therefore not be free, she walked by his side into the house. He had come to stay. As Dan would have expressed it —that put the tin hat on it. She would have to stay, because she had no money to go elsewhere. Dave would stay because he wanted to stay.

As Dave opened the door and she followed him in she paused, leaning against the door-stone. Just for a moment everything had been spinning. Then the floor that had rotated, the walls that had rotated were still again. She passed in, along the corridor, after him. Sarah had lit a candle and placed it on the table. The draught had caught it. It had a "shroud" on. There had been a "damp" on, significant of a change in the weather, which the natives always held would last at least three months, after a damp, whether it was for wet or fine weather. The candle-glow caught the trickle of damp on the dark green of the corridor wall, which gave cold, silvery trails where the damp was running, so that it looked as though snails had trailed over it. And in the graves there were snails and worms and things. Still, the dead would not know would not feel them creeping, crawling. One would sleep, unconscious of it all. Then she sat down would in a chair by the fire, shuddering. These wretched thoughts—

"Aye, I've come to stop," announced Dave.

Sarah's gaze went to Barbara's. The storm burst instantaneously.

"Tha's got him to do this, hussy," she accused, white to the lips. "I know. I've waited for this coming along. I know thee. Tha'rt like thy mother. It's in't blood. Shoo's bin today. Shoo's comin' back to see thee. I could find o' my heart to turn thee out wi' her. Tha' coom here after Dave. Tha'rt a nil 'un. Tha' can go wi' thy mother."

Then passion was reined in by diplomacy and remorse. The diplomacy was determined by Dave, who had rushed towards her, gripped her arm, and whose face was also white with passionate feeling. The remorse came swiftly at the sight of Barbara's face, stoney, pale, and with her over-large eyes looking shocked emotion at Sarah, then resentment, burning, fierce resentment, which faded, leaving her face pale and still as a dead creature's.

She stood up, leaning against the chair. Her voice came in a whisper almost.

"I—I thought my mother was dead," she said in the same, queer, strained voice. "I will certainly go with her if she has anywhere she can take me. By the way, I knew nothing of Dave's coming to stay for good till he told me on the road just now, when we met."

"Sit down. Tha'rt not going," said Sarah. "I—I take it back, Barbary,"

Tears at her own cruelty ran down her moved face. Barbara smiled.

"There are things one cannot ever take back", she said.

"Sit down," said Sarah.

She pushed Barbara into the chair. She sat down, silent, that odd smile on her lips and in her eyes.

"1 tell thee, Barbary, tha'rt not going," said Sarah. She stood staring at Barbara, who had sat down just as she had pushed her into the chair and whose fingers were tap-tap-tapping on the chair-arm as though she were playing a piano. She said it between a whisper and a sob. She would have given worlds to be able to unsay what she had said.

Barbara's eyes stared across into hers. The older woman quailed.

"You cannot stop me," she said. "I shall go."

"But I shall stop thee," said Sarah. Then: "Or Dave will."

"You can none of you stop me," answered Barbara with that dull, determined note in her voice. "She is a bad woman, then, my mother?"

"Barbary!" appealed Sarah.

"So long as she finds me a place somewhere where I can be quiet, I shall not worry what she is," said Barbara "I wonder—perhaps I shall find her kind, kind enough to leave me quiet. If so, I shall be grateful to her, whatever she is."

"Barbary!"

A knock fell on the door. Dave was going to answer it. Barbara read his intentions in his face.

"You shan't," she told him fiercely. "You shan't send her away without seeing me, or my seeing her. And I'm going with her if she has anywhere where I can sit and be quiet."

She went down the corridor. Dave looked at Sarah. Slow tears were flowing down her cheeks.

He snatched his cap up suddenly from its nail in the comer—the old cap he had worn at the forge. He stuck it on his head rather than put it on. His very lips were white. He approached her; She backed a little till she reached the chimney-piece. He brought his face very close to hers.

"You good people," he said with white heat, "you good people—blind, respectable, calling everything wrong because it upsets your ideas, not allowing of any circumstances altering anything, suspicious, watching for wrong, driving people to wrong as a refuge from your narrow-minded opinions—I wonder if the God who made you counts the numbers your ultra-respectability has decided to say—that for respectability if it is a hindrance to the human happiness which is wrong in humans but right in all his lesser creatures."

Sarah was staring at him like one hypnotized. The snap of his finger and thumb yet echoed on the air.

He strode out and brushed past Barbara and the woman yet standing on the threshold waiting to be asked in. He knew no Barbara would be there on his return, but he knew where she would be. Dan told him before he went for an "odd 'un" that Ruth Delling had come into some money and was living in a town a few miles away, and had been that day. And as he went it struck him that it was better, much better, after all, for him that Barbara went away from Rimton, since he could find her. Away, she was away from Sarah and Dan—those factors in helping her withstand him. She was worn, almost ghastly worn and weary. Dan and Sarah did not notice it the same since they saw her every day. At some moment, warm, human feeling would take the place of this chill despair. She would not stay with Ruth Delling long. He had seen Ruth's face by the light of the moon. It was enough; Barbara would go, because she had said she would go. Then she would leave her because she could not stand it. And then—she would not come to beg back of Sarah, who had said those cruel, irrevocable words; Then there would be only himself to flee to; Sarah had really, in her over-anxiety, driven Barbary towards the very path she had been cruel in fearing she would travel. The good woman, without understanding of human suffering and strain, was helping him to win Barbara. One thing was certain—much more waiting for Crichie to do one thing or the other, and—

He shuddered, recalling Barbara's face as she had stood by the chair.

And it came to him as he walked in a leafy wood, with infinitesimal small leaves murmuring above his head, how rigorously the comfortable and the happily, matched people set standards for the unhappy to live by. Walking in that wood, listening to the leaves, to the wind, seeing the glory of the radiant constellations where the leaves gave space for the night-sky, it came to him that every human being had the right to be happy so long as they hurt no one else. Joy was a holy, beautiful thing. Love, true love, whether blessed by bell and book or unblessed, was a holy and beautiful thing. Who was it said "Nay"? Those who were comfortable, Who was it said also poverty was a heaven-sent thing? Those who had it not. They judged for the other people who had the misery. A bird, an animal, a fly even on a window-pane, had no soul. Were humans, then, dowered with souls to have laws inflicted on those souls for their unhappiness, when, if there were a God, unhappiness would seem a cloud across the radiance of the world He had dreamed of and created? Fancy two sparrows having a divorce-case? He threw back his head and laughed—laughed at the wretchedness thrust upon the human race, on humanity, the crown of all created things, but which had, of all created things, only the divine right to be wretched and endure, because a number of its species had said: "This must be." His laughter echoed through the wood. As he went past them he startled two lovers. They were leaning warm cheek against warm cheek. This was original sin! This was what kept the world alive and yet was to be deplored. This was what he and Barbara had not to do, or they would shock everybody who heard of it. Of all creatures, man alone had a soul which seemed to have been specially given so that he could beat up against Nature, whilst every other living thing went disrespectable, happy and moral.

For was there any immorality in all the world like (hat of misery, either virtuous or not virtuous? And instinct—healthy, natural, beautiful instincts—how they had got atrophied by man's perpetual attempts to make himself believe he was happy when he was not, in the belief that if he was not he must bide it.

He walked on through the wood, hearing the leaves murmur, and repeating Ingersoll beneath his breath, saying the beautiful, happy litany of belief that each human born had the right "to stand happy and beloved under a free sky". That was reality. Yes. How all the philosophies thrust on people to help them bear unhappiness turned pale and bloodless besides such great, live, human litanies as those. There was hope in them. There was joy in them. There was progress in litanies like those. The rest were dust, simply dust thrown into the eyes of humanity, so that it should not see the indignity of pain.

He walked on through the wood. Barbara would be gone on his return, but he should follow, as the birds of the moors followed them mates.

Chapter Two

Barbara sat in the bay-windowed parlour. From the street came the clang of tramcars rattling past, the hoot of motor-horns, and anon the far-off echo of a train-whistle. She had gone to the door and from it several times this evening, had watched people passing, seen them through the tramcar windows, had heard their voices as they went by on the flagstones. Her mother had been out all afternoon. She had felt it a relief to see her get ready, "toffed up", as Ruth put it, and hear the door close behind her. But now even that companionship would have been a boon. She had not troubled to get tea. For seven solid hours she had sat in the parlour, and when sunset had been followed by the dip of the red October sun behind the grey house-roofs opposite, and evening mists had closed in, she had drawn the casement curtains together. Her piano had been sent from Rimton. It stood in the ultra-smart parlour. Once or twice she had sat down, attempting to play. The sounds had felt to go through her head, like the sounds of the clanging cars, the hooting of the motors. The silence grew so oppressive now that she sat down to the piano again and ran her fingers over the keys. The kitchen clock struck the half-hour. It was half-past nine. Surely her mother would be back soon now. She stuck at an aria from Balfe, finished it, and swung round on the seat and stared at the fire.

"Come in," she heard her mother's voice saying. "Aye, of course she's here."

The door was swung back, and she heard a man's footsteps.

Were they, then, to have another night like the last four nights had been?

Then she heard: "She's in there."

The door opened and Dave's face was looking in at her.

"Sit down and make thyself at home," said Ruth Delling. "I'll make supper."

Her footsteps retreated to the kitchen.

Dave had come in and sat down on one of the hair-seated chairs, after placing his 'cello on the big table under the window.

Barbara looked at him in silence.

"You can't go on staying here, Barbary," he told her.

"I do," she answered.

"But you can't."

"She's very good to me—really," Barbara told him. "And there is no other place I can go to."

"Sarah wants you to come back;" he told her.

"Are you there?" she asked.

"Aye."

"Well, I can't come."

"It's rubbish," he told her. "Barbary, if I cleared out and got lodgings, so you would come back, then folk would say I'd left because you'd come back, and make something o' that. But you can't stay here. I've come to take you back with me."

"I'm staying here."

"You're going back—to-night, too."

She laughed mirthlessly.

"I tell you, Barbary, you're going."

She gave no answer. They heard Ruth in the kitchen, half-humming, half-singing a comic song.

"Barbara, thee come an' set table," called her mother.

Barbara rose and was half-way to the door, when Dave stopped her, standing with his back against it.

"You're going back. I shan't leave here till you do," he told her.

"Barbara," called her mother, "come on an' set this table. If you want to spoon, come an' spoon in here."

Her laughter, coarse and good-natured, came to them. Dave's cheek flushed. He glanced at Barbara. Her face was immobile.

They went into the kitchen and Barbara set the table.

"You can allus tell when folk is in love," said Ruth as they sat down. "Help him to some of that pickled beef, Barbara. Aye, you can tell. An' she'd happen best go back with thee, Dave. I'm gettin' wed again myself this week-end, an' though I wouldn't mind her stoppin' here, well, he might. I were goin' to break it gentle, but since tha's come for her—"

She stopped, her mouth full of ham and tomatoes. Barbara was staring across the table at her mother.

"But couldn't I—just for a little while, stay?" she asked. "I'll do the housework."

Ruth winked at Dave, her mouth munching away.

"Hearken her," she said, "asking to stay with folk newly wed."

She went off into laughter, almost choked, and Barbara had to get up and thump her on the back.

"She'll come o' Saturday. She can stay till then," said Ruth magnanimously. "She could ha' stopped all th' time, but he mightn't like it."

There's nothing for it but to come back," said Dave quietly to Barbara.

"No. It seems not," she told him wearily. "I'll come tomorrow."

"You promise?"

"Yes."

She stared down at her plate, then lifted her head and caught the glad light in his eyes.

"I'll come now, after supper," she told him.

"Barbary!"

"Well, I'm right fain," said Ruth, "I were wondering how to break the news. It's a'reight. I'm goin' to be wed again. I'll send thy things on to-morn, Barbara."

Half an hour later Barbara and Dave were journeying back to Rimton. They stepped out of the train, walked through a few streets, and were walking in the country freshness between trees which loomed dusky shapes through the mists.

"Where've you been playing, Dave?" inquired Barbara.

He told her.

They discussed the programme's items, reading it by matches he struck, sitting on a low stone wall overhanging a stream. Then they went on again through the fresh, chilly night with its mists. The wind blew amongst the leaves that were beginning to litter the roadsides. Little lights shining here and there through the mists were like yellow stars on the hill-sides. Barbara looked at them shining, twinkling, every one the light of a home. Tears began to rain down her face silently. She stood still on the road, weeping quietly.

She was going back to Rimton, to go on waiting till Crichie got his partnership and sent her instructions. Sarah had promised never to say an ill word to her if she would come back. She was going. She had, despite the many things that frayed her already-frayed nerves in the bay-windowed house (including the hilarious nights which broke the neighbourhood's peace), been allowed to be there, without any attempts being made to influence her at all. Going back to Sarah, and where Dave was, she knew the struggle would re-continue.

"Barbary," said Dave,

He suddenly threw around her the arm that was not carrying the cello.

She made no movement away from him. It seemed good to have some human being to lean against. So, walking, they passed a road-lamp, and he looked into her face by its light.

Quite pale and with the tears still running down her face, her eyes were staring forwards into the darkness. He had planned to persuade her to go to the cottage at Rilsden rather than return to Sarah's, but it was scarcely the moment to plead a passion, or advocate their walking on through the night to get to Rilsden by two or three in the morning.

They walked on in silence, along the road between the great overhanging trees. Human happiness of each being near to each touched them both. A cyclist was coming down the hill.

He turned the corner of the road swiftly: almost ran into them. The glare of the acetylene lamp made a white disc of light which fell upon them. He noticed that Dave had his arm around Barbara. He flashed on, not noticing that as they had merely paused, dazzled by his sudden appearance, they again went on, steadily, towards Rimton. The tale as it would be told would scarcely be accurate; Dave thought of that. And the cyclist was a son of Sarah's greatest friend, who would take it as her duty to tell Sarah. And, though Sarah had promised to leave Barbara alone, to say nothing to her, as Dave had promised Sarah that he would not try to persuade Barbara to do what Sarah called a rash thing, he knew that Sarah's promise was worth as much as his own. Once back, the battle would start again, The simple natural thing was for him and Barbara to go to the cottage at Rilsden, to act as free, and end the tangle. Or, for Barbara to go away, right away from them all, have a holiday, by which time Goffers might have decided on the partnership, and the end would be in sight.

"Barbary," he began.

He had half-decided to tell her this was the best thing for her to do. Then he realized that to let her go, to help her to go, was not to see her for several weeks. There was comfort in just seeing her. She had been away many weeks now. He would think it out tomorrow at the forge.

They walked on and saw at the turn of the road the lights of Rimton, whose tenets and outlooks were the tenets and outlooks of Society, which made what should have been a simple matter a complex matter, what should have been a mere adjustment, a devastating, heartbreaking problem. And, coming on these lights, suddenly, out of the silence, from the road with its trees, Dave also felt the tenets and outlooks of Society, though to his mind all wrong, as things which must be abided by till slowly those outlooks changed with Society itself. For him and Barbara it was a question of waiting a little longer on the top of what had seemed an eternity of waiting. He thought of others, who must still "grin and bide it".

Then he stopped dead-still on the road.

"Dave?" queried Barbara.

"It's all right.—something just struck me," he said, and went on again.

He laughed, a laugh almost of enjoyment. Hope had flushed her spirit once more. Dave had not again spoken of the cottage at Rilsden. Sarah might cease to contend that she should return to Crichie. Goffers might give Crichie the partnership soon. If she could only be left quiet—

They were walking along in silence. Whilst Dave— Dave was staggering under this thought which had come to him suddenly as from nowhere. If Goffers did not give Dennison the partnership he expected, would Flora turn him down? It was possible. And would he expect Barbara back in that case? And might she go? She was being put through the mill. She might for a home and security, as thousands of others went back when things were hopeless. Going, the spirit of Barbara would perish.

They reached home, opened the door, and the first words they heard on opening the door were spoken by Sarah to Dan: "Shoo'll ha' to go back now when Goffers's has failed. T'other won't want him now. I knew everything would come out all reight. Shoo'll ha' to go back."

They went in.

"What's that about Goffers's? asked Barbara.

"Dan's got a paper, Bought it as he coom up through t' town. Sitha!" said Sarah.

Barbara took it. It shook in her hands. She stared down at the headlines. Goffers's had gone down.

She staggered to a chair. There was no partnership for Crichie. The muddle was a greater muddle than ever. She felt Dave's gaze on her face, a desperate, appealing gaze, from which she turned away. She went upstairs without supper, and heard Dan and Sarah discussing the new turn of affairs with avidity. They were glad, she realized bitterly. They thought she would go back.

Chapter Three

Barbara came down the stairs very quietly so that she should not rouse the rest of the household. She crossed over to the window, lifted the blind, and looked out on the early autumn morning. Night was rolling its curtains of darkness away. Dawn was sombre, but beautiful. She heard the sharp, sweet twitters of birds, saw them rising in a V-shaped formation against the sunrise sky.

All night she had lain awake, thinking of Crichie, Crichie battling with the hopelessness of a prospectless life, one amongst the City's nondescript workers now Goffers's had gone down. Flora would not want him now. She had seen them all, Peachley, Flora, the three boys, all sleeping—the little household at Hendon going on as usual, through Goffers's going down. And for herself and Crichie, there was the bond that now he would want her back and that she must go because Goffers's had gone down. Out of the impasse life had felt to be, her way had opened clear to her, the way of duty and sacrifice, the bleak way which wound ever uphill for years, which in prospect seemed endless.

"I heard you come down," said Dave a few minutes later.

"Yes. I am going back," she told him.

He gazed at her, appalled.

"Barbara, you can't," he expostulated.

They faced each other in the dim kitchen.

"Yes. I have decided," she told him. "Do not make it harder. It will be hard enough."

She went out to the wood-shed, brought in firing, and, kneeling on the fender, commenced to light the fire. The wood crackled noisily through the silence.

"But how can you be happy?" he asked dully.

"I shan't."

"Then why?"

"I'm thinking of Crichie."

"And what of me?"

Silence fell again.

"One can't pity people so big as you," she told him, looking up at him as he stood there with that stricken look on his face.

"Then—women love weaklings?" he asked with passionate scorn.

"I didn't say so," Barbara told him.

He looked at her as she knelt on the fender, fair hair dim and like a silvery cloud round her pale sad face, the lines of her lips compressed, her eyes steadfast in their determination.

"Pity is a poor thing," he told her, "to go on living with anyone for."

"You see—he's there—like a lost child, Dave," she told him.

He leaned down and drew her up in his arms, kissed eyes and mouth and hair. He let her go suddenly, realizing it was of no avail. Goffers's going down and the pity for Crichie's incapacity to face disaster was taking her back.

"That won't make you stay then? he asked.

"No. Besides, I shall have my home, as Sarah said, interests, things to do. Perhaps most people stay and try to make the best of things for those reasons," she told him.

"And you, Barbara, to go back for such reasons and the weak emotion of human pity!" he exclaimed. "Barbara, there's no justification for a man and woman living together unless they can't live asunder. All else is—blasphemy."

She eyed him, weary and worn, in the light of the grey morning.

"A great many people blaspheme, then," she told him.

They heard Sarah's foot on the stairs. She came down, looking at them, all in a fever of anxiety, and with it plainly written on her hard, wrinkled face, to find them down in the kitchen before her, and alone. But all she said was: "Oh, the fire's lit."

"Sarah, I'm going back," Barbara told her.

Sarah sat down in her chair and wept tears of joy and relief. Dan came down. The happiness in their faces, happiness that she would go back and be wretched, following the path of abnegation, was an irony to Dave, as his countenance showed. He went off, immediately breakfast was over, to the forge.

Barbara went across to it ten minutes before she departed. Dave looked up to see her standing in the doorway, silhouetted against the trees with their autumn colouring. She stepped over the threshold and looked round the place where Dave would spend the greatest part of his life. The glow of the smithy fire streamed over the walls, with the harnesses hung on big nails, awaiting mending, over the horse-shoes hanging up ready to be reached down, and—over Dave who would marry Nelly Greeby and toil here for her, herself passing by—a memory.

"Good morning, Dave," she told him in a low, sad voice, looked round the smithy once more, and then into the pain of his look, and was gone.

From the door of the smithy Dave saw Sarah and Barbara go down the road. The very back of Sarah, in her cape and bonnet and the long skirt, was exultant. He mused bitterly on these good people who would slaughter what they loved rather than see it moved out of a stereotyped path.

They had won. They and the way Barbara had been driven from Rimton, then back to it; and now Crichie's need, on the top of it all.

A few minutes later he was shoeing a horse. The smell of the burning hoof, the glow of the smithy, the sound of the hammer-blows echoing on the stillness of the morning air, the clacking of the stream as it ran past the great oak, familiar and' consoling, made him realize, amidst this heart-agony, that life dealt its devastating wounds, and to the toiler left one burden which never changed, one joy which helped one to forget—work. In twenty years he would still be hearing the stream go clacking past, noticing a robin on the fence that overhung it, seeing the oak, bearing its leaves rustle on the morning stillness. His heart would leap still to the roar of the bellows, his nostrils inhale the odour of hot iron plunged in water.

Barbara had gone by.

He listened as the horse he had shod went up the road, waking the echoes. Then he looked right along, far as the eye could see. Sarah and Barbara were two specks on the sun-glimmering road. The air was full of the sighing of autumn leaves. He went back into the smithy, took a harness from the wall and began to mend it. He looked once more dong the road. It was empty.

Barbara had gone by.

Chapter Four

The train sped along from hamlet to town rattled over bridges, went over rivers, plunged into tunnels, emerged again. Barbara sat looking out on it all, almost without seeing it. Tears blurred her vision. Crichie, seeing the furniture have to go, Crichie, moving into a tenement house, Crichie, through the years, fretting and beating against the harsh crudities of a poverty-limited life, above all, Crichie, without any prospect of anything different—she would have to live with that Crichie. Her dresses would bring quite a lot. She wondered if the sale of these, along with the furniture, would keep them until he got something. Tears ceased. She would have to plan all their lives out—this hard new life, with its things which would hurt him so. Perhaps she could get teaching. That would help. Only, no, Crichie would never let her go out to work. They would have to have lodgers. How he would hate that. Lodgers and the little house, and not even a lawn, possibly.

The train flew on.

She got out at Euston and thought of a taxi. No. They could not afford it now. She would go by Underground.

Rattled along between the tiled walls of the Tube, she passed familiar stations.

She got out. In a few minutes she would be home.

Home! The thought was an irony.

She went along the walk, past the railed trees, saw the sheen of the golden privet which hedged their garden, saw the almond tree.

She felt very old, and her head ached. She looked up at the windows. The curtains were drawn. What were the curtains doing drawn at this time of the day?

She dragged along the garden path, rang the bell, and heard Mary's footsteps. The door was opened. She saw Mary, her eyes red with crying.

"I—I came as soon as I could, Mary," she said. "Where's Crichie? And whatever have you got the curtains pulled across for?"

Mary burst into tears.

"Oh, Mrs. Dennison," she began. "I sent a wire. But you'd have left the North—"

"A wire?"

"Yes. You see, ma'am—there has been an accident—"

"Is Crichie dead?" asked Barbara.

Mary looked at her and wavered.

"Well, ma'am, he was badly hurt, and an hour since they wired from the hospital to say—

"Is he dead?" asked Barbara.

"I'm sorry to say, ma'am—" sobbed Mary.

Barbara waited for her to control her sobs.

"He died an hour ago," said Mary, at length, looking at her with compassion.

Barbara staggered to a chair which stood beside the hat-rack. She sat down, breathing hard. Mary was staring at her in unbounded amazement. She did not know if she should believe her own ears, but she had thought she had heard Mrs. Dennison murmur: "Thank God!"

THE END